2/90 99n

PERAHERA

Perahera

Julia Leslie

Heywood Books

© Julia Leslie 1983

First published in Great Britain
by Victor Gollancz Ltd
in association with Arrow Books

ISBN 1 85481 039 1

This edition published in 1989 by
Heywood Books Limited
55 Clissold Crescent
London N16 9AR

Printed in Great Britain by
Cox & Wyman Ltd, Reading

CONTENTS

To Mike Clarke
with thanks

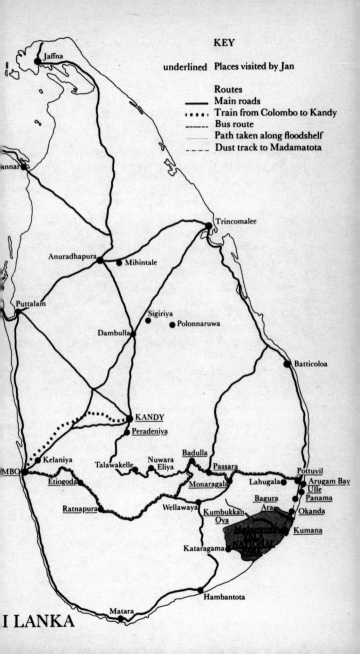

KEY

underlined Places visited by Jan

Routes
Main roads
Train from Colombo to Kandy
Bus route
Path taken along floodshelf
Dust track to Madamatota

Jaffna

annar...

Trincomalee

Anuradhapura   Mihintale

Puttalam

Sigiriya
Polonnaruwa

Dambulla

Batticoloa

KANDY

Peradeniya

Badulla

Kelaniya   Pottuvil

Talawakelle   Nuwara   Passara   Lahugala   Arugam Bay
               Eliya   Ulle
MBO   Monaragala   Panama

Etiogoda   Okanda
                           Wellaway   Kumbukkan
Ratnapura   Oya   Bagura
                                                   Ara
                                                   Kumana
                           Kataragama   Madamato... YALA
                                                   NATIONAL
                                                   PARK

                                        Hambantota
              Matara

I LANKA

PART ONE

13th–14th August 1975

Mrs Bandaranaike had total faith in her astrologer: he had told her husband, prime minister before her, the exact day on which he would be assassinated. Since his death that day in 1959, the stars had smiled. On 22nd May 1972, British Ceylon became the independent Republic of Sri Lanka, a socialist democracy with Mrs Bandaranaike as its first head of state. The future had looked good.

But on 1st August 1975, Saturn entered Cancer and the astrologer was worried. Saturn's entry into a new sign had proved catastrophic before: in Gemini to prompt the First World War; in Aries for the Second; in April 1971, Aries again to throw Sri Lanka into bloody insurrection. The gods alone knew what might happen this time.

Astrology apart, 1975 looked grim. Famine threatened. The island's economy was in chaos. The United Front government was becoming increasingly unpopular. July had been bad enough; August threatened to be worse.

A naked girl lay on her back on the hotel bed, waiting for the phone to ring. She had a young woman's body, lightly touched by the English sun, slim and firm. She was thinking of her ex-lover, hands moving automatically over pale breasts, smooth skin. She became aware of the hands with a start, pushed them angrily under her body, trapped by her buttocks on the bed. The movement pushed her shoulders back, her breasts forward. But her eyes seemed pained. She threw a worried glance at the phone, the telegram crumpled beside it, and continued to wait. The antiquated fan rattled above her, each slow circle sending a welcome breeze. Her limbs, still damp from the shower, were sprinkled with drops of water that drew attention to the skin. A small pool had gathered in the hollow of her neck. When the phone rang, she sat up quickly and it rolled over one breast to dash itself to pieces on her thigh.

'Hallo,' she said.

Her voice was anxious. Dark curls, newly washed to reflect the light, glinted chestnut. In their shadow, well-defined features spoke independence: a strong jaw softened by freckles astride the nose and green-flecked eyes that lifted at the corners.

'Can you hear me? Hallo!'

A shower of rattles and squeaks assailed her in reply. She held the receiver away from her ear then replaced it and tried again.

'Hallo!' she shouted. 'Hallo-o! Hallo-o!'

The response was far from human: a scraping sound as if someone were crawling along the wires to communicate. Without warning, it became a voice: faint, metallic, but a voice. She tried to catch its attention.

'Is that you, Dad?'

'Tom Nicholls here,' the voice croaked back automatically. 'McDair estate. Who's speaking?'

'It's me!'

'Jan?' Like an uncertain frog. 'When did you get in?'

'A couple of hours ago. You see . . .'

But he neither saw the anxiety on her face nor heard the urgency in her distant tone and his enquiries brushed her words aside.

'Did you have a good trip, dear?'

'Yes, but . . .'

'No delays?'

'Not much. I . . .'

'Where are you calling from?'

'Colombo.'

'Speak up, love. The line's infernally bad. It must be the rains. Where?'

'Colombo!' she yelled again. 'The Mount Lavinia Hotel.'

'There's nothing wrong, is there? Not feeling ill or anything?'

'Of course not, but . . .'

12

'Then why aren't you on your way up here?'

'I keep trying to tell you,' she shouted back, laughter mixing with exasperation, 'but you never let me finish.'

'Finish what? What's happened?'

'Christine isn't here.'

'Speak up.' His voice was brisk.

'Christine is not here.' She enunciated each syllable so that there was no mistake, but the words did not carry her concern. 'She said she'd meet me but she hasn't come.'

'There must be a message.' Brisk with common-sense.

'I've looked.'

'Perhaps she's coming straight to McDair.'

'That's why I rang.'

Her next sentence was drowned by explosive crackles subsiding in a sigh. It was some time before the line calmed down. As she waited, one hand returned unnoticed to her breast.

'Sorry, dear. You thought what?'

'I thought she might be with you.'

'Oh, I see.' A pause. 'Well, I'm afraid she isn't. Not yet anyway.'

'Oh.' She did not know what else to say.

'Why don't you come up?' her father continued. 'Christine's quite capable of finding her own way.'

But she persisted:

'Are you sure she didn't phone?'

'Quite sure.' But then he stopped. 'Come to think of it, there is a letter for you. It arrived this morning.'

'For God's sake,' she exploded, 'open it!'

That was just like him; so intent on his own affairs he didn't look beyond them. No wonder he was still in Sri Lanka when anyone with any sense had left. She checked herself: it was his life, after all.

She heard him pick up the phone again.

'Is it from Christine?'

He did not answer at once.

'I think so,' he said. 'But the ink's smudged – the damn thing looks as if it's been dropped in the bath.'

'Can't you read any of it?'

She strained to hear above the crackling wires, wishing she

13

could see it herself. She knew it was important. Why else would Christine write? But when her father answered this time, his voice had changed.

'Look, love. Why don't you come up here and we can discuss it in comfort?'

'Discuss what?' she cut in quickly. He was hiding something; she recognized that tone of voice. 'What is it?'

'The letter, dear. It's odd, but . . .'

A harsh medley of sounds destroyed the rest. When it stopped, the disembodied voice had gone. She replaced the receiver. But when she tried to get through again, the operator told her the lines were down.

She gave up then and lay back across the bed. The fan had dried her body but she did not move. Nor did her hands resume their journey across her skin. Paul was forgotten now. She interlaced her fingers across her waist and thought hard. First, a telegram brought her to that hotel; now a letter waited for her at McDair. Why?

She caught the first bus the next morning. She had wanted to take the overnight train but the monsoon ruled that out. The floods that annually swamped the island's fertile south-west triangle had torn the rail track apart: no train would reach the hills for days.

That explained why the bus was so full. Spare hands and legs lurched out of the open doorway as the vehicle executed a shaky right-hand turn out of the Colombo depot. Beneath the printed sign restricting the number of standing passengers, the aisle was jammed with six times the official quota. An eight-hour journey ahead of her, Jan was lucky to get a seat. With her elbow wedged white against the glass, her shoulders hunched forward to make room for the other seven sharing that five-person back seat, she was more comfortable than some.

'Excuse me,' said a voice in the familiar sing-song accent of the Sinhalese. 'When did you come to our country?'

A young man sat next to her; a student judging by the books on his lap, and with the delicate beige skin that denoted a Burgher, of Dutch or European descent.

She smiled.

'Yesterday,' she said. It seemed weeks ago already. She had spent the time worrying about Christine.

'You like Colombo?' he asked shyly.

She remembered how the evening had crawled by. She had strolled through the city, barely noticing where she walked. She kept wondering what her father had been about to say. In an effort to be constructive, she had started writing a letter to Paul. It began as a letter of explanation, letting bygones be bygones, but had ended in a stream of reproach. She had torn it up and gone back to worrying about Christine.

She remembered the Burgher youth beside her.

'Oh yes, I like Colombo,' she said, 'but I like the rest of the island more.'

He was waiting for her praise. The ancient cities. She had made out Christine's itinerary herself. With her four-week holiday to Jan's two, she could do her sightseeing alone. The royal capital of Anuradhapura. Mihintale where the Buddhist doctrine was first preached and the conversion of the Sinhalese began. The cave temples of Dambulla. The rock citadel at Sigiriya. Polonnaruwa, capital city of the Chola dynasty from South India.

'Yes,' she said again, to please him. 'I never get tired of your country.'

Christine could have seen the lot in a week. Then Kandy to see the temple and the lake – Jan had promised to take her to the Perahera festival later – and finally, an east coast beach to mop up the sun. She had suggested Arugam Bay and told her to look up her old friend, Mohan, of the Pottuvil Police, if she wanted to be shown around. It sounded easy enough, even for a stranger to the island, a girl alone. Surely Christine could look after herself? But Jan remembered the way her father's voice had changed, and she wondered.

Her train of thought was disturbed by a wave of movement that separated the passengers like a comb parting hair: heads craned left or right while standing passengers bent double to peer at the devastation on either side.

Acres of paddy suffocated under a reddish swirl. Homes lay submerged. Row upon row of kilns stood useless, bricks disintegrating. Men floated on rafts or tiny canoes, searching, ferrying. Women and children huddled beside cooking pots and sodden clothes.

'It's bad,' said a woman with a round face and neat flat features. She spoke Sinhala, over the foreigner's head.

'Every year the same,' replied a man beside her, her husband perhaps. 'It started when the planters came.'

His voice held resignation, not complaint. Jan did not argue. The island owed its current wealth to those determined pioneers and yet she knew what he meant. She had discussed it with her father often enough.

When the coffee boom collapsed in the 1880s, the surviving planters had turned to tea, 400,000 acres of it. They had added a flourishing rubber sector in the foothills, cocoa plantations, and more coconut estates on the coast. But the massive crop enterprise had meant a wholesale alteration of the landscape: vast tracts of primary forest uprooted; hillocks levelled; grassland fired. Tea was planted even on the steepest slopes. Consequently, the monsoons had swept away the vegetable mould laid by centuries of leaf fall and left the top soil bare. In the hills, water flushed that soil away. In the lowlands, river beds rose and a tidemark of destruction was left behind.

A voice intervened on her behalf.

'My father,' began the young Burgher who had addressed her before, 'he is a professor at the university and he says it is our fault too.' He smiled at Jan as if he sensed that she had understood; he had eyes like Paul. 'When we clear the forest for our chenas, we do the same thing.'

'It is the way our grandfathers taught us,' growled an older man with tangled blue-black curls.

It was true. And what alternative was there? The soil was often too poor to support more than one crop: those inadequate plots had to be abandoned; fresh forest was felled and the rains had a free hand.

Another voice spoke up, a man whose slant eyes and high cheekbones indicated Chinese origins, a descendant of early traders perhaps, or of the emigrants who for two centuries had flowed from the overpopulated provinces of China.

'Something should be done,' he announced. His chin jerked towards the window.

'It would not be so bad if we helped each other,' muttered someone to her right.

A murmur of assent rumbled along the back seat. The voice grew more confident, louder. People further forward turned round to join in.

'My sister lives in Talawakelle,' it said. 'Rocks have fallen on the roads and no one can get through.'

Jan nodded to herself. The hill country always suffered most. She wondered about McDair: she had been so worried about Christine she had forgotten to ask.

'My sister tells me all the prices have gone up. The roads are blocked and no trains are coming through. So the shopkeepers refuse to sell for less.'

'It is always the same,' chimed in an older man with grey hair scraped into the traditional knot at the back of his head. His mouth turned down in distress and his head bobbed from side to side. 'Remember the curfew,' his voice rose shrilly, 'this last curfew or the one before. Did not our own brothers in the markets put their prices up?'

'Yes, father!' a woman agreed angrily. She clutched a baby asleep on her lap while a larger child stood in the grip of her parted knees. 'I was in Kandy for the last curfew . . .'

Excited voices cut in on one another. April 1974. With prices high and the numbers on the edge of starvation rising daily, the opposition had tried to exploit discontent by organizing rallies: another curfew had been imposed. Jan had been in Kandy then too. She had watched the heated haggling in the market as curfew hour approached, the shopkeepers playing keenly with the people's fears. The Ceylonese were their own worst enemies; it would be the same this time.

'Even in '71 things were not so bad!' One voice, louder than the rest, claimed Jan's attention. 'People complained in private then. Now everyone is talking!'

As voices rose with comparisons, Jan watched the fire of argument ignite each pair of eyes. Centuries of foreign invasion had bequeathed startling alien irises to skins of coffee, mud and mahogany brown: from the palest albino blue to a rich sea-green, from brown cats' eyes flecked with yellow to an inscrutable black merging with the pupil. They were all angry.

Despite the new law forbidding 'loose talk' about the current crisis, opinions were vehement. Jan sympathized. Who could fail to draw comparisons with 1971? But the impassioned debate made her uneasy.

Tension, unrest, revolution. She pushed the unwelcome thoughts away. She had come for a holiday. After that confrontation with Paul, she needed it. The decision had come shortly before she was due to leave: the relationship simply did not work; she was moving out for good. Paul had been stunned. Then a curtain of resentment had blocked out all response. Jan remembered that heavy hostile shadow as she had packed.

A voice interrupted her thoughts.

'I think you understand Sinhala,' suggested the student tentatively, in English.

She nodded.

'They are right,' he continued quietly. 'It is not a good time to come. Perhaps there will be trouble again.'

'Like in '71?'

'No revolution.' He smiled sadly as if he wished it could be helped. 'Without Wijeweera that is not possible now. But trouble all the same.'

She nodded again, automatically. Wijeweera was in prison, his Peking-based revolutionary party disbanded or dead. The Janatha Vimukthi Peramuna: the People's Liberation Front. The student was right: if Wijeweera and the JVP could not do it in 1971, no one could.

She looked away to discourage further conversation. Coconut palms and bananas heavy with fruit swung by. Ropes snaked from palm to palm, the toddy tappers' trapeze. Rubber estates stretching for miles, half coconuts fixed as cups to collect the bleeding milk. When the bus slowed down, dots of white became frail swastika wheels, the common temple flower.

She had promised to bring Paul with her some time but kept postponing it, wanting to keep this part of her to herself a little longer. That had been the trouble all along. Paul had always wanted too much. When he asked her to live with him, she had been touched. But after a month of indecision, she had moved back to her own flat with Christine. She felt more comfortable that way, living her own life, spending several luxurious nights a week in Paul's big bed. Their love-making was better too. She had tried to explain. She remembered his sulky face and how she had made love to him with such deep feeling and evident effect that she had felt sure he must have understood. She sighed now, angered by her own stupidity. She should have known it would not work. The memory of his body lingered on: the damp weight of him, her fingers in his back, his urgent breathing in her ears.

'Look.'

The young man pointed past her. A hillock wore the startling decoration of Christ crucified and, in pastel blue and pink, a grieving lifesize Mary, a legacy from the Portuguese. He smiled.

'You are Catholic?'

'No,' she said. It was the easiest answer.

Through Etiogoda, with its lush papaya trees. Across the mud-flushed river and into Ratnapura, the bedraggled city of gems. The bus halted in several inches of water, prospective passengers wading to the door. On again, past primitive mines where blackened men in loin-cloths, trousered in mud, peered down flooded shafts.

The humming rhythm soothed her, the bus a giant cradle rocking her to sleep. She dozed.

When she awoke, the road was rising and the air had cooled. Beside her, three young men leaned together in sleep. The student's head rested gently on her shoulder, reminding her of Paul. Outside, paddy had given place to avenues of flame trees and the start of the tea country. The first of many factories wore its name emblazoned onto corrugated iron.

She looked at her watch. In another hour, they would reach what she called real tea country, not this poor quality stuff with its glimpses of couch and brown earth between the rows, but the lush uniformity of each bush merging into the next with the smoothness of a giant lawn. McDair was like that. She never tired of those green waves, nor of the scent of tea drifting up from the factory. She smiled, remembering how she had button-holed her friends about it, refusing to accept their indifference. Paul had tried to understand but only Christine had shown real interest: which was why she had invited her.

Christine was her closest friend. Growing up in English boarding schools with her parents abroad, Jan had valued her friendship. Part of her never forgave her father for putting McDair first, before his only child, before his wife's precarious health. When her mother died, Jan blamed him and turned to Christine in defiance and distress. As the years passed, Christine's family became her own, Christine herself more a sister than a friend. They rented a flat together, shared the practicalities of daily life, and discussed each other's problems. Not that they always agreed. Christine often displayed an impulsive flightiness that irritated Jan, whereas her own reluctance to commit herself to anything or anyone made her friend despair. But they got on. In recent months, they had made a foursome: Christine and Andrew, Jan and Paul. She knew Paul had been jealous of their friendship, and rightly so. For now at last, long after the rift with her father had healed, she was going to show Christine the island where she had been born, where her roots still stubbornly grew.

She felt a twinge of unease. Surely Christine had arrived at McDair by now? She must have done. Jan settled her head more comfortably against the corner of the seat, closed her eyes, and resolved not to worry.

The bus squealed into the Badulla depot. Tom Nicholls grinned. He was a fine-looking man, fit and tanned from many hours of walking through the estate. His hair was still dark, although it started further back than it had. The eyes, alight with pleasure, were Jan's.

Her worries forgotten, she stepped out of the crowd into a hug. Jan was aware as she kissed him that the affection she now felt was all the more precious for those wasted years.

'Fancy coming all this way to meet me when you're always so busy!' she teased.

'Not to mention all the things that are bound to go wrong in my absence,' he laughed. 'The clerks will succumb to a paralysis of fear!'

'The labourers will go on strike!'

'Or perhaps that old feud in the lines will be carried one step further: someone hit on the head with a shovel. Not such a joke,' he added, 'with nationalization so close and everyone's nerves on edge.'

'You needn't have come,' Jan insisted. 'There are plenty of buses.'

'You only visit me once a year,' her father smiled.

Things had changed since the old days. Once there had been over two thousand foreign planters on the island: in 1945, when Tom took up his first assignment, there were six hundred. But by the time his wife died in the spring of 1972, the number had dropped to thirty. Now there were eight: in Passara district, Tom Nicholls was alone. Weeks went by without a visitor; months might pass before he saw a European.

Jan watched him fondly as he stowed her luggage in the back of the landrover. She was glad she had come. This might well be her last visit: it was only a matter of time before McDair was taken over and her father forced to leave. His vulnerability saddened her. With each year, the prospects of a new career somewhere else grew dimmer, and yet he stayed. When she asked him about the future, he talked about the present or the past: the sun setting over the Uva hills; the swallows nesting each year in his front room; the care he lavished on those acres of tea and the two thousand hardy Tamils who worked for him. He loved the island more than he had ever loved England and besides, he would say, what would happen to McDair if he left? So he stayed.

He folded his body behind the wheel, beamed a boyish grin at his daughter, and eased the vehicle onto the road.

Jan looked at him.

'Is Christine at McDair?' she asked.

He shook his head, his eyes on the road.

'Blast, I was sure she would be. Haven't you seen her at all?'

'No, love, I haven't.'

His smile was reassuring. Square brown hands cradled the steering wheel, his body relaxed.

'It's pretty soporific at this time of year,' he said. 'I expect she's forgotten what day it is.'

'Then why the telegram?'

He glanced across at her. For a moment she thought he looked worried.

'What telegram?'

'Just before I left London; telling me to meet her at the Mount Lavinia instead of at McDair.'

'That's all?'

'Yes. On the thirteenth, it said – that's yesterday.'

'And you don't know why she changed her mind?'

'No.' She paused. 'But it must have been important if she was coming all the way from the east coast. It would have been much easier to meet at McDair.'

Her father frowned but said nothing.

'It's so unlike her,' Jan exclaimed. 'Christine may be unreliable but she'd never fix a meeting and just not turn up!'

Her words carved a rising pattern of anxiety. Then she paused, remembering.

'Did you bring the letter?'

His hand reached across to pat her knee. The gesture was strangely out of character.

'No, love,' he said gently. 'There was nothing to bring. Someone must have left it in the rain: it's quite illegible.'

But Jan had noticed that he did not look at her.

'You said there was something odd about it.'

'Well, I was wrong, wasn't I?' His voice was firm. 'Just a trick of the imagination as you'll see for yourself when we get home.'

'Are you sure . . . ?'

'Quite sure, dear. Now why don't you stop worrying and tell me what you've been up to. I haven't seen you since last April, remember.'

Jan smiled at that. She knew better than to pursue a subject her father had closed. But she felt calmer, too, reassured by his insistence. She chatted about her life in London; about the job she had just landed on a local newspaper and how she had got it on the strength of a series of articles on Sri Lanka. She did not mention Paul. Much as she loved her father now, she had grown too far away from him for that. They had never discussed her boyfriends, nor had she even mentioned the man she had once thought she might marry. She smiled wryly to herself. A part of her had never intended to marry him, the same part that she identified with her independence, and with Sri Lanka. Now, as the landrover rumbled into the dark, thoughts of London

22

vanished under choppy waves of tea. Jan felt as if she had never left.

'And McDair?' she said. 'Are things running smoothly?'

Her father made a face.

'The rumpus in the British press hasn't been much fun,' he said.

She nodded with feeling. The controversy formed a painful postscript to the disquieting history of Tamil labour in Ceylon. Without permission from the Sri Lanka government, a film crew had made a documentary on estate conditions and broadcast it on London television. The tender British conscience was inflamed overnight.

'Of course it's high time people back home realized what's entailed by the low price of tea,' Tom Nicholls admitted. 'But it's been hard this end: no one enjoys being the villain.'

She sympathized. To the conscientious planter aware of his luxuries, labour conditions were a constant embarrassment. Most of the barracks-like quarters had been built before the war. Even at McDair where the lines were more modern, they were hopelessly overcrowded.

'God knows, I've argued for improvements,' her father expostulated. 'But without cooperation from other estate managers, without approval from London and the local tea board, my hands are tied. I can't even increase their wages without permission.'

His knuckles whitened on the wheel. He needed somewhere to anchor his anger.

'And my director's only interested in the factory, the quality of tea and production figures!'

'You told me,' Jan said gently. 'In your letters.'

It was a frequent topic. She wondered when he would see that it did no good to stay. Thunder groaned beyond the windscreen and her father paused for it to die away. When he spoke again, his voice was calmer.

'As someone said the other day, if consumers back home paid 1p more per cup, and the companies took 2p less; if the local elite extracted less on the way out and the Ceylonese government redistributed the gains more effectively; then the Tamil labourers just might have two good meals a day!'

'But what about you?' she asked. 'Does this mean you'll have to go?'

For as Sri Lanka's foreign minister had stressed, British sterling companies owned most plantations, hired the labour, controlled the auctions, shipped out the consignments, blended, distributed and consumed the tea. Sri Lanka gained a token ad valorem tax and some cesses. Ceylonese agency houses had also come under attack: drawn from the island's elite, they were the goslings of the British goose that had laid the golden egg and it was in their interests to maintain the status quo. Outrage had sparked off a new nationalistic fire and perhaps, Jan thought suddenly, a far greater political awareness than before. Something must have triggered off the angry excitement she had witnessed in the bus that day. The uneasiness she had felt then returned as her father replied.

'Yes, the government can't put it off much longer.'

She watched him with concern but his expression was self-assured. He turned to her and smiled.

'At least the fuss has made that easier to accept,' he said.

Her father was changing gear, manoeuvring the vehicle round a group of people standing in the road. As the lever clicked back into top gear and the landrover twisted on its tarmac spiral, she could see the lights of Passara below and above, like a reflection, the stars. They would soon reach McDair.

McDair. She remembered Christine. She wanted to pursue her fears, but her father was already speaking.

'I'm losing workers to the chena farmers. They're offering five rupees a day plus food, which is a damn sight more than my chaps get.'

'I thought there'd been a seventy per cent wage increase.'

'So what?' her father retorted. 'Forty cents a day once covered everything they needed with money to spare. Now sugar is seven rupees a pound – ten on the black market. They can't even afford their rations, let alone clothes, soap, salt, cooking oil and all those other things we call necessities.'

She watched him, worried by his tone.

'I heard some pretty tough talk on the journey up,' she said. 'I didn't know how much of it to take seriously.'

Tom Nicholls frowned.

'I'm not sure either,' he said. 'The atmosphere's definitely changed over the past few weeks and I'm beginning to wonder what's going on. Something's brewing, that's for sure.'

'What do you mean?'

'I can't put my finger on it; perhaps it's the tensions caused by the food situation. Perhaps they've lost faith in their politicians. Perhaps I'm imagining it, but I don't think so.'

He fell silent. Jan inhaled the heady night: they were in the heart of the estate. The factory squatted below the road. The bungalow waited above. The landrover slowed to take the right-hand curve, then climbed through an avenue of flowering cassias. Jan peered through the darkness for the familiar signs of home: the old swimming pool where dragonflies hawked; the summer house where she liked to watch the birds and read; the ominous mara tree.

She leaned forward suddenly. It was dark but she thought the mara tree had gone. Her father was watching her.

'I was afraid you'd notice,' he said.

'You've cut it down.' Her voice was accusing.

'I had to, love. Those blasted bambaras come back to it year after year and each time there are more.'

'They don't do much harm,' she protested. 'A few stings here and there.'

'Well, this time they went too far. They attacked my clerks as they walked down for lunch: no one turned up for work at two and I thought I had a strike on my hands.'

Jan gave a gasp of laughter and gave in. Of the five varieties of bee in Sri Lanka, she knew the bambara was most feared. Only the bambara attacked persistently, giving chase for long distances. Only the bambara bore such animosity that if one were killed, the rest pursued to the death. Only the bambara could kill. Even as a child, staring up at the mara's death-hung branches, Jan had known the tree would be felled one day.

They had arrived. She sat for a moment, listening to the highland night. The fine old bungalow, built to last in Burmese teak, looked out over hillsides of tea. The idyllic setting had been chosen by a heartbroken planter so that he might gaze through the hills towards Nuwara Eliya where his errant wife cavorted with her friends. For Jan, the bungalow resonated with the suppressed passion of the past. Her father's predecessor had blown his brains out there. When she told Paul about that hole in the sitting-room carpet, he had been shocked. But as they walked up the steps together, Jan knew her father had not thought of it for years.

'You sit down,' he was saying, 'and Kandiah will bring us tea. And your letter. Then I'll ask him to run the water for your bath.'

Jan obeyed.

The envelope was a plain buff colour, the sort available anywhere on the island. Her name and the McDair address were written in pencil, in large square capitals. She lifted it into the light and frowned. That was not Christine's writing. She turned her attention to the letter.

'Well?' said her father. 'Is it from Christine?'

'Yes.' Jan seemed doubtful. 'At least I think so. I can't make head or tail of it.'

Watery ink seeped incomprehensibly into the page. But this was Christine's writing, she felt sure.

'You see what I mean?' Tom Nicholls spoke as if he wanted to bring the incident to a close.

But Jan was trying to read the letter. The first words were easy enough: 'Dear Ja . . .' Indecipherable blue smudges followed, interspersed with white patches encircling the occasional miraculous word. One such patch held the date: 12th August, the day Jan left England. Others provided disconnected words: '. . . please . . . reserve . . . terrible . . . *soon* . . . you must come . . .' Then these too petered out.

Her eyes gave up and raced back to the beginning. 'Please' do what? 'Reserve' what? What was 'terrible'? Why was '*soon*' underlined so vehemently? Jan realized with dismay that her father had been right the first time: there was something odd about this. The urgency scared her. Why had Christine not rewritten the letter more legibly? She checked the envelope again: no smudging there; and those pencilled capitals were definitely not Christine's.

She scanned the page again. Above an uneven splodge that

could only be her friend's signature, she slowly traced out the following words: '. . . nine days . . . only nine . . . must hurry . . . please Jan . . .' She swallowed. What had happened? What was happening now? Where was Christine?

In her anxiety, Jan flicked the envelope back and forth between her fingers. A slip of paper fell out onto the table. She unfolded it hastily and read.

The note was written in painstaking pencilled script:

Dear Jan,
   I found this letter in Christine's pocket after the accident. She told me you were friends. She had been in the water some time so it is hard to read, but I thought you would like to have it. I hope I have done the right thing.
   Your friend was a fine person. Please accept my condolences for her tragic death.

                                        Yours, Mohan Weeragama,
                                              Pottuvil Police

'Jan! What's wrong!'
'Oh, my God!'
Tom Nicholls stared aghast as his daughter burst into tears.

The bland façade of the undertaker's stood at the end of a tree-lined drive in Colombo's smartest suburb. Jan, her father's hand constantly at her elbow, was numb. Despite herself, she looked for signs of death and found only carefully nurtured life. Heart-shaped coleus, a flush of crimson edged in green, glistening with silver hairs. Canary-coloured mussaenda like costume jewellery pinned on salmon bracts. Allamanda on the garden walls, and the scent of frangipani hanging hot in the drowsy air. Her fingers clenched. A mortician had no right to such beauty, such life.

A gentle pressure on her arm made her move towards the entrance. Vases of plastic-smooth anthuriums on naked stalks welcomed them at the door. Incongruously, Jan thought of Paul. He had brought her anthuriums on her last birthday. How pleased with himself he had looked, standing there on her doorstep with Sri Lanka's flowers in his arms. She had almost loved him then. She shook her head distractedly.

27

A slight chubby-faced Sinhalese in a dark suit was greeting them between the ornamental urns. His hair curled with tight control while his face wore the curbed smile one expected of a mortician.

Jan knew Sando da Souza by sight. She had heard it said that no one was more suited to his profession, for who else could combine real sympathy with impeccable good taste? Her father described him as self-assured, thoroughly westernized and smug. Five years earlier, his marriage to the daughter of the richest Chinese family on the island had caused a sensation. Tom Nicholls called it a rare compliment, in recognition of his business acumen perhaps, for his success was indisputable.

Da Souza approached with a discreet smile and shook hands. His skin seemed dry in the midday humidity as if he might slough it to grow a glossier one, but the clasp was brisk and sympathetic. His voice was low.

'Miss Jackson is ready. You wish to see her now or . . .' – the pause was perfectly judged – 'shall we continue to the airport?'

She hesitated, her lip between her teeth, then nodded quickly. Da Souza led the way. At the threshold of a darkened room, he let the foreigners pass.

She had not wanted to look at first. Christine had drowned. She had been in the water some time, Mohan said.

But she looked beautiful. Jan felt weak. She had had a sudden vision of Christine emerging from her bedroom during one of Andrew's weekends, a towel round her waist, with proud naked breasts and heavy eyes. And now she would never love anyone again.

She pulled herself together. Her friend lay against pink cushions in a gleaming satinwood casket lined with silk. The yellow dress recalled summer parties in England and stopped short of her toes. Jan allowed her gaze to rise. The wide blue eyes were closed, the smooth skin and long pale hair the same. Or almost. The mouth was not quite right. And there was something almost plastic about that flawless skin. She shivered suddenly. How much of that still beauty was due to the embalmer's art?

She felt her father's arm round her shoulder as he ushered her out. Grateful, she leaned against him. In the fresh air, away from the paraphernalia of death and that nagging hospital smell, she felt stronger. They waited in silence. The satinwood lid was set in place, the casket carried outside.

The vehicles formed an unlikely cavalcade: the hearse, Tom Nicholls' worn landrover and a black Mercedes complete with uniformed chauffeur and British diplomat.

Jan hardly noticed the rest. She was thinking of Mohan's oddly formal letter. Beneath the courtesy, she sensed an undercurrent of something else. A conspiratorial touch? A whisper of alarm? She could not define it and that bothered her: it hugged the edges of her mind, taunting her sorrow for her friend.

The plane lifted into the sky and Christine was gone.

They were accompanied to the landrover by the occupant of the Mercedes, a tall lean Englishman with the nondescript good looks and colourless appeal that so often represents the British nation abroad. He kept a tactful silence until they reached their cars, then introduced himself.

'My name is Bob Saunders,' he said gravely. 'British High Commission.'

The smile was gentle, the pale eyes earnest.

'You have my deepest sympathy,' he added quietly.

Tom Nicholls thanked him. Jan nodded. She was thinking of Christine's parents meeting the plane at the other end, imagining the distress that unreal beauty would bring.

'If I can be of any help during the rest of your holiday, Miss Nicholls,' he continued, 'you have only to ask.'

One hand reached into a pocket to reappear with a printed card. He held it out to her, almost shyly.

'This is my address,' he explained. 'If you're ever in Colombo and need somewhere to stay, or a meal, please feel free to give me a call.'

She was touched by his concern. She accepted the card and found herself scrutinizing his face, wondering if she should tell him about Mohan's letter. His eyes were kind, their pale directness softened by white eyelashes curling like a girl's. But neither they nor the courteous manner concealed the strength of character in that elegant face. Jan felt she could trust him. More important, he would know what to do.

But she hesitated and her father interposed a formal farewell.

29

She wondered if he had done it deliberately, to stop her making a fool of herself. Saunders waited but the moment had passed.

She smiled her thanks and they parted, each to his respective destination: Bob Saunders to the stern sea-front buildings of the British High Commission; Jan and her father back upcountry to McDair.

During that drive, she decided. She would go to Pottuvil. She knew Mohan too well not to suspect that there was something behind that note. Why had he sent her the letter at all when it was so hard to read? Something must have prompted him and she wanted to know what it was.

Besides, she felt responsible somehow. How could she face Christine's parents, the younger brothers who had accepted her without a second thought? For she had insisted that Christine spend her holiday in Sri Lanka, she had sent her to sunbathe alone on the east coast. After all that Christine had meant to her, she had unwittingly sent her to her death. But she couldn't let it go at that. She had to find out what had happened. It was the least she could do.

At the back of her mind, Jan knew there was something else too: she wanted to keep herself busy. For she was beginning to feel the strain of the last few days. She did not want the time to brood.

Her father tried his utmost to dissuade her.

'Look, love,' he said, 'Christine's dead and there's nothing you can do. Why upset yourself any more?'

'But the letter?' she protested, working herself up. 'She was trying to tell me something important. Only nine days, she said. That was three days ago and . . .'

Jan stopped then because her father braked hard. She could not continue because she had started to cry. Even as she let herself go, the tears surprised her. She had not realized quite how brittle her composure had become. Grief rose into an engulfing wave that made her shoulders shake.

Her father put his arms around her, holding her awkwardly as if out of practice, his concern real. She let him comfort her. She even listened as he tried to talk her out of it. But nothing he said changed her mind. She knew she was being unreasonable: a

30

dozen unconnected words on a sea-soaked page meant nothing. And yet –

'You don't know Christine,' she insisted.

Didn't know what a good swimmer she was, how well able to take care of herself. Everything – the telegram, the missed rendezvous, the accident – was out of character. And the fear in that letter? Christine was not the sort to be needlessly scared. No, nothing that had happened made sense so how could the reasonable explanation be true?

Her father let her run on until hysteria exhausted itself in fatigue. Then he turned to her and said:

'You realize what you're saying, don't you?'

She looked at him.

'That Christine didn't have an accident.'

He waited as if he did not want to spell it out. She sat still, her face pale. He had to say it for her.

'That she was killed,' he said, deliberately low-key.

Still she said nothing.

'Well, I can't believe that,' he said at last, 'and I don't see how you can either.'

His tone was final. But she had faced the implication now and was not so sure. He seemed to read her thoughts.

'For God's sake, Jan!' he exclaimed sharply.

She felt sorry for him then. For she had always been stubborn, even as a child, and had so often caused him pain.

She knew she had little to go on: a few smudged words, Mohan's uncommunicative note and a growing hunch that Christine's death was no accident. And behind all that, driving her on, was the desire to do something, anything, to keep her mind from turning in on itself. Nothing could shake her resolve.

The next morning, she left for Pottuvil.

PART TWO

16th–17th August 1975:

the east coast (1)

It was just her luck to be going east in August when the land was parched. To the west, storm clouds hurled against the hills; to the east, they were transparent, bequeathing only shadows to a cracking ground. As the bus grumbled into the clearing that served Pottuvil as a depot, Jan mopped her face again. Sweat cooled her shoulder-blades and the backs of her legs. Her dress was soaked.

In the deepening twilight, the village formed two lines, one on each side of the road. When she first came to this part of the island, that was all it was: a T-junction, a transit stop. The road to the west hit the hills; to the north, it ran along the coast to Batticaloa and Trincomalee; to the south, tarmac turned to dust at Panama, twelve miles away. She had often come this way with her father, to fish in estuaries or lagoons, to spend weekends at the rest-house in Arugam Bay and swim in its sheltered sea. Bird lovers came for the sanctuary at Kumana, eighteen miles south of Panama; wildlife enthusiasts for Yala game reserve. And in recent years, in the fishing village of Ulle, three miles south of Pottuvil, a fluctuating nucleus of Western beachcombers challenged the surf on the point or sunbathed naked on the sand. But few stopped in Pottuvil. If it had not been for Mohan, Jan would not have stopped either.

She waited her turn to leave the bus. The journey had tired her. All she really wanted now was sleep. But first she had to find Mohan. Her watch told her where he would be: in the Muslim boutique by the curd stall, deep in a bottle of arrack. She was right.

As she walked in, Jan sensed the familiar waves of depression lurching across the room. That hunched figure in its outdated khaki uniform could only be Mohan.

She nodded to Muhammad, the fierce proprietor, waited for the handlebar moustache to dip in acknowledgment, then walked across to her friend. He sat in the corner at the furthest of the three small tables. Above his head, a glass bottle preserved sayings from the Koran. She pulled out a chair and sat down.

Mohan's head rose blearily, eyes half closed. A moment of doubt then the film of misery cleared. The heavy moustache, trained with wax to droop towards his chin, lifted in a smile.

'You have come?' he said softly. 'I did not think you would.'

It was almost a reproach.

'I thought it best,' she said.

She spoke casually but there was no mistaking the change of expression on the big man's face. He drew a subtle skin across the first, replacing friendship with a sincerity that did not fit.

'A bad business,' he said, 'but over now. We must forget.'

It was no time for questions. She would have to wait. The friendliness in her voice was deliberate but real.

'You're drinking arro, Mohan, and you know that makes you sad.'

He opened his mouth to defend himself then saw the raised eyebrow and laughed.

'Of course, I'm sad,' he said. 'Who would not be in this hellhole, away from his family and friends? With only these Muslim buggers to talk to?'

His head jerked contemptuously towards Muhammad, surly, silent at his counter. Jan smiled.

But, for her own reasons, she sympathized. During all her time on the island, the only trouble she had ever run into had been in a Muslim area. It was something to do with their women being so well guarded and the parallel assumption that bare-armed unaccompanied Western women were whores. She remembered the circle of Muslim youths taunting her, how she had tried to explain, how she had had to fight her way out, saved only by their genuine surprise that she did not want to play and the timely arrival of some friends. In Pottuvil, largely due to Mohan's patronage, she felt safe, but Muhammad's black eyes flickering constantly to their corner always made her nervous.

'I am a Sinhalese Buddhist in a Muslim village,' Mohan was saying. 'Can I be happy here?'

'What about your buddies in the police?' she replied. She knew what he would say.

'All Tamils!' he complied and spat with exaggerated contempt before he too grinned.

She laughed. But Mohan had told her about his first posting and she knew that old wounds cut deep beneath the repartee. He blamed the violence on Solomon Bandaranaike. Born and bred an Anglican, Bandaranaike had proclaimed himself the champion of Sinhala Buddhism against all alien elements, specifically against the Tamils. Religious and racial chauvinism had torn the island apart. Bandaranaike gained a massive victory in the 1956 elections but the violence cascaded on. She remembered Mohan's face, seamed with guilt and horror as he dredged his past. A Sinhalese teacher had been killed in Jaffna and her dismembered body sent to her family in the south. In retaliation, an entire family had been burnt alive. The madness reached its peak in May 1958 in the province where Mohan was stationed. Jan knew he had seen, felt and no doubt done things in those days that he could never forget.

She watched him pour out another glass of arrack. Now memories were transmuted into condescension. As a Sinhalese among Tamils he distrusted and Muslims he could not understand, Mohan was alone. In the melancholy hours of evening, his longing for a friend consumed him, an involuntary radiation of despair.

That was how they had first made friends. Jan had walked in from Ulle for an evening meal and they had shared a table. They had liked each other at once. Their meetings became a habit: whenever she was in the area, Jan would make a point of letting Mohan know and they would meet for supper. She had described her life in England, shared with him her ambivalent feelings for the island and McDair. She had even told him about Paul once, explaining how difficult she found it to commit herself to anyone. He shared with her the traumas of his past, the irritations of his current job, the gossip of the village. Their friendship had grown. She soon noticed that Mohan stopped his heavy drinking when she arrived, and the customary depression seemed to lift. When he was not depressed, he displayed a robust sense of humour and she found him excellent company.

34

She also knew she could count on him if she had to. Sometimes, she sensed something more personal beneath the talk, but neither of them drew attention to it. Now, looking at Mohan's broad affectionate face, Jan realized for the first time how fond of him she had grown. Whatever the delights of Ulle and Arugam Bay, she would not have spent so much time on the east coast if Mohan had not been there each year to welcome her.

'Your wife,' she said at last. 'Is she well?'

He nodded. Conversation fell into its usual pattern. The life of a police sergeant away from home. His preoccupation with news of his family in Kandy, most of whom were in the police force too. Mohan's father was responsible for the family tradition. Retired now, the old man was absorbed in his beloved bees: he collected all varieties, from the sweet honey bee to the dreaded bambara, and many a beleaguered household had given thanks for that.

Jan had heard a lot about the old fellow and, without ever meeting him, judged him an incorrigible if well-meaning rogue. If you want a secure profession, he had said, certain even in hard times to bring in the income your family needs, then join the police. Mohan had often had cause to thank him. His young wife was in the police force too. Not for the first time, Jan wondered what she was like.

She scooped the vegetables she had ordered onto her plate and listened. Her fingers pinched string hoppers apart, kneaded them into the curried mush and spiced coconut, and lifted them to her mouth. When Mohan felt silent, she asked:

'What news in Pottuvil?'

Her tone was flippant, in case. Mohan's reply was a shade too casual.

'Quincey's here.'

Jan pouted in automatic distaste. The Rt Hon. Quincey Senevisuriya. The name meant power, tradition and – the crux of the island's political problems – nepotism. The UNP had been dubbed the 'Uncle-Nephew' party. Mrs Bandaranaike's United Front was nicknamed the 'United Family'. Four of her brothers – from the feudal Ratwatte clan – held important posts; as did her two daughters and her son-in-law. Both the president and the minister of agriculture were related by marriage. Then

35

there were Solomon's relatives, a bevy of Bandaranaikes led by the determined finance minister, Felix. And Quincey. Married to the premier's first cousin and unofficial third-in-command of the party, he was a prominent member of this strong and privileged group.

He was also, if half the tales were true, a scoundrel. Nothing was ever proved; nothing except the customary rich man's evasions of the republic's laws. But Jan did not like him. Her reasons were more personal. In Ulle, once, she had seen him deliberately run over a dog asleep on the side of the road. He left it mangled but alive. Bound by their belief in karma, the villagers had refused to put the creature out of its misery, so Jan had done it. The experience had haunted her for months. She had never forgiven Quincey. She summed him up as vicious, power-hungry and mean; and he frightened her.

She watched Mohan's hands toying with the bottle. His dark-ringed eyes seemed troubled. She tried to help.

'Has he been misbehaving again?' she said.

The Sinhalese looked at her for a second, then his eyes dropped.

'Your friend was with him,' he said, 'before . . .'

Jan did not like that pause.

'Christine?' she said.

He was silent, stolid.

'Please, Mohan.'

He sighed then and spoke, his fingers moving restlessly, touching now the bottle, now the glass.

'I saw nothing,' he began slowly. 'But she went with him to Yala. The next morning, she was dead.'

'Yes?'

Mohan did not answer.

'What are you trying to say?'

'Nothing.'

But the retort was too quick. She waited. One hand dug into a pocket and re-emerged.

'When I was making my report for Colombo,' he explained, 'Quincey gave me this.'

His fingers fidgetted with a crumpled hundred-rupee note.

'No need to mention his name, he said.'

'He tried to bribe you?' Jan struggled to understand.

The magenta note had vanished. Mohan concentrated on a stale breadcrumb, pushing it across the table with his thumb.

'He didn't try,' he said sheepishly. 'He succeeded. You know Quincey.'

'You said nothing in the report?'

The broad shoulders shrugged eloquently.

'What could I say?' he asked. 'They went to Yala. That's all.'

'Then why the hundred rupees?'

Again that shrug.

'What's a small bribe?' he said. 'For us.'

He was aroused now, on the defensive. Jan was careful.

'Yes,' she said quietly, 'if it were ten. But a hundred?'

He frowned, unable to pretend.

'That's what worried me,' he said. 'Politics is a touchy business, especially these days. And Quincey's always keen to smooth his own path. But a hundred? It's as if . . .'

Mohan's voice trailed away. His eyes were fixed to the table, his face set. Jan tapped him sharply on the wrist. The eyes swung back, surprised to find her still there.

'As if what?' she demanded. 'You must tell me.'

But Mohan had been drinking all evening and it showed. His eyelids collapsed to half mast. To look at her, he tipped his head back and peered out beneath those lowered blinds. A lumpy shadow jerked from the side of his nose towards his throat. He was finding it difficult to concentrate. She leaned forward to catch his attention.

'Mohan, listen,' she commanded. 'You read Christine's letter, didn't you? You could have thrown it away but you didn't. You sent it to me. Why?'

She watched him free himself from the mist climbing into his brain. He cleared his throat noisily and blinked.

'I left it to Kataragama,' he said thickly. 'I am a Buddhist but here where Kataragama rules, I bow to him.'

She waited.

'I promised him: if she comes, I'll tell her; if not . . .'

His hands spread with vague expression.

'If not?' she prompted.

'Then I'll know it doesn't matter,' he finished sadly.

37

Jan remembered Mohan's advice in the past; it was something else he owed to his father. 'Don't you mess with Kataragama,' the old man used to say. For the god had a whim of steel that even Buddhists feared. The Buddha preached enlightenment but the gods still governed the earth and were worshipped and placated in the old manner. In Kandy, Kataragama was the most terrible of four guardian deities; on the east coast, he reigned supreme. Jan understood how binding Mohan's vow had been.

'And I came,' she said gently.

'Yes.'

He sighed as if it was more than he could bear. But he obeyed.

'Christine was a lovely girl,' he said. 'She often came in here for a chat. I told her once she saw too much of Quincey.'

'She *liked* him?'

Jan's disbelief was evident. and her disapproval. Had Quincey bothered Christine as he had once bothered her? Trying to win her over with his big-time talk, enticing her to his bungalow for drinks in the hope of a fumble later on? She shivered slightly as she remembered. Surely Christine had not fallen for that? Mohan shrugged.

'He took her for drives and gave her dinner. He brings his own cook from Colombo, you know, and his own provisions. And he talks well.'

Mohan kept his eyes on his hands.

'She spent her last night there, you know,' he said, then added as if by way of excuse, 'Servants always talk.'

He paused, his eyes bloodshot. Jan was confused, hating Quincey, unaccountably angry with Christine. What had she been playing at this time? If she'd had to sleep with the man, why the hell couldn't she have been more discreet? No wonder Western women were seen as whores. But she said nothing, reminding herself that Quincey did not leave a girl much choice.

'She'd been asking him to take her to Yala,' Mohan continued. 'Said she'd never seen a national park. He took her the next day. But when she came back she was different. Smaller somehow. Scared.'

'You saw her?'

His head jogged sadly from side to side, the Ceylonese nod.

'She came in here,' he said. 'She must have made some excuse to Quincey because I could hear the jeep running outside. She asked me to wait. Not more than an hour, she said, two at the most. She wanted to give me something, a letter.'

His eyes swivelled up to hers.

'Of course, I said I would. Said I'd wait all night for her,' he added with an uncomfortable attempt at a smirk.

'And she went back to Quincey?'

He nodded.

'I waited but she didn't come.'

'But . . .'

'The next morning,' his voice droned past her. 'When they found her, I was shocked but I accepted it. Then I read that letter and remembered: those words and her face that night said the same thing. She was frightened. But I don't know why.'

His lips were rubbery, out of control. He was grasping the table, his body hunched as if the spine had gone. Jan reached out a hand.

'There was nothing you could do,' she said. 'Perhaps it was an accident after all.'

Mohan did not hear her say good night. She rose to leave and the heavy head nodded as if he understood. She shook him gently, told him to go to bed and forget about it, told him there was nothing to forget. Clumsily, he clasped her hands in his, planted a moist kiss on the back of each one, and gestured wearily that she should let him be. She felt a sudden wave of affection for him. But Mohan was past conversation now. She put out a hand to touch him, glanced up to find Muhammad's black eyes watching, and changed her mind. At the doorway, she looked back at the crumpled figure, then left.

It was a beautiful night as she turned south to walk the three miles to Ulle. A light shoulder bag carried all she would need: soap, toothpaste, a small towel, a change of underwear, another unremarkable dress, and a bikini in case she found the time to swim. Beneath her sandalled feet, the tarmac that melted every day had reset. Above, a humped moon shone against a velvet sky. Jan stared at it, trying to calculate when it would be full. August 21st, the Esala full moon, when the Kandy Perahera reached its peak. She had promised to take Christine that year.

39

She conjured up a picture of her friend's face, but Quincey's kept superimposing itself on top. A few yards ahead, the call of a jungle nightjar rapped out like a marble bouncing rapidly on ice.

Dawn rose stealthily over Arugam Bay. In her borrowed fishing hut, Jan felt the night air quicken, woke from a nightmare with a start, and got up.

She walked south, remembering, and wanting to forget. The scared tone of Christine's letter. Her beautified death. The hundred-rupee note like a conjurer's trick in Mohan's hand. The ugly thought of Quincey making love to her friend. The images had clogged her brain until she slept, then brutally invaded her dreams. She needed to forget them for a while.

Ulle cast its usual spell. Fishing boats, hollowed out jakwood trees with crooked outrigger arms, lay like beached fish whitened in the sun. The stillness of deserted sands. Only old Muttuvil leaned against his grandson's boat, ready for another day. His head inclined towards her unsurprised. Jan waved and continued round the point.

The corner turned, she stopped, toes curled down to hug the sand. The sun poised solid gold above the sea. A tiny figure raced across it, riding a metallic wave that curled towards the shore, his surfboard flinging sparks of colour at the sky. As Jan watched, he hung for a second, a pinned insect on a burning globe, then vanished. The sun seized her eyes.

It was then she saw him. He had stopped forty yards away to scan the waves. He had evidently not seen her: the strapping frame wore a uniform honeyed tan and nothing more. She studied him, admiring. He was tall and well made, his stomach tight and brown, without that chaste white mark of swim trunks she had always found on Paul. Then he strode towards her and she saw he was not wholly naked: a saffron cloth encircled his forehead and a startling square of sticking plaster sat astride his nose. She chuckled, curious to see what he would do, and walked on.

He faltered. One bleached eyebrow jerked in surprise. Then he saw her smile of mischief and his features folded in an embarrassed grin.

'Hi there!' he called as they crossed paths.

He gave a boyish laugh and gathered speed. His body moved easily, like one used to exercise naked in the open air. She turned to watch him, enjoying his smooth back, muscled buttocks and loping legs. She smiled. How easy it was to be bowled over by a fine body and a cheeky grin. She felt more cheerful now.

A honking cry made her look up, shading her eyes from the glare. High above, two white-bellied sea eagles soared on black-edged wings. She remembered the nest she had found the year before and decided to look for it. A set of wild boar tracks led her across heaped dunes, past uprooted shrubs and small trees. She followed cautiously, but found instead a black-naped hare frozen into Dürer-like precision, and langurs, with wizened black faces framed in white. She went too near: in one concerted flash, white-tipped tails curled into angry question marks, they cantered away.

The question marks reminded her. She looked at her watch: seven-thirty. Another hour and the sand would be white hot, the sea ablaze, the trees a shimmering mirage. She would sweat in earnest then, even in the shade.

She wished she had not come. Her father's disbelief stemmed from logic now, her own suspicions from shock. She promised herself she would not stay long. A few questions to satisfy the doubts, a few answers to explain what did not yet make sense, and she would go.

The eagles' nest forgotten, she cut across the dunes towards the shore. But a scrap of eggshell caught her eye and she stopped. As she stooped to investigate, a pleasant voice addressed her.

'They're turtle eggs, aren't they?'

She looked up into a smiling face, sticking plaster still perched across his nose. He held white flakes carefully, as if they were alive. Jan found the gesture endearing. Against the white, his hands looked brown and big.

'I was looking for turtles when we met before,' he said with a trace of an accent. 'I thought I saw one out at sea.'

The smile grew wider. She could tell he thought her attractive. The idea spun a thrill of excitement down her spine.

'I'm afraid I didn't notice you,' he added.

She laughed easily.

'Don't apologize on my account,' she said.

His hair was drawn into a knot revealing a fuzz of beard on cheek and chin, a shade lighter than that on the taut skin across his chest. The saffron cloth was wrapped about his loins. She laughed again.

'Is that a loincloth or a bandana?' she said.

The sun had burned white wrinkles round his eyes. They came and went as he smiled, flashes of sketchy lightning on a tan sky. His eyelashes were long and like his eyebrows bleached white-blond, but straight and sharp. The fuzz belied his years.

'A dual-purpose garment, miss,' he grinned. 'I'm on my way to the baker's for tea and thought I'd better put it on.'

'Very fetching,' she said with a smile. 'And the plaster?'

He laughed and shook his head.

'Not so pretty, I admit,' he said, 'but I had to think of something to protect my nose.'

He had an engaging laugh. They left the scraps of eggshell and walked towards the village together.

'What brings you here?' she asked.

'A surfie without a board,' he replied with mock pathos. 'It's my third summer here. And now, after less than a week, I've broken my board. In real life, back in Heidelberg, I'm studying law.'

'Your English is good,' Jan commented.

'My mother was English, and she was always keen that I should keep it up.' He turned to Jan. 'And you?'

She hesitated. Crabs scuttled across her toes, yellow legs like knitting needles.

'I came to meet a friend,' she said at last, moving on.

'Anyone I know?'

She wondered whether to tell the truth. He was a stranger still but she liked him. She glanced up at his face, then looked away. To her right, coin-bodied soldier crabs spat out pellets, neat and round. To her left, a fiddler held aloft a giant claw. But her gaze saw neither.

'Christine Jackson,' she said. 'She was staying at the rest-house over there.'

She pointed over the bay. Her movement disturbed clock-york plovers unwinding at the water's edge. The crest of a wave thudded down, spattered her with spray that sizzled and bits of shell that chipped into her skin. She hardly noticed. She was waiting for his answer: for some reason, it seemed important that he should understand.

He stopped. She noticed that his smile had gone. He was watching her with concern.

'I did know her,' he said gently. 'I'm sorry.'

She nodded vaguely. She appreciated his sympathy, both the words and what was left unsaid. But Muttuvil called her then and she was glad.

The gnarled hands were fiddling with a net. He cleared his throat, spat a gob of phlegm into the sand and threw out a string of guttural syllables.

'He says his grandson found it past the reef,' Jan explained. 'They think it's Japanese.'

She smiled and waved, calling to the old man in Tamil, indicating the bakery up ahead. Then she walked inland to retrieve her things. The German waited. Briefly, Jan thought of washing at the village well, but tea seemed more important. As she returned to the beach, she found herself watching her new companion closely.

He seemed thoughtful. He picked up a dried seed pod from a clump of spinifex at the edge of the sand, toyed with it awhile, then dropped it. There was something futile about the gesture. He made no attempt at conversation now. They completed their walk in silence.

At the baker's, too, neither of them was in a hurry to talk. Jan tried to collect her thoughts. Was it foolish to want to tell him what was on her mind? She liked him, yes, but was that enough?

She signalled to the baker to bring two teas. Baby Singho merely clicked his fingers at his son. In the August heat, the man's bulk impeded both speech and movement, possibly thought as well: for all he ever had to sell was bread and tea.

'My name's Wolfgang,' her companion said suddenly. He pronounced with a V, and the vowels were short as in 'shotgun'. He had removed the square of sticking plaster from his nose and the skin beneath was peeling from the sun. She wondered about his age. Late twenties perhaps, a few years older than she was.

He had the kind of healthy good looks that made it hard
judge.

'Jan Nicholls,' she replied.

'I'm sorry about Christine.'

She nodded. Her hands fidgetted with the glass of plain te
'black water' Baby Singho called it for there was no milk or suga
these days, and that morning no jaggery either.

'Do you know what happened?' she asked.

He hesitated.

'She must have gone swimming that night,' he said with
shrug.

His eyes were very blue. Jan noticed that the right pup
expanded more than the left: if she concentrated on one then th
other, she had the impression of talking to two different peop
at the same time. The effect was oddly appealing.

'Christine's an excellent swimmer,' she said quietly. 'H
father built a glass cabinet for the cups she's won.'

'And the currents here aren't really very strong.' He ha
spoken in the same steady tone.

They looked at each other in silence. Her eyes were guarde
still. She had to talk to someone – about the telegram, the lette
Mohan's bribe; about Quincey and her fears – and she truste
Wolfgang; but she could not decide. She found herself leanir
back, staring at him, thinking hard.

'I still can't quite believe it,' she said.

Her eyes slid past his face. Beyond them, in faded black an
white, the baker and his stern-faced wife stood beside an ol
man's corpse. The photograph showed none of the trimmin;
of richer folk: no golden candlesticks, no ivory tusks or en
broidered silk canopy. A shelf was nailed below and on
rested a bowl of flowers and a stick of incense. So different fro
Christine's funeral; the polished grain of satinwood, pir
silk, yellow dress and pale blonde hair. She shivered. W;
Quincey responsible for that?

She felt a hand clasp hers.

'Are you all right?'

Wolfgang's face was anxious. Jan looked at him. His bro
was furrowed with concern but everything about him – from t
lines of his jaw to the fingers that held her own – was stron

broad square shoulders, the outline of muscle moving the skin beneath, and above an honest face. She was glad they had met. And she knew he would help her if he could: she could read that in his eyes.

'I'm meeting a friend in Pottuvil for breakfast,' she said. 'Would you like to join us?'

Wolfgang smiled.

Jan waited on the bench outside the bakery while Wolfgang changed. Squirrels fumed overhead, the mark of Shiva on their backs. Beside her, a pile of newspapers yellowed in the sun.

Front-page photographs of Republic Day rallies caught her eye. May 22nd, celebrated with pageants and military parades, ranked with the festivals of the gods. She skimmed through the usual biased report and sighed. Power alternated between the UNP and the Bandaranaikes' SLFP or United Front, but there was little to choose between them. Now Mrs Bandaranaike had extended her government for an extra two years without elections. Prices continued to soar. Eleven families still controlled over half the private investments. In a population of thirteen million, 800,000 lacked jobs. On top of that, the rice harvest had been halved and the poor suffered famine conditions. The politicians' roars sounded hollow against the facts.

She was still deep in thought when someone called her name.

'Jan, my dear! How are you keeping these days?'

The voice was familiar but Jan did not recognize it till she turned. Quincey. She remembered Christine and felt a sudden rising panic that vanished as quickly as it had appeared. It left an icy residue of apprehension. She raised one hand in greeting.

His landrover was parked on the other side of the road in front of the fishing cooperative. Behind it stood a van, its back doors open as two men loaded the night's catch, supervised by the Mudalali, the richest merchant for miles.

Quincey waved again. He was wearing an off-duty sarong, and round his neck a glittering gold chain. He was far too big for this heat. Sweat shone on his chest and shoulders. Jan watched him adjust the sarong, stretching out the tube of damp cloth to let cooler air swirl down inside, then tucking it tight at his waist. She had to admit that the garment suited him. It accentuated his disturbingly physical good looks, the powerful structure of his body, the gleaming skin. She did not even want to think it, but she could see why Christine had fallen for him, if she had.

Quincey was looking across at her, surprised she had not moved. Then he beckoned peremptorily. Jan stood up. Her hands made vague attempts to straighten her dress, as if it mattered that she had slept in it. She did not want to speak to him but saw no choice. Quincey was not the kind of man you snubbed. She adopted a casual air and strolled across. But she was scared. She was wondering which of them would mention Christine first.

He did. He must have known someone would tell her of his interest in her friend.

'My dear, I'm so sorry about Christine Jackson,' he said. 'She was a marvellous girl.'

Jan wondered if he was thinking of the night they'd spent together, wondered too if he realized how much that weighed against him in her mind. Christine's last night with him. The thought disgusted her.

'A dreadful business,' he continued, shaking his head. The sun ricocheted into Jan's eyes, reflected off the gold around his neck. 'Such a pretty girl, such a horrible way to die.'

As he spoke, he used the hem of his sarong to wipe his face. The movement revealed strong legs and ankles. Jan nodded. She was growing increasingly nervous. Those small black eyes were watching her too closely. His next remark explained why.

'I'm surprised you could face coming here after such an unpleasant incident,' he said. 'Will you be staying long?'

'I always visit Mohan when I'm on the island,' she replied rather quickly. Then she remembered the magenta note in Mohan's hand and wished she'd kept her mouth shut. Quincey was still watching her.

'How about you?' she said hastily. 'Are you well?'

Quincey allowed himself to be side-tracked but his eyes continued to bore into her own.

'Right as rain, my dear. A few days at Arugam Bay and I'm ready for the fray. Just as well too, in the circumstances.'

'Things are pretty bad, aren't they?' she said vaguely.

But Quincey needed little help. The sound of his own voice and the persuasiveness of his opinions were enough.

'Ah, the degenerating effects of British rule!' he boomed. 'By the time you left, we couldn't fend for ourselves. Now the welfare system we inherited is beyond us: we can't afford subsidies and yet the competition for votes means we can't abolish them!'

'You cut the rice ration,' Jan interjected.

Quincey seemed to have forgotten about Christine and she had no desire to remind him.

'Look what happened!' he retorted. 'No economic effect and a drastic drop in popularity. Too little and too late.'

He laughed. He was enjoying himself, exercising his rhetoric.

'Don't misunderstand me,' he said, 'but your democracy has no place here. It has left us divided and in ruin!'

He beamed complacently as only a rich and powerful man in the East can. His air of authority was born of a line of patriarchs whose power, even in British days, had never been seriously challenged. Even now, when things had changed so much, there was little he could not have or do or make someone else do if he wished. Jan wondered what he wanted from Sri Lanka, and how long it would take him to get it. Then she changed the subject. She did not like the look in those eyes.

'Are you buying some fish?' she asked.

'That's right,' he said. 'The Mudalali promised to keep me a paraw. Always ready to do me a favour, aren't you, old chap?'

The question was superfluous. The Mudalali, a gaunt man with tight black skin and opaque eyes, spoke no English. To his inferiors, he was a small-minded tyrant; with his betters, maddeningly impassive. He was engrossed in the loading process and ignored both Quincey and Jan.

As the men carried crates past her, she inhaled the stench of raw fish mingled with another smell that bothered her but that she could not place. The Mudalali rapped out a question in Sinhala. One of the men spat a thin red stream onto the ground, lifted the lid of the crate he was carrying and replied. As the Mudalali spoke a second time, evidently a command, Quincey interrupted.

'You don't speak Sinhala, do you, Jan?'

47

She hesitated, so briefly no one could have noticed. Then something in his face made her lie.

'I'm afraid not,' she said. 'My father insisted I learn Tamil Sinhala seemed even more difficult so I gave that up.'

She laughed vaguely. Quincey laughed, too, an ugly sound that matched his character, if not his looks. She shifted uncomfortably. It always sounded as if his laughter was hiding something not in the least amusing. She wondered if it had anything to do with Christine.

Then she saw Wolfgang. He waved and she turned to Quincey to say good-bye. She felt his eyes follow her as she walked away. The curious pressure on her back was unnerving.

Half an hour later, Muhammad served three breakfasts: two egg-hoppers each, three plain, and a cup of hot sweet tea. Mohan's brow was furrowed to fight a headache but even he looked pleased.

'Now this,' he crowed, 'is what I call a good meal!'

Wolfgang dipped a hopper into the yolk and murmured his approval to Jan. She was not listening.

'What's the matter?' he said cheerfully. 'Did your friend upset you back there?'

She did not answer at once. Her eyes followed two black armoured beetles rolling a sphere of cow dung through the dirt. One lay spreadeagled across it, front legs kneading saliva and dung.

'That's Quincey,' she said without looking up, 'and we aren't friends.'

The second beetle stood in a handstand, back legs arched to push. She was speaking to Mohan now.

'He was watching us when we got that lift on the cart,' she said. She straightened her shoulders as if to dislodge those eyes from her back. 'He knows I'm up to no good.'

Wolfgang laughed.

'Judging by appearances, it's him that's up to no good, not you,' he said. 'Isn't that right, Mohan?'

The policeman nodded gravely, his mouth full. He seemed to be concentrating on keeping his moustache clean.

'It depends on your point of view,' he said indistinctly.

48

Jan brooded over the beetles. They zigzagged together, heaving the dung over stones, between plants, under leaves and refuse; direction did not matter so long as they got there fast. She shook her head impatiently.

'Did you see his expression?' she said. 'And something else too. The Mudalali spoke to his men in Sinhala and I swear Quincey looked worried. He asked me if I understood and I said no.'

'Well?'

Wolfgang had resumed his breakfast, his fingers sticky with egg. Mohan said nothing but he was watching her.

'Because it worried Quincey, it worried me,' she said. 'So I lied.'

Both men were looking at her now. She recalled the words one by one, trying to remember them exactly.

'The Mudalali said: "Is that fish for the European master?" The man looked and said: "Yes." Then the Mudalali said: "Put it at the back. He will collect it at Moneragala." That's all.'

She looked up at the faces opposite, one a honey tan framed untidily in gold, the other a melancholy milk chocolate neatly hedged in black. She wondered suddenly if Wolfgang had a wife too, then pushed the trivial thought away. For he was puzzled, staring at her with unmatched eyes, alerted now. Slowly he turned to Mohan, waiting for his answer. They would have to tell him soon.

The policeman was hesitant. He glanced quickly at Wolfgang, then back to Jan. The furrows on his brow deepened.

'The Mudalali's no good,' he said in the tone of one who had explained it all before.

She remembered now. Pottuvil's local kingpin had made shrewd use of economic pressures, buying land from those in debt, expanding at their expense. The committees set up to enforce the rights of labourers and tenants were dominated by the very man from whom they needed protection. The cooperative scheme was the same.

'He's Quincey's man,' Mohan continued, 'and Quincey pays well for his services.'

He coughed, embarrassed. He had forgotten the relevance to himself. Jan hardly noticed. She was still watching Wolfgang. A half-eaten hopper lay forgotten on his plate. His voice was sharp with curiosity.

'In God's name, what is going on?' he said.

Mohan raised an eyebrow in Jan's direction and she nodded. So they told him. From the telegram to the hundred-rupee note to Quincey, they told him everything they knew; and more, they told him what they feared. Murder was what they meant. Jan watched Wolfgang as he listened, nodding from time to time as if everything they said was reasonable. But the growing hardness round his jaw was more than concentration. They had gained an ally. Jan felt her breath escape in relief. She had wanted him on their side. With new determination, she took up the discussion where they had left it.

'There's a co-op at Moneragala,' she said. 'And I wonder who that "European master" is.'

She thought she knew most of the foreign residents. Was it one of the old guard, like her father, or a newcomer to the island? She leaned forward suddenly. With Wolfgang's support, she felt more adventurous, reckless even.

'Can I use your motorbike, Mohan?' she asked. 'I just want to have a look. Maybe I can find out who it is.'

He did not seem particularly happy about it but that might have been due to his moustache. He would have gone with her if he'd expected any trouble, she knew that. And as for the bike, he had taught her to ride it himself.

'You'd better hurry,' he said. 'The van will have left by now.'

'Thanks,' she replied. 'I'll be back in no time.'

'We, you mean.'

Wolfgang had risen from his seat. Jan smiled at him, glad of the offer, and turned to leave. But Mohan stopped her. Eyebrows raised, he looked from one to the other as if they had forgotten something important. For a crazy moment, Jan thought he might be jealous.

'If . . . ?' he prompted.

Then she understood.

'If the great god Kataragama wills,' she obliged with a laugh as they walked out into the glare.

*

As if to deny its ordinariness, the town's name was overtly picturesque: Moneragala, 'peacock rock'. For this had once been jungle where the peacock, Kataragama's vehicle, roamed wild. Now forests had made way for men.

'Over there.'

From the boutique opposite, Jan pointed to the fish stall. A bus drew up to disgorge its passengers, adults and children stumbling out of the narrow entrance. Behind them was the van.

They watched the crates being unloaded. The driver stayed and talked. When at last he drove away, they sauntered over, escorted for the last few yards by a stomach-retching smell.

'Fresh from Pottuvil, madam.' A burly man in a blood-stained apron eyed Jan speculatively.

She was wondering if he was on Quincey's payroll too, but she nodded and looked around. An apathetic assistant was unpacking the fish, washing off ice and sawdust, removing head, tail, fins and guts, listlessly slapping them onto a blood-pink slab.

'Which do you want?' said the merchant.

Jan glanced quickly at Wolfgang then studied the fish. Several kinds of paraw: long bodies, sea-green and silver; flat broad ones tinted green and gold. A goli with humped body and fighter's mouth, its green-blue back and yellow belly more like a painting than a fish. She gestured to a row of long grey shapes.

'The seer?' she said.

'For you, madam, 4.25 a pound.'

It was a good price but her expression denied it.

'Have you nothing cheaper?' said Wolfgang.

He was clearly enjoying himself. Jan stifled a smile.

'The goli is 3.50. The dalla only 2.25.'

The merchant's hand waved over a coppery creature with green-black vertical stripes and a row of spines down its back. Jan's gaze went further and found another crate tucked into a corner.

'And these?' she said casually, lifting the lid.

Again she smelled that mixture of raw fish and something else. But no shock registered on the man's accommodating face.

'A special order,' he said, 'for Mr Andrews. He likes the best

51

and' – the hands spread expressively – 'when a man pays, we are ready to serve.'

Andrews. The name was familiar but for the moment Jan could not remember why.

'Excellent fish,' Wolfgang's voice was understanding, 'and gutted too. Your assistant is quick.'

The comment was deliberate. The man's actions seemed almost sluggish. The merchant snorted.

'The Mudalali prepares them himself!' he said.

Jan pointed to her choice. They were still waiting for change when a more important customer arrived. The merchant moved quickly past them, wiping his hands on his apron. The doorway framed a squat silhouette.

'Jan!'

She looked but saw only opacity and bulk.

'Yes?' she said, peering at where the face should have been.

Then she remembered. Teddy Andrews ran a tea estate not far from Moneragala. She had met him with Quincey once, and had disliked him on sight. He said he wanted to retire to Scotland but she had heard no more. She greeted him politely.

'I recommend the dalla,' she said. 'Only 2.25.'

'Don't ye worry about me, ma dear,' he replied expansively. 'This rascal and I are old friends, aren't we, laddie?'

As if in deference to his hosts, the outlandish burr merged into the sing-song intonation of the Sinhalese, making a mockery of both.

'Take ma feesh to the jeep,' he ordered and watched the merchant scurry away.

As he talked, his hands strayed up to pat his hair into place. Against the light, the delicate trellis trained across his pate formed four-inch arms and between them a ludicrous sunlit gap. Then he moved and the sun shone blandly on his face. Luxurious whiskers, thick black eyebrows and curling hairs on legs and arms all compensated for the absence on his skull.

His business transacted, Andrews withdrew. From behind, his belly hidden, the high waist and coltish legs gave him a youthful look. He wedged a knitted hat over the network of hair and waved.

'Well!' Wolfgang shook his head. 'Who on earth was that?'

'I've only met him once,' she said, 'but I know about him through my father. They rarely meet.'

'Your father doesn't like him?'

'They couldn't be more different.' Her tone was final.

'They've both stayed on,' Wolfgang reminded her gently.

But Jan was adamant.

'They both had the choice,' she said. 'Pull out while the going's good and you're young enough to start a new career, or stay and keep your fingers crossed. My father stayed. He loves this island and obeys her laws.'

'And Andrews?'

Jan's voice took on a hard edge.

'Andrews came for the easy life and he's determined to keep it for as long as he can. According to Dad, he works as little as possible, makes the most of his perks, and tries to think of ways to make his money multiply.'

'Legal ones?'

'Who knows?' she shrugged. 'Dad thinks he means smuggling. Gems probably. I wouldn't put it past him either.'

She caught Wolfgang's eye then and stared.

'The fish?' she said slowly.

He nodded.

'They were gutted but not topped and tailed.'

'And so many of them, too,' she said. 'He couldn't eat them all.'

They were silent, wondering. A pair of cock sparrows quarrelled overhead, the black markings on their chests standing out like the medals of Sinhalese legend. Jan's eyes followed them. Was that Quincey's game? The reason Christine died? It was hard to believe.

She saw Wolfgang watching her. He seemed to be waiting for her to decide. Should they go back, report to Mohan? Or go on to Maitland? For a moment, she hesitated. Her eyes glanced at Mohan's bike, then up the road that Andrews had taken, back to Wolfgang. He looked ready for anything, his face alight. Jan felt excitement urge her on. Why not? They had Mohan's bike. She knew the tea country well. And the exuberance of new friendship gave her a confidence she had not felt before. They might even find out what was going on.

53

'I visited Maitland some years ago,' she said at last, 'when it was run by someone else. It won't have changed much.'

They had lunch at Moneragala first, paying for it with the dalla. Then they bought a torch. As they left, the moon glowed above the stalls, oddly luminous in the afternoon sky. In the direction of Maitland, the hills were draped in cloud. Jan hoped it would not clear that night. She also hoped they were not being too stupid. Andrews might look a fool, but Quincey was dangerous. Wolfgang countered that it was better than watching others surf and she was reassured: it would do no harm to look.

Some time later, they sat on a boulder of pinkish quartz, waiting for the sun to sink. Brittle gums on a scorched ridge behind testified to patna fires. Below, Maitland was on the edge of sleep. The mottled flow of brown and green, interwoven with silver grevilleas and threaded by a tarmac band, was broken twice.

'That's the bungalow.'

'And the big building over there?'

'The factory.'

Their voices sounded odd in the dusk and they talked softly. Jan found herself telling him about Christine. Not the Christine she had seen in Colombo, gift-wrapped for the plane, but the friend she had known and loved. She told him of their escapades as schoolgirls: bicycle races on the pavements, climbing trees after kittens, teaching their classmates to play bridge for money and being hauled up before the school for gambling. So many half-forgotten episodes that meant so much. Jan smiled through the memories. Wolfgang's responses caught her mood. For a while, she listened to his tales of childhood shared with his sister. Then, as the light dimmed, they fell silent.

Night spread an intimate spell. Jan sensed a sudden need to feel his body next to hers and moved closer. He smiled, made room for her, put his arm lightly round her waist. His touch reminded her of Paul. She found herself wondering what he would do if she turned to kiss him. She could not reach his mouth unless he bent to help. She considered it for a while, thinking of the bronze body she had seen that morning, the gentle hands; then she turned to see. His mouth bent to hers.

The muscles in his arm tightened, his free hand tracing patterns by her chin. His lips were smooth. It was a long kiss, kindling desire but in no hurry, gentle and curious. Jan felt a thrill of pleasure knowingly postponed. When it was over, they sat still. Her head fitted neatly in the hollow of his neck.

Without speaking, they watched the sun melt into a cleavage in the hills. As it sank, violet tentacles reached out to break its fall, clinging to clouds and mountain tops, yielding inch by inch. Darkness swelled the hills. Still neither of them moved.

At last, Wolfgang stood up and helped her to her feet. They started down, their steps kicking up the scent of moist earth and decaying leaves. Their exuberance returned. To their right, a highland nightjar throbbed. The lack of moon was comforting. And he was still holding her hand.

The bungalow crouched against the hill. It was old now and blind in one eye, a single light shining in the night. Outside, a generator hummed; inside, behind drawn curtains, energy was devoured.

As they approached, the eye developed a cast: Andrews sat at the door. His fingers clutched a half-empty bottle of Three Coins beer.

They left him, hugged the outer wall, creeping round the house. Sitting-room. Dining-room. Study. A room they could not see into. A spare bedroom with an unused look. Beyond this, an outside corridor ran from one side of the house to the other, linking two gardens and separating an out-house from the main building: the kitchen, perhaps the servants' quarters too. Jan placed a hand on Wolfgang's elbow.

'Wait,' she whispered.

A man emerged from the out-house, bare soles echoing like suction pads. When he had gone, they crossed the lit corridor and ducked into the shadows by the kitchen wall. Round the next corner, they found a window and on the table in front of it, the fish.

Wolfgang got there first. He laid his cheek against the wall, flattened his body and reached into the light. But the kitchen door opened and his hand whipped back. A servant placed a tray on the sideboard, his back to the window. Quickly, Wolfgang seized the nearest fish and retreated.

In the shelter of the trees, they paused. Wolfgang sniffed. Beneath the smell of fish, there lurked that other smell, familiar but strange.

'That's odd,' he murmured.

She watched his fingers grope against the slippery flesh. The fish bulged and fell slack. Wolfgang's hand was empty.

'It was a lot to ask,' she said. 'He picked them up at twelve.'

But she could not keep the disappointment from her voice. Wolfgang flung the fish into the darkness. It landed with a thud.

'What next?' he said.

'Another look at Andrews?'

They worked their way back to the front. Andrews was still there, fidgeting, looking at his watch. Jan looked at hers: seven-fifteen. The bottle was empty. He seemed to be expecting someone and one hand wandered repeatedly over a bundle on his lap. He reached up to press a knob on the wall. Seconds later, the servant padded into the room, adding his silhouette to his master's. Andrews' voice drifted clearly through the night.

'Tell the tea-maker to come at once,' he ordered. 'I'll be in the study. Then you can go. I want the generator switched off at ten-thirty. Good night.'

He rose and left the room, taking the package with him. Jan led the way back to the study window. The curtains leaned inwards in the breeze. They watched.

He switched on the lamp at his desk, seated himself in front of it and opened the package. Several plastic packets lay inside. There was a knock and the door opened. A dapper Ceylonese in Western clothes walked in.

'Come along, man,' said Andrews. 'We havena got all night.'

The tea-maker was carrying what looked like a bundle of sticks. He pulled up another chair and the two men bent to their task. They took a packet each, opened it and poured white powder into hollow wooden tubes. Neither man spoke.

Jan watched, wondering what to do. They had to find out what that powder was. She stepped back, pulling Wolfgang with her.

'Can you knock over the vase in the front room – loudly?' she whispered. 'Make it look like a cat?'

Wolfgang nodded and disappeared.

Two minutes later, she heard the crash. In the study, a vicious expletive escaped. Both men leaped towards the door. A packet collapsed, spilling powder on the desk. Jan leaned over the sill but could not reach. She cursed her own short-sightedness. She should have made Wolfgang do this bit. Then, looking round wildly, she saw a lacquered walking stick against the wall, seized it, licked one end and stretched. It reached, the tip of the stick soon white. By the time the men returned, she was back in the shadows.

They stopped away from the house to examine their find. A powder pyramid on her palm. She showed it to Wolfgang, a scared expression on her face.

'Is it what I think it is?' she said quietly.

It was. Wolfgang's face made that clear.

'Expensive high-grade No. 4 heroin,' he said. 'Produced specially for the West.'

Their bubble of excitement deflated. Suddenly, it was no longer a game.

'How do you know that?'

He hesitated.

'I played with it once,' he said, 'and learned.'

Jan realized how little she knew about him. She saw his grin gleam in the darkness and hoped it would not matter.

'No gems anyway,' he pointed out.

They were silent for a while. Her hand clenched and un-clenched over the white powder. She was remembering Quin-cey by the fish van. Was this why Christine died? Not gems, but heroin. It seemed even more unbelievable. But she remem-bered Mohan's words and the hard cold look in Quincey's eyes.

'Do you know where it's from?' she said at last.

'That quality?' Wolfgang made a face to indicate an educated guess. 'The Golden Triangle, I should think.'

She remembered what she had heard. The Golden Triangle, spreading across the blurred borders of north-eastern Burma, northern Thailand and northern Laos; providing seventy per cent of the world's illicit opium; and manufacturing heroin.

'How it gets here is more difficult,' he added.

But she was thinking of Muttuvil's net. If Japanese trawlers could come in so close, so could others.

'By boat to the Mudalali,' she said. 'Then Andrews. But where does it go from here?'

They turned together to stare at the factory shining tinnily below. It was the obvious place to look: twenty-five per cent of Sri Lanka's tea was exported direct to England; much of the rest was auctioned in Colombo for export abroad. But Jan shook her head.

'It's impossible,' she said. 'For a start, you couldn't put anything in a tea chest without being seen: by the packer, the men who make the chests, the labourers who put the tea in and the tea-maker who checks each chest before it's sealed. Dad and I discussed it once.'

'The tea-maker is in on this,' Wolfgang reminded her.

'Well, even if he managed it without being seen, the weight of the chests would be wrong. And what about the spot checks at both customs and the auction rooms?'

She was convinced it would not work, but Wolfgang continued to stare at the factory pulsating below. She watched his face. There was something different about him now, a hard quality she had not noticed before. He seemed tougher, more determined, as if he too recognized that the game was over. For some reason, it made her feel more secure. She followed his gaze to the factory.

An electric light stood at each corner. Men came to the main entrance in twos and threes, knocked and were let in. A hand-held lantern drifted clockwise round the building then disappeared into an out-house behind.

'What's going on in there?'

'Not much,' she said. 'The leaf is being withered in the lighted section upstairs. Those men are the night shift: they'll sleep inside. Once the withering's done, they start work.'

'Can anyone walk in?'

Jan smiled at the hope in his voice.

'I'm afraid not,' she said. 'The supervisor checks each man and locks the door after him. The rooms not being used are padlocked – and there are bars on all the windows.'

She was about to go on but a crisp silhouette in Western clothes had broken into the light. They watched him walk towards the door.

'The tea-maker,' Jan muttered.

But Wolfgang was already weaving a downward path through the tea.

Five minutes later, two extra shadows attached themselves to the stack of firewood just beyond the light. Jan looked anxiously towards the factory. She was searching for the obligatory fire-escape from the top floor.

'There it is!' she said suddenly, pointing. 'To the left of the main door.'

There was an open window at the top.

'If we could only get over there without being seen.'

Wolfgang pointed to their left.

'The fuses,' he said. 'When I break them, we run across.'

His hand scuffled after a stone but she caught his arm.

'I'll go,' she said quickly.

'Over my dead body,' he replied, without turning round.

It was an automatic response. She shook her head, both touched and irritated. The last thing she wanted was a hefty German falling over things he didn't expect to be there.

'Look, I know my way around in there,' she said, her voice sharp with tension. 'You don't.'

He turned to look at her, surprised at her tone. She tried again, keeping her voice neutral this time.

'I'll be OK, I promise,' she said. 'I was brought up in a factory just like that. And if anything goes wrong, I'd much rather know that you're waiting out here with the bike, all ready to run.'

He hesitated, his face an appealing mixture of concern and pique. But then he saw the sense of what she said, and smiled.

'You're right,' he said, patting the hand on his arm. 'I'll get the bike. And if you need me, just yell.'

She nodded, relieved. Then she tensed herself to run.

A stone sang out against the sky and disappeared. Then a second. With the third, the glaring lights flicked off, the vociferous motors stopped and she ran. Unreal lights lingered on the retina, non-existent sounds tingled in the inner ear. In that eerie world of after-images, Jan felt her way to the corner, gripped the railing and began to climb. Her sandals made no sound. It was

59

an odd sensation, climbing in the dark, like being in a dream Then her head collided with the window frame and she bit back a cry.

Seconds later, she crouched inside, her eyes straining. Ahead the leaf hoist menaced like an empty gallows; the withering room beyond. She listened. Someone was shambling around in there, stumbling into machines, swearing. Another voice sympathized. They were speaking Tamil.

She shrank back against the sill. There was a click and a ray of light shot out. It picked out the leaf hoist, sneaked behind it and reappeared, hovering above a hole in the floor. The two men descended. In the glow of torchlight, they looked like goblins dancing on a shifting earth.

The clattering ceased. Jan listened in dismay. The two voices had been joined by a swarm of others: the labourers were awake

She tiptoed to the staircase and listened again. Two loud voices found a third; the tea-maker's, she was sure. A three-part disharmony against a choral hum of speculation. He produced his keys and the three men rattled and clinked their way through two sets of doors into the engine room. Sounds were fainter for a while. Finally, both clinking and voices returned and drifted outside, leaving an audible vacuum below.

She started down. The sound of breathing was broken by an occasional grunt as someone turned in his sleep. In the shelter of the stairs, she paused. Several humps rose against pale cement in between, empty blankets lay like skins sloughed off in haste. With exaggerated care, she tiptoed past.

On the other side of the room, hidden by a monster dryer, she looked around. She was suddenly confused. Where was the weighing machine, the ready-sliced plywood for packaging tea Had Andrews moved that section somewhere else? Could that be part of Quincey's plan too?

Where the line of storage bins had been, a blank wall was broken by a door. It was open, a padlock with a key in it hanging from the handle. Was this where the tea-maker had been when the lights had failed? Before entering, she looked outside Surrounded by blanketed labourers, in a ring of kerosene lamps by the broken fuse, the tea-maker shouted orders to a man on a ladder, like two scarecrows gesticulating to a flock of crows. She closed the door behind her and switched on the torch. Shadows danced.

It was a narrow room, built as an afterthought. A series of padlocked bins formed one wall. Sealed chests opposite. The work bench in between littered with the debris of the packer's craft: plywood rectangles for the sides of a chest, squares for top and bottom; wooden battens to join and strengthen; plain and scalloped lengths of aluminium foil; tissue paper to protect the tea; nails, rivets, staples. She wondered where to start.

A pile of battens newly wrapped in tissue caught her eye. She picked one up, unwound its paper shield, then frowned. Most battens were made of albizia but this was sapu. Why?

Jittery shadows obscured her view. She put the torch on the counter and held the batten in its beam. One end came loose in her fingers, a deep hole drilled inside. That explained it: albizia would have snapped.

She tipped it over her hand. White powder again. Each batten was the same: hollowed out and filled with heroin.

She replaced them, breathing heavily, then raked the bench with the torch beam. She was looking for something. All tea chests had short battens; only those going abroad needed the long ones down each side. She found them; solid albizia this time. England, then.

A movement behind her made her jump. As she whirled round, the torchbeam caught the surprised face of the foreman, the rest of his body still hidden by the door.

'Who is that?' he said in Tamil. His voice was rough.

She froze. The man moved into the room, putting up a hand to shield his face from the glare. Stunned, Jan followed him with the torch.

'Who is it?' he said again, uncertain now.

Then she panicked. Seizing the metal container of nails, she flung it in his face. The corner tore a jagged line across his cheek. He staggered back, his hands daubing at the bloody gash. She pushed him hard. His feet slipped on the rolling nails and he fell. Jan fled, heading stupidly for the main door, wrestling with the lock. She could hear him stumbling in the darkened room, calling out angrily for aid. Several sleeping forms stirred. Some sat up.

She remembered the fire escape then and ran, cursing her disabling fear. As she raced to the top of the stairs, she felt them shake. Footsteps clattered up the metal rungs behind her, guttural voices urged each other on. Terrified now, she found the window. She saw the men gathered in the circle of light outside, heard the pursuit behind, and plunged recklessly over the sill. It was a noisy descent but she was past caring about details now. She was praying Wolfgang was there.

She hit the gravel too hard. Her foot slipped, one knee grazed against the bottom rung. She swore, picked herself up and ran on.

'Wolfgang!' she yelled.

She was still running, still calling Wolfgang's name, when she heard the bike. Swooping out of the dark, it carved a bold half circle in front of her pursuers, knocking down the two leaders and barely missing three more. The rest faltered, taken by surprise. Quickly, Jan scrambled on behind him and he accelerated showily away. She did not look back.

Only then, with her arms tightly round his waist, her cheek against that solid reassuring back, did she realize what had happened. She breathed deeply, murmured Wolfgang's name some more as if for reassurance, eyes tight shut. She was shaking.

By the time they reached Pottuvil, it was well past midnight. Mohan was waiting on his verandah. When he saw them coming, he clasped his hands together and raised them to the sky. Then he hurried to meet them.

'What happened?'

He was anxious, his eyes fixed on Jan's exhausted face. She was moved by his concern and reached out a hand to reassure him. In the light from the verandah, she could see he was excited about something too. He was about to speak but her hand pressed against his chest to keep him still.

'Could we eat first?' she said.

Mohan gestured to the chairs on the verandah and disappeared. He returned with a bottle of arrack, three glasses, two plates of string hoppers and prawns, and a bowl of buffalo curd.

'Short bites,' he said.

They were too hungry to be polite. At first, Mohan stood but
the tension became too much for him and he sat down. The
rattan chair creaked with impatience. At last, unable to contain
himself, he spoke.

'Much has happened since you left,' he said, stroking his
moustache. 'Lucky I was here.'

Pride throbbed in his voice and his brown eyes glowed. Jan
watched him with affection. Even his moustache seemed to
tremble with excitement. She swallowed her mouthful and
smiled to show she was listening.

'Three new developments,' he said, flexing his fingers so that
the joints cracked. 'First, something is up tomorrow night. I
delivered the message myself.'

He waited, clearly expecting a response. Jan obliged.

'What message?'

Mohan took his time. He wanted to be sure they appreciated
his contribution.

'There's no phone in Quincey's bungalow,' he said, 'so he
uses ours. The message came this afternoon.'

He paused to be sure of his effect.

'The ranger at Okanda invited him to dinner tomorrow
night.'

He looked expectantly from face to face as if he had told a
riddle and was waiting for someone to supply the obvious wrong
answer. Wolfgang fell into the trap.

'Doesn't sound suspicious to me,' he said. He was still more
interested in the food.

'Ah,' Mohan sighed with satisfaction, 'but then you missed
the second development, too. You weren't on the beach this
evening at nine o'clock.'

'Boats?' Jan leaned forward abruptly. 'Is that what you saw?'

The staccato questions startled him. He paused to draw back
the satisfied air she had destroyed. She almost apologized.

'I would have been conspicuous at Muhammad's without my
bike,' he explained, 'so I went for a walk. I went down to the
beach and walked to Ulle – it wasn't as far as I'd thought.'

The uncharacteristic exercise made Jan smile but Mohan
was unperturbed. He must have known she would take him
seriously soon.

63

'When I got to the co-op, I was tired and sat down. I wa
invisible sitting there in the shadow of that boat but I didn
think of it then. I was watching the waves, trying to see how fa
back the moon made the edges white. Then I saw them.'

He knew they were listening now but he waited a bit longer
make sure. Their eager faces gratified him immensely.

'Yes?' said Wolfgang.

Mohan sent a nod in Jan's direction.

'Boats,' he said. 'They had no hurricane lamps – or if the
had, they weren't lit – and that made me curious.'

'This isn't the season for night fishing,' Jan cut in.

Mohan bent his head in acknowledgement.

'Just what I thought,' he said, 'so I watched.'

He took a deliberately refined sip of arrack, licked his li
with an actor's appreciation and used the tip of his smalle
finger to rescue his moustache from his mouth.

'Four boats,' he said, 'and no fish. Crates, lots of them a
heavy too – I could hear the men panting as they carried the
up the beach to the co-op. And the last load was a man.'

Mohan could not have hoped for better effect. Jan understo
his excitement now. The tale puzzled her but she kept quie
trying to piece it together with what she knew.

'I sneaked after them,' he was saying. 'In the courtyard, thr
bullock carts were being loaded with crates. Then an argume
broke out. The man's head was bandaged: it seems he was bad
hurt and had to go north to the hospital. But the crates we
going south, to Okanda.'

There was a definite gleam in the policeman's eye as he sa
the name.

'Someone said there'd be trouble from Quincey if he died, s
with a lot of swearing and panting, the loads were redistribute
A few minutes later, two carts apparently carrying straw turn
left towards Okanda; one turned right to Pottuvil; and everyo
disappeared. The Mudalali blew out the lamp and went insic
From start to finish, it took less than fifteen minutes!'

Mohan was impressed. This was his first brush with orga
ized crime and its efficiency amazed him. His admirati
almost made Jan smile. Then he remembered the thread of
story and concluded on a rising note.

'The crates went to Okanda, the ranger lives there, and Quincey joins him tomorrow night. It must be important.'

His friends were silent, digesting his news. A lever clicked in Jan's mind and a connection she had not been looking for came clear. Okanda was the point of entry into Yala. Quincey had taken Christine there before she died. Now with painful clarity, Jan recalled her last smudged words: '. . . reserve . . . terrible . . . soon . . .'. She had thought it was a verb. Now it made sense: Yala game reserve.

Mohan misunderstood. He head shook in commiseration.

'I'm sorry you had no luck,' he said. 'A wild goose chase is never fun.'

'Oh, but we were both right,' Jan replied. 'I just can't see the connection, that's all.'

They told him what they had found. Mohan's face mirrored his thoughts: surprise, excitement and crestfallen dismay; their story was as thrilling as his own. With a shock, Jan realized that he was jealous after all, jealous of Wolfgang and the success that he and Jan had shared. She said nothing. They had enough problems already.

'It seems simple enough to me,' Mohan said at last. 'The heroin comes from the Golden Triangle or somewhere up there' – his hand waved vaguely – 'by boat to Ulle. The Mudalali puts it in the fish. From the co-op to the fish stall, from the fish stall to Maitland, from Maitland via the tea to London. Simple! And all master-minded by Quincey!'

Jan disagreed.

'Two cartloads is a hell of a lot of heroin,' she said. 'And why take it to Okanda? That's twenty miles in the wrong direction; forty unnecessary miles.'

'Perhaps they're storing it,' suggested Wolfgang. 'Andrews would look a bit silly collecting a ton and a half of fresh fish.'

'Okanda's a good hiding place,' Mohan agreed. 'Not many people round there.'

She allowed herself to be persuaded. The truth was, she was too tired to worry any more. They moved the chairs aside and Mohan laid mats on the floor. She noticed that he put hers at the opposite end of the verandah from Wolfgang's, his own halfway between. Was he protecting her from Wolfgang, or from herself?

65

She could not tell. Wolfgang caught her eye with a smile but she let it pass. Too much had happened too quickly in the last few days. Now fatigue had jumbled it all together in her mind. She needed time to sort everything out; above all, she needed sleep. But as Mohan leaned forward to blow out the lamp, she remembered something.

'You said three developments, Mohan. You've only given us two.'

The drowsy atmosphere prickled awake. Mohan hesitated. In the lamplight, Jan could read the flickering emotions on his face: doubt, a touch of embarrassment, and distress. His troubled voice projected over her head.

'When I took Quincey that message, he asked me where you'd gone. After that hundred rupees, he thinks . . .'

The policeman stopped and started again.

'I told him I didn't know. He said he'd seen you on my bike and wagged his finger at me in a knowing way. He scared me. It's as if . . . as if he's having a joke at our expense, and knows he'll get the last laugh.'

He paused and the heavy night rushed in to fill the gap. A soft-skinned gecko scuttled down the wall to glare at the moths round the lamp. It waited on flattened toes until frustration swelled and spoke: the voice of gods, an omen good or bad. Mohan shuddered. There was a whoosh of expelled air. The lamp flared and died.

'Be careful, Jan,' he whispered. 'Quincey is evil – and he knows we're onto him. I don't know how but he knows.'

It was some time before she slept. In her dream she was visited by a doll-like Christine whose casket turned into a chest of powdery white tea; and Quincey climbed in and brewed himself a cup and sipped and laughed.

PART THREE

18th August 1975:

the east coast (2)

When they woke next morning, Mohan had gone. Jan returned
to Ulle with Wolfgang. Later, they would check out the hospital, and Okanda. When they had found out all they could, when
she was sure there was no mistake, she would go to Bob
Saunders at the British High Commission. But first she needed
a swim.

They sat in the shallows, luxuriated in the heat, the abrasive
texture of sand, the caress of waves tipped with foam. Behind
them, fishermen chanted and stomped, hauling in a net whose
horseshoe arms stretched a quarter of a mile. Jan's eyes kept
returning to Wolfgang. The sun had turned his hair a gleaming
gold. Below, taut skin glistened wet, drying in the heat to streaks
of salt. She was surprised by their closeness, tentative in her
pursuit of it. For she knew more urgent things came first. But
she realized he felt the same, and was pleased.

'What made you think of taking heroin?' she said at last.

She was gazing inattentively at the fish that chewed her toes
and the froth of bubbles hung about her waist. Below that
jewelled chain, her limbs were green and cool; above, the skin
began to burn. The salt made her grazed knee smart. She looked
up and found Wolfgang's eyes on her body. He smiled un-
abashed.

'I wanted more than acid could show me,' he answered
lightly. 'Trees walking, people melting before my eyes, multi-
coloured elephants bursting out of walls to say hello.'

She laughed. Her experiments had gone no further than the
ganja she had smoked with Mohan, but she thought she understood.

'Any luck?' she said.

He shook his head.

'Not really, but nice all the same. Drifting off into the void like an island that has cut its roots. But God didn't speak to me, which was sad.'

His smiling face was close to hers and she had a sudden impulse to kiss him again. She spoke instead.

'Why did you stop?'

His smile vanished and he looked away. The sun bounced off tiny pupils, leaving sharp white flecks that glittered.

'Someone died,' he said. His voice was hard, sorrow poignant beneath.

Silence separated them. She wished she hadn't asked. She wanted to touch him, to restore the connection she knew they both felt, but she did not move. She had remembered her dream of Quincey. Her eyes drifted to a silver web hung from a coconut frond overhead. She watched the spider moving clockwise, hooking damp strands into place. But she was thinking about Quincey, and the heroin.

'Is it feasible – what we've found?' she said, almost to herself.

Only a week ago, she had been reading up on drug smuggling, for she had already acquired something of the journalist's magpie mind, filing away stories in her head, never knowing when they might turn out to be of use. But this story was complicated. Arrests included students, a Mexican general, Third World diplomats on missions abroad, even the Laotian ambassador-designate to France. An Australian ring flying from Sydney to London via Hongkong. Consignments shipped to Buenos Aires then smuggled over successive South American borders to the States. Filipinos shuttling from Bangkok to the West. The details proved the magnitude of the heroin iceberg: smashed in one place, it soon broke surface somewhere else.

'I don't see why not,' Wolfgang replied. The hardness had reached his face. It gave him a sculpted quality.

Now that the Suez was open, Sri Lanka was even more likely to link Hongkong to England or the States.

'The profits are vast,' Jan added, recalling what she had read.

Ten kilos of opium worth $500 became one kilo of heroin worth $30,000 in the West. Diluted for sale at $5 a shot, that same kilo fetched $225,000. Quincey would be the vital middle man.

'But who do you think's behind it?'

'As far as I know, there are three main syndicates now,' Wolfgang replied. 'The Corsicans who started in Marseilles and have now taken over Saigon; the Sicilian-American mafia dotted about the Asian capitals; and the Triads, various Chinese secret societies controlling most of Hongkong, Bangkok and parts of Saigon.'

'Any idea which it might be this time?'

'None at all.'

But Jan was thinking of the Chinese restaurants and hotels in every major town; Chinese 'Dental Mechanics' with grisly pink-gummed signs; close-knit communities all over the island. Was there any connection? And could Quincey, a Sinhalese, be involved? It seemed pretty far-fetched.

'Quincey's a politician,' she said, 'not a gangster.'

Wolfgang looked depressed.

'The drug trade couldn't survive without the authorities,' he replied.

Jan knew he was right. The most important drug organization in Thailand was the police force. In Laos, the government tolerated all smuggling – gold, guns and opium – while their own refineries produced morphine base and heroin. In Vietnam, the navy took care of the smuggling, the army of the distribution, and the political leaders of the overall control.

'They all want money,' he explained, 'and Quincey's the same.'

Jan wondered what the High Commission would do when she told them, whether anything could be done. For if one country stopped producing opium, another took over. When one method of transportation was blocked, another began.

She sighed. Heroin addiction in the West marked the return of the karmic boomerang. European merchants had introduced opium to the East in the sixteenth century. In the seventeenth, the British East India Company imported Bengali opium into China, becoming the first major narcotics dealers. By the nineteenth, every European colony had its official opium den. Perhaps, Jan reasoned sadly, it was only fair that Asian heroin now undermined the West. The boomerang had returned; the karmic debt was being repaid.

'GOVERNMENT RURAL HOSPITAL': the board hung askew, its hand-printed legend liberally splashed with droppings. A house crow perched on top, slighter than its black cousin, with a smaller beak, glossier wings and a distinctive smoke-grey neck. As they approached, it flew off cawing indignation.

Jan and Wolfgang were escorted by Mohan's nephew. Neemal was well mannered, shy and eager to please, one of those endearing young men to be found all over the island, always anxious to find a foreigner on whom to practise their English. Mohan had instructed him to give them a thorough tour; they even wanted to talk to patients in the wards. Neemal had been overjoyed.

Jan was glad he was there. It made her feel less conspicuous, less of a callous tourist. For two hundred people milled over the hospital steps. A woman with a drawn face clutched a scrap of paper in one hand, a fractious child in the other, the baby's head adorned with open boils. Grubby bandages decorated an ankle here, a calf there, a knee or finger over there. Some limped, leaning on friends. Others squatted on turned-out feet, rocking to and fro. Others merely sat not caring, staring while the crowd ebbed and flowed from door to door.

She hesitated, waiting for Wolfgang to join them. He was watching children playing with ant-lions outside, dropping sand into conical pits. The game clearly amused him. A surge of affection made Jan smile. His face could look so young. Beside him, a scruffy child picked three yellow flowers; carefully, as if they were precious gems, she placed one in her hair, two like toe-rings on her feet. Regretfully, Jan turned to the hospital.

'Are there always so many people?' she asked Neemal.

'Oh yes,' he said brightly. 'If there is sickness, more people come.'

His grammar was fine but like so many of the new generation he had not mastered the acoustic differences between Sinhala and English. He missed the subtle rhythms and intonation, and

70

assumed that each syllable should be heard. The result was delightful.

'The nearest hospital is twenty miles to the west,' he was saying. 'To the north, thirty miles. To the south, there is nothing this side of Yala.'

No wonder, she agreed, that Pottuvil astride the east coast junction was overwhelmed. It also meant that the injured man had to be there. Jan was anxious to find him: he might be persuaded to talk. But she was wary of seeming in too much of a hurry. She looked around nervously. Any one of these people might work for Quincey.

Inside, others pushed and jostled, leaning their weight against those in front, arms reaching over intervening shoulders, an unthinking mass trying regardless of probabilities to do the same thing at the same time.

'Out-patients,' Neemal explained. 'They must register their names with the clerk.'

He pointed an elegant brown finger but the clerk was hidden by a stabbing cloud of arms.

'For twenty-five cents, they get a piece of paper with a stamp on it,' he said. 'Then they go to the doctor over there.'

But the doorway he indicated was obscured. Jan was reminded of her GP at home, the comforts of his surgery. She found the comparison both encouraging and sad.

'And if you have to be admitted?' Wolfgang asked.

Neemal led the way to the wards, telling them what he knew. Like most Ceylonese, his faith in doctors was absolute. Jan remembered the uproar a year earlier when Britain ruled that Ceylonese doctors would need further training before they could practise in England. But nurses merited no such pride: to obtain undiluted medicines or the use of a bed-pan, Neemal confided, patients had to resort to bribery. Jan did her best to look interested. She was wondering how to approach the injured man. She glanced at Wolfgang, needing his support.

The first building housed two six-bed wards. The side walls stopped at waist height, rounded off and crumbling at the edges; the end ones enclosed office rooms and supported a thatched roof. Sparrows looped in with the breeze.

Neemal started with the women's section. A shrivelled old

lady lay in one corner, face and knees to the wall. A girl stared at the ceiling, her crumpled forehead anticipating the next abdominal cramp beneath her hands. Three women gossiped as they might at home, while the patient in the nearest bed enjoyed the sympathy of friends. Neemal introduced them to each one. Not until they had traced each family tree complete with details of residence and occupation were they able to withdraw.

They entered the men's ward. Jan felt her palms grow damp. All six beds were full. Three had dysentery. Another sweated from an unknown fever. The fifth had cut his leg chopping wood. The last nursed a septic hand. But not one had a bandaged head. Wolfgang looked tense. He turned to Neemal.

'What if a seventh man comes in?' he asked.

'They put mats out there.'

Neemal pointed to a verandah running alongside the two wards. An old man crouched there, hugging the wall as if in pain.

'If it rains, they go on the floor in here,' he added. 'But that is not common: in our country, men are not sick as much as women.'

'There is another man,' said a voice. It belonged to a middle-aged patient with a pockmarked face and a nose flattened many years ago. 'He came in last night. The doctor said he was too sick to lie out there so he went in the big ward.'

Jan's apprehension increased. That would be the third ward, also for women. She wanted to go there at once but forced herself to stay and talk.

'And the old man on the verandah?' she said. 'Why doesn't he have a mat?'

'The Sinhalese?' answered the man with the pugilist's face. 'His sickness is of the heart not the body. His wife died this morning giving birth. His karma is bad.'

Jan gazed with pity at the hunched figure. The life of the coastal villager was tough. She spoke to him in Sinhala, a soothing formula for comfort, but he did not seem to hear.

She turned to leave, then stopped. Quincey barred their path. A pair of white shorts above long socks, and in the opening of his shirt the gold chain glistening with sweat. He was looking at her oddly, his fixed expression suggesting he was puzzling something out. With a shock, Jan realized what it was. She had said she did not know Sinhala. Had he heard her talking to the old man?

'Hallo,' Wolfgang said.

He was prompting her. But it took Jan a moment to pick up her cue. She managed it at last.

'Hallo,' she said weakly. 'May I introduce my friend, Wolfgang. From Heidelberg. Neemal is kindly showing us round.'

Quincey's face relaxed into a rubbery grin as he looked Wolfgang up and down. But his eyes looked through the jovial mask unchanged.

'Yes, I do believe I've seen you around,' he said. 'Though if you don't mind my saying so, some of you hippies are damned difficult to tell apart.'

Wolfgang did not smile. 'It's mutual, I suppose,' he said.

Quincey roared with laughter, one hand sending a hefty slap across the German's shoulders. Wolfgang flinched. Jan wished they could leave: that violence had not been entirely unintentional. And the laughter had not reached his eyes. But Quincey was still talking.

'Now don't you believe everything this young whippersnapper tells you,' he was saying. 'This hospital may be all right for superstitious villagers but an educated chap wouldn't put up with it.'

Wolfgang moved out of his reach and nodded. His face was flushed with anger, his lips pressed tight. She prayed he would not do anything rash. She had to get him away. But Quincey had not finished. He turned to Jan. The full impact of those eyes was astounding. She just managed to stop herself stepping back. She tried to act normally.

'You know Jeff Baker?' he said. 'He collapsed in the heat once and was brought in here. But the bed was too short and he kept hitting his ankle on the railing. When the skin broke, someone put a second-hand dressing on and the next minute the poor chap had gangrene. Didn't think it was his karma at all!'

Quincey's large frame quivered at the memory. Jan tried to smile. It was a good story and she did not doubt its veracity, but Quincey frightened her. Beneath the laughter, those eyes were cold. She wished she knew what he was thinking.

'You make me glad I'm fit and well,' she exclaimed too loudly.

'You mark my words,' he replied. 'Keep clear of this hospital if you value your health!'

He laughed as if the ominous words were arbitrary, the meaningful tone unintentional or a joke. Jan was unnerved. Was Quincey threatening her? She glanced at Neemal: he was subdued but had not tuned in to any threat. She dared not look at Wolfgang.

'Well, I won't keep you,' Quincey said. 'In fact, since you're ready to leave, I'll escort you out.'

Again she heard that tone, saw the close look in his eye. Was she imagining it? Quincey had moved to one side and was waiting, clearly expecting them to submit. He was used to getting his own way. Jan felt her resistance disintegrate.

Wolfgang came to her rescue.

'We'll go when we're ready,' he said.

The deliberate rudeness made Jan start. Without thinking, she put her hand on his arm to caution him. Quincey's eyes followed her: he knew she was afraid.

'They haven't seen the other ward,' Neemal insisted bravely.

The boy sounded anxious to avoid trouble, but his words filled Jan with dismay. Appalled, she waited for Quincey's response. Wolfgang cut in first.

'Come on then,' he said pointedly to Neemal. 'We may as well see everything while we're here.' Jan was slow to respond; his arm coaxed her away. 'Perhaps we'll see you later,' he added over his shoulder to Quincey; it was intended as a taunt.

The politician inclined his head gravely, his face set. Jan could see he meant it. She was wishing Wolfgang hadn't been so rude. Quincey was bound to suspect something now. Again, she felt those eyes on her back. Her hands were trembling.

As they walked towards the third ward, she tried to calm herself. Neemal was repairing the damaged image of his country's doctors. He described to Wolfgang how an American surgeon demonstrating a gall-bladder operation once gave up halfway declaring the patient too far gone to survive; in true Hollywood fashion, a Ceylonese took over and the man re-covered. Jan found herself growing stronger as she listened; she much preferred his story to Quincey's.

The third ward was larger but much the same: a row of iron bedsteads down each wall; thin coir mattresses and off-white sheets; low walls to let the breeze in; the same white-washed barrenness. There were four patients, two asleep, their bodies rising and falling in drowsy rhythm. The third stared unblinking. The fourth was a girl who smiled shyly, her eyes flickering to a bundle at her side, a baby with a rumbled face. Jan's answering smile was cut short by Wolfgang.

'The man must be over there,' he said, pointing. 'Behind that screen.'

She looked across the ward. On the walls, foot-high numbers untidily daubed in red dripped streamers to the floor. A screen obscured the number 10. Jan hesitated.

'Do you think we can see him?'

But she had already started walking. When she reached the screen, she paused. She had heard something: a breathy sigh and a scraping sound, perhaps a foot shifting against the end of the bed. Was the man in pain? She felt ashamed and called out softly in Tamil for permission to enter. There was no answer; not a whisper nor the rustle of bedclothes. She called again.

'Perhaps he's sleeping,' Neemal suggested.

She poked her head round the screen to look, gasped and stepped back onto Wolfgang's foot. She did not bother to apologize.

The man was dead. Beneath a blood-soaked bandage wound like a batik turban round his head, his eyes stared. They were too late. As Jan stared back, ghostly fingers palpated her spine and she shivered.

Wolfgang found her a chair out of sight of those eyes and she sank into it, holding on to him for strength. Neemal went to fetch the doctor.

Jan breathed deeply. She was aware of the other patients watching her from the far end of the ward, wondering what was going on. She wanted to leave but kept thinking of that sigh. Her skin prickled with fear.

'Did you hear something?' Wolfgang's voice was soft. 'Just before you went in?'

She looked up at him, a shocked expression on her face. So he had heard it too. She nodded. Then she realized he was loosening his fingers from her grasp.

'Where are you going?'

'To have another look.'

His tone was reassuring but his eyes were not. She could not let him take his hand away. So she went with him instead.

The man's eyes were scared. Had something frightened him before he died? A superstitious fear of hell to come as the pundits had described? The karma to be reaped the next time round? Or something tangible? She edged closer. Death had not come easily.

Suspicion took root and grew. Her eyes dropped to the wall behind the bed. Scratches marked the whitewash. Wolfgang followed her gaze, stooped and found a heap of red and white dust below. Something had scraped past, chipping it in haste. A careless shoe as someone leaped over the dividing wall? They looked at each other. Wolfgang's face was blank. Had Quincey got there first?

A noise made them turn. It was the doctor, a well-meaning worried man, and Quincey. Neemal followed behind. As the doctor felt for a pulse, two pairs of eyes met across his back: Quincey's shone a black challenge; in Jan's, fear and shock were undisguised.

The official filing away of a human life began. She listened to the cold details that defined a man and felt the hollowness of death.

'Profession – fisherman,' the doctor intoned as he filled in the form. 'Nationality – Sri Lanka citizen; place of birth – Hongkong.'

She glanced up startled. Hongkong? She looked at the dead man again. Now his eyes were closed, the oriental features were obvious. She stared, remembering her conversation with Wolfgang: boats bringing heroin from Hongkong; and the Triads.

She felt weak. The Triads were more than a mafia. Originally from southern China, they had fled from Communism to Hongkong as the Huk Sai Wui societies, the Black Associations. Soon they monopolized the heroin trade: they provided the raw materials, the specialists required for the opium-morphine-heroin, transition, and the necessary organizational skills. By the early seventies, they constituted a vast monolithic syndicate feeding the pipeline to the West.

But, as Wolfgang had explained, while other Triads dealt largely with 'brown sugar' – No. 3 smoking heroin – only the Chu Chow concentrated on No. 4, ninety-eight per cent pure. They were also far more difficult to trace. When there was a crackdown on police corruption in Hong Kong in '73, all the Triads had been forced to look elsewhere. Jan had read about the move to Malaysia, the recruiting drive in Macao, the infiltration of Amsterdam by the 14K, even the fears for Britain at the hands of both the 14K and the growing Wo Shing Wo. Had the Chu Chow opted for Sri Lanka? And if so, where exactly did Quincey fit in?

As they turned to leave, he was watching. His eyes were still hard but the challenge had been replaced by a question. She hoped he could not read the answer in her own.

Outside, a scrawny grey-necked crow raised its hackles, jerked its tail and croaked a gin-sodden caw. Jan tried not to run.

Evening shadows lengthened as the sun lowered itself on to the Uva hills. A soft lilac spread from the clouds into the lagoon. A flock of parakeets flew north. Low-slung pond herons, one last black-faced tern, a cormorant or two: each in turn dematerialized into the dark. The sea's blue turned black. For some, the day had ended; for others, the night began.

South of the lagoon, in Ulle, Jan and Wolfgang crouched in the back of the Mudalali's van. The smell of fish was intolerable. She hoped the plan was worth it, prayed it would work.

North of the lagoon, in Arugam Bay, Quincey climbed into his landrover and started the ignition. The vehicle spluttered, shambled down the drive and turned south. Red eyes gleamed on the road, nightjars unfolding out of his path. Tarmac sneaked away from the headlights' pursuit: it would run for ten miles, then at Panama yield to a dusty track. But he had to pass through Ulle first.

Mohan was ready for him. Ten rupees had persuaded Baby Singho to disable two bullock carts in the middle of the road.

Now he and his sons, well lit by kerosene lamps, shouted obscenities at each other across the debris. In the back of the van, Jan was listening. She nudged Wolfgang. So far, so good. The next move was up to Quincey. And Mohan.

They could hear the landrover approaching fast. A dog ran barking into the road, a self-appointed sentinel no one needed. Quincey's horn blared angrily. Jan tensed. For a moment, she thought he was going to plough right through the mess. But the landrover slowed down. Even Quincey had to stop for this.

He poked his head out of the window and yelled. He was in a hurry, his temper tight. The engine was still running. Baby Singho responded with the servile alacrity demanded of their respective positions, but without much effect. His shouts increased in volume, each order contradicting the last so that the two carts jerked first this way, then that, never budging from the centre of the road.

Quincey exploded. He switched off the engine, leaped out and slammed the door behind him. His commanding figure outlined in the headlights, he directed the operation himself. Baby Singho and his sons scurried to obey.

No one noticed Mohan leave the shadows of the co-op wall. They were too busy enjoying the drama on the road. He was carrying a newspaper curved into a large funnel: the funnel was filled with sand. Stepping quickly past the landrover's rear lights to the driver's side, he lifted the flap over the petrol cap, unscrewed the lid and emptied the funnel inside. There had to be enough sand to settle on the bottom of the tank and block the filter. Then he returned to the shadows.

As he passed the van, he tapped on the back window. Wolfgang pressed his hand against the pane in reply: it was their turn now. Her face pale in the darkness, Jan turned towards him. He placed a finger on her lips to keep her still, then kissed them. He was listening hard.

Outside, Quincey had cleared the road. Still flinging curses at Baby Singho, he returned to the landrover. He switched on the ignition, put the vehicle in gear. But he was forced to wait, revving the engine impatiently as Baby Singho darted across the road to retrieve his lamp. At last, he let the clutch out.

Jan could feel Wolfgang's body beside her rigid with excitement. He was listening intently. Had Quincey's impatience already used up the petrol in the pipe? How much more would draw through that filter? Enough to cover a mile or two, or none at all? Unable to see, they listened as the landrover pulled away. It travelled thirty or forty yards at high speed, then began to cough. Wolfgang's head nodded at the tell-tale sound. The vehicle jerked a few times, then rolled to a halt. The filter was blocked.

They waited, listened to the repeated rasp of the ignition, the repeated whine as the engine failed to catch. Quincey would be checking his petrol gauge now. Would he suspect anything? And how long before he finally gave up?

Not long. Hurling imprecations at the sky, he looked back and saw the van. That was all it took. Seconds later, a surprised Mudalali handed over his keys: Quincey had commandeered his van.

Wolfgang squeezed Jan's hand. Suspense was making his fingers shake. But his plan had worked. Unaware of his passengers in the back, Quincey would lead them to the crates. The last few pieces of the jigsaw would soon fall into place.

But Jan still wished she hadn't come. With a sinking heart, she watched the darkness unroll behind. It was all Wolfgang's idea. After that last brush with Quincey, she had had enough. God knows, she was petrified of the man. She wanted to go straight to Colombo, to the British High Commission. Mohan had agreed: it was foolhardy to go on alone. But Wolfgang had persuaded them. To catch a man like Quincey, he insisted, they needed proof; what better than a plastic packet from the stock at Okanda? That, plus the exact knowledge of their hiding place, would clinch the whole affair. Saunders could do the rest.

Jan remembered the intensity with which Wolfgang had put forward his plan. His face had been flushed with excitement and resolve. The heroin had angered him; the incident in the hospital had made him determined to find the truth. He was an obstinate man, she could see that now, and he was developing a bitter hatred for Quincey. It was obvious he would not give in. Of course, he had been prepared to go alone. Mohan had even suggested it; he was on duty so couldn't go himself. But Jan could not let him take that risk. Tenacity apart, Wolfgang understood neither local language, nor did he know the area as she did. Two summers' worth of swimming was not enough. It would have been crazy to let him go alone. She wished she could have persuaded him not to go at all.

The blackness outside was broken only by the gleam of an animal eye, the brief spark of a beedi, the hysterical call of the koel as it wound itself up the scale and paused as if uncertain how to stop. But she knew where they were. The road sliced through marshy ground, through forest so dense that few cared to enter after dark, over a makeshift causeway, past an abandoned tank. To the left, Pankandahela rock and a cluster of ruins. The Ragamweli tank over there, its thousand-year-old bund still intact. A path drifting off to the right. Another abandoned tank, another causeway, yet another, then the lights of Panama. She mouthed the name to Wolfgang. He nodded. Ten miles gone: another ten before Okanda.

The tarmac gulped and died. By a whitewashed dagoba, the van swung right onto a raised track winding between paddy fields. Dust swirled up against the windows. Quincey must have been regretting his landrover: he had to manoeuvre each bump and dip. Jan prayed he would make no mistake. An accident this side of Panama meant a night in the open waiting for the first bullock cart from Kumana, and their almost certain discovery.

They entered the ancient kingdom of Ruhunu. To the left, thick jungle reared to hide the sea, to the right extended for miles inland; and in their midst the remains of palaces, dagobas, paddy fields and homes. When the Tamils invaded from India, the Sinhalese took refuge here: Ruhunu lasted over two thousand years, all of them BC, and then was swallowed by the jungle. Jan had trekked through there looking for ruined statues, lop-sided pillars, meditation caves. She had no desire to test her nerves out there at night.

She remembered Mohan's parting words: Take care, he had said, for those are the jungles of Kataragama. In his holy city the other side of the national park, Kataragama was worshipped by Tamils as the son of Shiva; by forest tribes as the god of hunting; by Buddhists as their god of war; even by Muslims. In the height of the drought, at the Esala full moon, pilgrims came from all over the island and beyond to make terrible vows to this most dreaded deity.

It was not surprising she was infected by Mohan's fears. Which other god expected his devotees to skewer their cheeks and limbs with metal shafts, pierce their tongues, attach ropes with heavy weights to fish-hooks in their backs and suspend themselves like butchered meat? Who else asked them to walk on live coals, lie on beds of sharpened nails, or roll in screaming zeal through the dust to his shrine? Death in the service of Kataragama meant life everlasting. Conversely, the life of anyone who passed through his domain without obeisance was at risk. Instinctively, Jan muttered her request: that Kataragama keep them safe that night.

The van braked. She saw the edge of a verandah decorated with the mementoes of a ranger's life: antlers and buffalo horns; sun-bleached skulls, some forward-pointing like crocodiles, others grotesquely elephantine. Okanda. They had arrived.

Quincey called out and a pair of feet descended, topped by a striped sarong. The ranger offered Quincey a drink. They went inside. Wolfgang waited till their steps had died away, then turned the handle.

'Stay here,' he whispered. 'I'll see if it's safe.'

This time, she obeyed. The truth was, despite the reek of fish, she was glad to stay hidden a little longer. All too soon, once Quincey and his friend had settled down to dinner, Wolfgang would be back. Then she would have to be brave again and go. She was not looking forward to it. Creeping around Maitland at night was one thing; tracking Quincey quite another. Again she wished they had not come. Unfortunately, once Wolfgang put his mind to something, he was a difficult man to stop. His stubbornness had come as a surprise. In other circumstances, she might have been amused.

The noise of the engine startled her. The van was jogging under Quincey's weight, jogged again as the ranger climbed in the other side. Two doors slammed. The van lurched forward and crossed the boundary into the national park. A man closed the barrier behind them.

Jan froze in horror. Where was Wolfgang? Then she realized: Quincey was driving on, not back.

Panic-stricken now, she fumbled with the back door. But her hand stopped. She had seen Wolfgang running: round the far corner of the building, across the verandah steps, after the van. He had not noticed the man at the barrier. Her fingers clenched round the handle. The man stepped forward into the light. He was carrying a gun. Wolfgang faltered. Then he stared theatrically after the disappearing van, one arm outstretched. The man turned to look and Wolfgang hit him. Jan watched his body swing with the weight of the blow, determination contorting his face. He caught the guard on the jaw. His head snapped to one side. There was blood on Wolfgang's knuckles but he hit him again. The man fell back, slammed his head hard against the barrier post, and lay still. As Quincey accelerated out of sight, Wolfgang began to run once more.

But the van had left him behind.

Still inside, Jan cursed her own cowardice. Why did fear always paralyse her limbs? She should have jumped clear while the van was still gathering speed. She could have warned Wolfgang about the guard. She could have saved herself. Now, through her own stupidity, she was hurtling through Yala at the mercy of a man who filled her with dread.

She loosened her fingers from the door handle. What would Wolfgang do now? He could check out the ranger's home undisturbed, but then what? Could he find his own way back? It would take him all night to walk. And what would Mohan do when he found out what had happened? He would be angry certainly, rave at Wolfgang for his negligence, strike him, perhaps – but what would he do? What could either of them do to help her now?

She ran her fingers through her hair in desperation. The smell of fish made it hard to think. But she had to. She was on her own now.

First, why hadn't Quincey stayed at Okanda? Second, where the hell was he taking her now? The track continued for eleven miles across the plains to the banks of the Kumbukkan Oya and the isolated hamlet of Kumana: were they going that far? Why? And how would she get back? No one walked beyond Okanda without a gun. She forced herself to concentrate.

The journey from Panama was measured by seven lagoons: Panakala, Kunukala, Helawa, Bagura. . . . But first a river, the Bagura Ara. Quincey over-revved the engine in his determination to cross but in the dry season even he could not bog the van down. Soon they were executing a slow zig-zag across the Bagura plains.

Jan struggled to remember. Over there lay the desolate Leanama country where the last of the Nittewo, herded into a cave by Veddahs, were smoked to death. Three lagoon mile posts remained: Andarakala, Itikala where flamingoes gathered, and Yakkala. Picturesque names sprang to mind: *kiripokunahela*, 'the hill by the lotus pond of milk-like water'; *kanbisaunge galge*, 'the cave of the blind queen'; *aliya kema*, 'elephant rock'. They spoke of history, of legend and of every day.

Jan tensed suddenly. The van had stopped. She saw lanterns, a clump of coconut palms, fifteen to twenty huts. Kumana, the trackers' village. Trackers like Banduwa who served the intrepid Dr Spittel; like Karolis whose back bore the scars of a leopard's teeth and claws; like Garuwa, his arm torn from its socket by a bear on that very track. But those men were all dead now and in Kumana times were hard. Had one of the new generation made a bargain with Quincey?

A shadow disengaged itself from a coconut palm. Quincey's clipped questions carried into the back.

'He is there? . . . When? . . . Who else? . . . And food?'

The man's answers were absorbed into the engine. Jan crouched, hardly daring to breathe. For the men from Kumana could hear the shadows move and know what moved them. Quincey's final command rapped out.

'Get in.'

Jan tensed. Would he get into the back? The moon shone obliquely through the window, encasing her in black. Her hand curled round a spanner. Soft footfalls came closer, breaking crisp earth. Her mouth went dry. She was staring at the dim square where the silhouette would come.

'Hurry up, man.' Quincey's voice followed him. 'In front here, quickly.'

The shadow floated by. Jan breathed out and her hand uncurled. She was sweating.

83

They drove on. Her mind whirled as she tried to keep track of where they were. This was the route that pilgrims took each year to attend the festival at Kataragama's city. They walked ten miles a day: Panama to Okanda, Okanda to Bagura, Bagura to Madamatota on the banks of the Kumbukkan Oya. Would Quincey cross the river too?

But the van swung right, inland. The denser darkness falling away to the left marked the river bank. Jan suddenly understood why Quincey had been so angry about the landrover: there was no track now. The van was bumping along the flood shelf created in the wet season when the water rose, following the bends of the river like a skin. They were plunging deeper into the jungle.

Again they lurched off to the right. In the back, Jan looked out at the blackness of trees growing close together and a smoky darkness high above. The night was studded with moving fireflies and stationary stars, the moon not yet risen above the hedge of trees to blot them out.

She shivered suddenly. Sky, stars and fireflies had disappeared. Rock walls closed in to hug the van. The noise of the engine reverberated as if they had entered a subterranean vault. She held her breath.

The next moment, they were freed. The sky splintered into lantern sparks and she breathed again. The engine coughed and died. They had reached a clearing.

Three men jumped down. Muffled voices and crunching feet dribbled off to the right. A flash of new light, a greeting, then nothing. They had vanished.

Jan waited for a long time, easing her cramped limbs, straining her ears for the slightest sound. Should she wait for Quincey to return and take her back to Ulle? Or should she follow him and see why he had come? She opened the door and looked around.

Silence blanketed the clearing. A landrover stood at the edge. Beyond it, a giant rock seemed to divide, its great sides forced apart by a shaft of light.

She was afraid, but now intensely curious too. If only Wolfgang were there. Following Quincey was his idea: he would know what to do. Despite herself, she smiled, for she knew he would not dream of skulking in the van. He would find out what was behind that rock. Curiosity fought with fear, and won: she wanted to find out too. But she would have to take care. She intended to be back in the van by the time Quincey was ready to go home.

She let herself out, crouched as low as her aching bones allowed and ran, willing her feet to skim the brittle ground. Leaf skeletons sucked of moisture by the drought exploded into fragments. She flattened her body against the rock but nothing moved.

Praying no one was there, she poked her head into the lighted gap. A narrow corridor stretched forty yards then stopped, the light round the corner illuminating the grain of the rock face. She hesitated. If she walked down there, she would be spotted at once. There had to be a safer way.

Her eyes searched the rock. Above her head, the corridor wall tilted back and stopped: the passage had no roof. If she could climb up there, she would overlook the other side.

She placed her back against one wall, her feet on the other, and jerked clumsily upwards. It took all her strength. When she looked up, the top of the corridor sagged outwards. To her left, almost out of reach, a small tree had lodged itself in a crevice. She seized it, pulled herself up. It held. One leg scrabbled against the rock and then it too found the ledge. A moment later, she was lying on the top, catching her breath, listening.

A concise history of earlier visitors was written in scattered dung: tiny brown pats left by sunbathing monkeys; blackish capsules of porcupines in search of water; mongoose droppings; all hardened in the sun. Jan crawled past them. Inch by inch, she wormed her way to the other side. The moon was rising now and the slightest silhouette against the sky would be obvious. When her fingers felt a downward slope, she raised her head.

Thirty feet below, the corridor opened into an inner clearing. Rock as sheer as the face she had climbed enclosed it on three of its four uneven sides. As the light from the lantern bobbed and probed, the shadows of the fourth receded into a cave. At its entrance, a man played with a knife. From time to time, he looked up automatically at the well-lit corner, then down again at his hands. His tuneless whistle was reassuring.

Jan felt quite safe on that rock, like a cat gazing into a goldfish bowl: exhilarated by her apparent power, frustrated by her inability to jump in. Quincey and his men were inside that cave. A guard barred the entrance. A circle of light protected both cave and guard. She would have to wait. Now that she was there, she was determined to find out what was going on. She could picture Wolfgang's face when she told him.

The tongue of the kachan scraped the rock. Paper leaves crackled, twigs jangling like drum sticks. The cicada rose to a crescendo that almost drowned the mosquitoes' whine. She lowered her chin to the rock and watched. She hoped it would not take long.

Some distance from the cave, hidden by ferns, water splashed: rain had forced runnels into the rock and they ran into a pool, joining forces with a spring. No wonder they had chosen this place. Even now in the dry season, water bubbled along a ledge towards the cave, its silvery path adorned with rusty patches deposited on pale grey stone. Jan's throat tightened; she could almost taste the metallic liquid on her tongue. Her eyes followed it, noting how it twisted and turned and then, at the edge of the cave, appeared to hold breath and plunge. As it fell, water flicked visibly like sparks from a fire, reaching inwards.

Her eyes kept returning to that cave. What would Wolfgang have done? But the walls on either side offered no shelter, no encouragement for bravado, no excuse for bluff. Occasionally, when someone emerged from inside, a second lantern threw the jagged hole into relief, but it taught her only that the entrance was small and, beyond it, Quincey had found a place so situated that an observer outside could see no light within.

Three times, a man appeared. She thought it was the tracker but the light cast disfiguring shadows and she was unsure. Each time, the mutter of conversation was followed by a splat of bare feet against wet rock as the man returned inside. Once, the guard jerked his head at the beedi trailing from his fellow's mouth and the two squatted together, smoking in turn, not exchanging a word. The fourth time, the man brought a plate of food and the clearing echoed with the sounds of hunger appeased. Jan swallowed enviously. But the longer she watched, the more curious she became. Whatever was happening in there?

It was a long wait. Rare moments of activity were separated by silence broken only by the call of a night bird and the scuffling of knife on wood. The guard was carving a buffalo head: deep nostrils and that peculiar forward thrust of the neck. Every now and then, he reached across to a bottle hidden in the shadows, took a hefty swig, and wiped his mouth on the back of his hand.

Jan's eyes drifted over his head and stopped. Tucked under a ledge above the cave hung the bambara's drooping combs, each one completely hidden by a moving, glistening mass of bees. She counted six such clusters, each one a grave warning: death by suicide for them in their thousands; death by multiple poisoned daggers for their foes. For the second time that night, she begged Kataragama to keep her safe.

Her lips were still moving when the conspirators emerged. The guard hid his bottle and stood up. Jan's ruffled hair pressed into the sky.

Quincey came first, awkwardly as if afraid he might slip. A striped sarong identified the ranger. Then came the tracker and another man similarly dressed, similarly taciturn, also from Kumana perhaps. Two men followed together: a Ceylonese in Western dress and a European. Jan felt a stab of disappointment: there were no Chinese.

The European was speaking. If Jan had not recognized him already she would have done so now, for the man spoke Sinhala with the broad vowels and burred 'r's of his native Scotland. Baggy trousers clung damply to his legs while beneath an unbuttoned shirt pink skin protested at the jungle humidity. Without the hat, those carefully nurtured arms of hair stood upright: Andrews' appearance was at once distasteful and absurd. It occurred to Jan that he would have told Quincey of the break-in at Maitland. Had Quincey guessed who was responsible?

But she was staring at the sixth member of the group. With his neat appearance, tight curls and lush good looks, Sando da Souza exuded an air of tactful confidence that was out of place. Jan stared in bewilderment. What was a mortician doing here?

87

Then she saw the last figure and forgot her question. This man wore yellow robes. She blinked. A Buddhist priest involved in heroin? Surely not; yet there he stood while Andrews' voice bounced off the boulder walls. Jan studied the pale skin unused to the sun, the patched robes of chosen beggary, the shaven head; hollow eyes that in that jungle seemed closer to the ancient worship of trees than to the Buddha's spirituality; and a mouth that belied those eyes, aloof, composed. A monk then, mixing with the worst scum a money-oriented society could produce; a monk working for Quincey. Jan detected sadness in his face.

The guard unhooked the lantern from its spike of rock and walked ahead. At the bend in the corridor, he stopped to let them pass, holding the lamp up high to light their way. Jan watched them go. Every footfall crunched, parched earth and stiff leaf corpses crumbling beneath their weight. No one glanced up.

As each face passed into the light, Jan knew something was wrong. Quincey's blank mask hid nothing of his anger. It made the ranger nervous, his eyes fluttering repeatedly to that unforgiving back. Behind him, Andrews' hirsute face twitched, discoloured front teeth nibbling at his lip. Da Souza watched them, his contained smile seeming to conceal a greater amusement. Jan was baffled. What could have happened to anger, frighten and amuse four such different men? Only the trackers were impervious. The monk drifted behind, apart, but his face too betrayed emotions albeit embryonic ones of which no layman would have been ashamed. Even the guard was affected: his eyes sped from face to face for he, like Jan, had missed the crucial confrontation.

She drew up her knees and scuttled back across the rock to overlook the larger clearing outside. Eight men stood distractedly together. Something was definitely wrong. Despite da Souza's amusement, Jan could see it was serious.

'I'm sorry, old man.'

Andrews appealed to Quincey in English; perhaps to bypass the others, perhaps to gain sympathy from one who had been educated in a British public school. The stratagem, if it was one, failed. Andrews began to bluster.

'He'd have had to know eventually,' he said. 'Where does he think the money's coming from, eh? Not from his Lord Buddha, that's for sure.'

His head jerked towards the monk and he laughed derisively. Quincey stared at him, unmoved. Perhaps he had noticed that Andrews' whine did not match the bravado of his words; perhaps he was merely following his own logic. Standing there surrounded by his men, he made an imposing figure. It was clear to Jan as she watched them that Quincey was master here.

When he spoke, he reverted to Sinhala, but he addressed them all.

'If he feels he must tell him, he will.' He turned to the monk. 'Is that not so?'

'It is so.' The monk spoke without expression.

Quincey nodded gravely as if he sympathized.

'Then you may go,' he said. 'But think well before you act.'

Was there an undercurrent of menace in those words? She was not sure but something in da Souza's eyes frightened her. The monk placed his palms in the age-old gesture of salutation, bowed and left. Jan stared with the rest as he vanished, a saffron-robed will-o'-the-wisp, into the night. The huddle of men seemed less significant without him.

'What can he do?' said the ranger at last. 'He'll be angry but even he can't stop us now.'

'He can,' Quincey retorted brusquely, 'if I let him. But I shall make sure the twenty-first goes as planned. You' – he indicated one of the trackers – 'stay with me. The rest can go.'

They were summarily dismissed. Not even da Souza argued. Four figures moved towards the landrover: one gross and crumpled; another furtive; the third neat and upright; the last an easy animal gait. Four pairs of eyes – three below, one above – watched as the vehicle rolled away.

Jan's eyes shifted to the van, then back to Quincey. She was staring in dismay for she had only just realized what she'd done. The two men blocked her escape. She could not even leave the rock unnoticed now. And if Quincey drove away, she would be stranded. She felt the paralysing fear begin. A voice recalled her.

'You have everything you need?'

The question was a formality and the guard saw it, nodding with an alacrity born of fear. He backed away with his lantern into the gap. At first, the blackness he left behind was absolute, then the moon stepped up her voltage and Jan could see. She heard the guard resume his whittling. Quincey was deep in thought.

'I will take you to Kumana,' he said at last, spitting out each word. 'The bhikkhu will pass that way. Follow him. If he goes north of Panama, he is going to Kandy. That must not be.'

The command was a staccato burst. Jan shifted uncomfortably. Quincey's venom was never wasted.

'It must not be,' he repeated. 'You understand?'

'I understand.'

The words came low like the promise of a serf. Jan thought of that wraith of ochre flying through the trees, and shuddered. Questions shot with fear spun through her mind. What was Andrews' crucial blunder? Who were they so anxious about in Kandy? What had Quincey planned for the twenty-first? But as the two men walked away towards the van, one panic-stricken question overthrew the rest: what in heaven's name should she do now?

Fifteen minutes later, she was still lying on that rock. The guard had stopped whittling. He was applying himself to the arrack as if making up for lost time. The van had gone.

Jan was gradually getting used to the idea. Panic subsided as she tried to think. She kept wondering how far Wolfgang had got, whether he had reached Panama, when he would tell Mohan. What would they do? More important, what would they expect her to do? She shook her head in disgust. Not what she had done, that was sure. And what would they think when they saw the van return without her? Would they imagine her dead, or merely stranded by her own inefficiency in the jungle? She was not looking forward to explaining herself. How could she have been such a fool?

A melancholy wail rose behind her as an animal searched for water and found baked mud. The guard stopped drinking to listen. It gave her an idea.

There was still one way to salvage her friends' respect. She could bring back the proof Wolfgang had been looking for: a packet of heroin. She had to take a look inside that cave. It might even provide a clue to Quincey's words. She brightened for a moment. Perhaps she could solve the riddle, produce the proof, and recover her lost face in one. It was worth a try. She considered her plan. Having something to do made her feel braver. For one thing, it postponed the problem of getting out of that jungle.

The pellets of mongoose dung suited her purpose best. She lined up several on the rock in front of her. She would need a weapon, too, in case. But there was nothing up there. She scoured the clearing below, saw a large rock with a jutting edge, memorized its position. Then her arm swung in a low arc. In the corridor, beyond the guard's vision, the dung broke on impact. He sprang up, one hand darting into the opening of his shirt, then stopped. A slow smile spread over his face, its looseness betraying the arrack.

This time, she threw the dung so that it pattered distinctly further down the passage. The guard picked up a torch and padded with surreptitious clumsiness towards the sound. He was more than a little drunk. She lobbed one last missile as far as she could into the undergrowth on the far side.

He was unlikely to be back in a hurry: boredom would suggest he make the most of the diversion; drunkenness should make it difficult to return. She calculated on ten minutes at least.

She wasted not a second more but slid from crevice to foothold to crack to the ground below, crouched briefly to regain her balance, cast her eyes back up the way she had come in preparation for retreat, and ran. Her fingers scooped up the stone pinpointed from above, its rounded end fitting neatly into the palm of her hand. Seconds later, she was inside the cave. So far, she was safe. But she would have to move fast.

Her eyes saw little at first. Something soft swished a caress across her face, making her recoil: bats. Her nostrils wrinkled at the smell. Her ears began to accept the echoing space and, chipping into it like chisels on a massive wall, the rustle of insects, of lizards and beetles, scuttling along moist crevices in the rock.

She remembered the stream and dropped to her knees to

check the ground. The rock was wet. Water splashed her groping hands. She edged forward. Bat droppings had made the surface dangerously slippery. Then she saw it: water leaned over the lip of the cave to collapse into a pool twenty feet below.

A noise outside stopped her dead. Foot scuffed rock and expletive flew. She huddled against the cave mouth. She had miscalculated badly: her watch told her he had been gone less than three minutes. Perhaps he had not left the corridor at all. Her fingers gripped the stone.

Then she froze. Three feet away, the guard had struck a match to light the beedi clenched between his lips. The flame illuminated a heavy face adorned with the brief moustache worn by every hero in a Tamil film. A pair of black eyes glittered, the white surrounds streaked with red, then merged into the night. He was no taller than she was. Her muscles tightened, her hand easing round the stone for a better hold. She had never hit anyone seriously before. Never used a weapon of any kind. Her nerves were taut. She waited, watching the man she had to strike. Her eyes never left his face.

And he knew. He was reaching for the bottle, one arm poised, when he stopped. He could have heard nothing and yet his head turned as if he felt her hostile spirit lurking there. The head swivelled slowly, a puppet with only one string. She stiffened. His eyes were wide as if he saw something he could not believe. She looked down. The luminous dial on her watch was glowing a witches' green.

There was no time to think. She switched the stone to her left hand, tore the watch from her wrist and flung it away. It skittered noisily across the cave floor: there was a brief silence as it dropped through the air, and a splash. The guard blew out the lamp.

Swamped in black, Jan edged backwards into the cave. The splash worried her: she prayed the floor did not plunge on that side too. In faint silhouette, the guard crouched at the entrance, gun in hand. She cast round for escape, found none. He began to walk forward.

She flattened herself behind a shoulder of rock, hoping he could not see her, hoping he would pass and she could take him by surprise. Her fingers tightened fiercely on the stone. If he came within reach, she would hit him. She had a sudden memory of Wolfgang lashing out at the barrier guard with his fist. It gave her courage. She steeled herself for the blow: if it was going to work, it would need all the strength she could find. She knew she would not get a second chance.

The guard crept by. She waited till she saw the back of his neck, then let him have it. The stone cut into his flesh without a sound. In the split-second it took for the man to react, Jan realized her hand was wet: she had hit him hard. But not hard enough. Two black shapes twisted together on a polished stage. Four arms scrabbled in the air. Someone slipped. There was a deafening report: bats panicked and the ceiling disintegrated into frantic wings. The heavens split open and fell.

The dust settled. Jan woke to feel hands on her body. Hot breath, laden with arrack, rasped across her face. The guard stood astride her, insolent fingers searching her, hard with cruelty. Blood oozed along his jaw from a gash on the back of his neck. His features were distorted by a drunken rage.

She tried to move and he hit her. He slapped her savagely several times, then held her by the throat and slammed her head against the rock floor. She felt the skin split. Warm blood matted her hair. She lay still, half conscious. From a great distance, she heard him laugh. She knew she should get up, fight back, run away; but she could not move. Those waves of paralysing fear had begun. Terror crept up from the base of her spine, defusing all resistance.

The guard misunderstood her response. Perhaps he took it for compliance. For he ripped her shirt open and placed rough hands on her skin.

Something snapped in Jan's head. A new kind of panic took over, stampeding her brain. She brought her foot up hard, a vicious kick calculated to shift his genitals to his throat. The impact shocked them both. The guard doubled up, his face inches from her own. A bubble formed at the corner of his mouth; his eyes screwed tight in pain. As his weight lifted from her body, she struck him. Suddenly aware of the bloody stone still clutched in her hand, she lunged at him again. Drink made his reflexes slow. She saw his eyes widen in surprise and pain, and he lurched away. His head fell hard against the cave wall. A moment later, his body slackened and lay still.

Jan was sobbing aloud. She looked at the stone: it was painted a viscous red. She let it fall in disgust. Then she saw him move. Briefly, one hand convulsed. She remembered the dog Quincey had run down, the one she had had to kill, and turned away. From outside came the angry buzz of bambaras disturbed.

At last, common sense prevailed. She had to know if the guard was still alive. If he regained consciousness and found her there, the horror would start again. She dared not let that happen. Quickly, to give herself less time to think, she moved towards him, checked his pulse, his heart. Nothing. The man was dead. She stayed kneeling, unable to move. Relief and shock were jostling for first place.

Eventually, she made herself stand. Her legs shook. She stared at her hands: they were caked with blood and dirt. Supporting herself on the cave wall, she made her way to the entrance. In a daze, she found the guard's matches, lit the lamp. Then she went to the stream and washed. The cool water on her face cleared her brain. She left the wound on her head, not wanting to touch the matted hair, and concentrated on the rest. Much of the blood was not hers.

Then she went back. The guard's body rested at an unnatural angle on a carpet of limestone debris. She looked at it dully. She felt numbed of all response. Had she meant to kill him? She was no longer sure. But death bred death. First Christine, then the injured fisherman in the hospital, and now the guard. The threat hung even over the living: over the bhikkhu skimming through the trees; over herself.

She shook her head, remembering where she was, what she was supposed to be doing. She must check out the cave, find the heroin, then go. She did not want to be caught there now.

Raising the lamp above her head, she saw a channel two inches deep above the cave mouth; a drip-ledge chiselled centuries ago to keep out the rain. Fragments of brick scattered on the floor by grooves where walls had stood. Square sockets, empty now of pillars they once held. Shallow depressions

94

scooped into the floor. The light shifted, bringing into relief an ancient script. Were these hermit cells for meditating monks? But there were sketches, too, crude outlines of stubby men and unlikely animals, and a bow with an arrow balanced on the string. Was it a prehistoric home? The cave was perfect: for primitive man, for hermit monks, and as the hide-out of a criminal band. A drumming pulse started up at the back of her head but she ignored it, lifted the lantern more firmly and began to look.

She scoured that cave from front to back and back to front, and found nothing. Then she did it again. She crept to the edge of the stream and stared at the slimy walls, the water heaving queasily below. But as she turned to go, she stubbed her foot on a rope and, when she stopped to check, found two: a rope ladder dropped over the edge into the dark. The lamp illuminated it rung by rung. At the bottom, floating on the surface of that Hadean pool, bobbed something small and square: a raft.

She climbed down. The effort made her head hum. Cautiously, holding the lamp in one hand, she transferred her weight to the raft. Bats swooped over the oily water, leaving expanding circles where their tongues had touched. She wondered what secrets the pool concealed: drinking vessels perhaps, ornaments or arrow heads; fragments of monastic pottery beside a wild boar's skull; or a human skeleton, someone who had stepped too close. The thought made her grasp the ladder more firmly and in that instinctive movement, she found it: a heavy nail driven into the rock face and a rope running horizontally, leading the way. She balanced the lamp on the raft and pulled.

As she moved across the pool, a black patch appeared in the far wall. Invisible ten yards away, it swelled into an opening. The gap was barely wider than the raft and two feet high. The tunnel roof scraped her back. The lamp spluttered. Years of airlessness choked her nostrils. Then she was through.

When she looked up, she gasped. A single lotus bloomed amidst plate-like leaves on a black table of water. The wall behind glistened green and yellow, liquid pink and brown, unholy blue; every shade pierced with specks of mica that glittered like fool's gold. Far above, the night spun a dusty moon-beam through the cavern roof.

A noise made her jump. On a ledge to her right, a six-foot monitor lizard slithered out of sight. With its close-set scales and flickering tongue, it resembled a prehistoric monster. She waved the lamp towards the ledge in case it thought of returning, then exclaimed in surprise: at the back, concealed in an alcove in the rock, was a large tarpaulin. Quickly, she tethered the raft and felt her way across.

The tarpaulin drew back easily. Underneath, piled on top of each other as far back into the rock as she could see, were the crates. She stared in amazement. Mohan was right. But where would even the Chu Chow find so much heroin to ship at once? And why risk so much on one consignment, one route?

One of the crates was open and she knelt to look. Metal joints creaked: the lid fell open. She frowned. The crate was filled with long and bulky packages.

She lifted one out: it was cold, heavy. As she unravelled the plastic-coated wire that served as string and folded back the heavy plastic wrapper, her imagination tripped over itself. Then all she could do was gape: for there, wallowing in a layer of protective grease, lay a submachine-gun.

For a moment, she did not move. The shiny coating glistened in the light and she stared as if it were a modernistic work of art she could not understand. She was thinking of Christine, remembering the fear in her letter; the fear Mohan saw before she left with Quincey; and the plastic beauty of her punishment. It took an effort to break the trance.

She felt each package and found the same. She opened another crate to make sure; then a third, a fourth. Each one contained weapons. Most were new, modern M60 machine-guns that had never been fired. Others were older, well-used M1 Garands, Russian AK47's, more M60's. There were boxes of cartridges; ammunition of all sizes; sticks of dynamite in polythene bags; hand grenades. Then more guns: brand new M16 rifles, .45 calibre automatics, .38 revolvers, even some lethal-looking shotguns.

She sat back on her heels and tried to think. No heroin at all; only arms. What could it mean? Heroin at Maitland – they had not imagined that, had they? – and arms here.

'What's the connection?' she muttered.

There had to be one. The guns were loaded on to carts in the Mudalali's yard; the heroin stashed in fish in his van. According to Mohan, the Mudalali was Quincey's man. Quincey was by the van during the loading; he was at the hospital when the fisherman died; he had been at the cave that night. Andrews at Maitland and here. There had to be a connection. For God's sake, she thought wildly, there were enough arms there to start a revolution!

The thought floated on the musty atmosphere. A revolution? She remembered the excited talk on the bus, her father's hunch that something big was brewing. April 1971 all over again? Was that what Quincey wanted? Surely not; and yet, faced with that pile of crates, even that seemed possible.

She stood up. Quincey was mad. And this whole crazy business was beyond her. Whatever Wolfgang said now, she was going to Colombo; she would tell Saunders; leave the rest to him.

But when she saw the raft, she remembered: she was in the middle of the jungle. The beauty of that underground cavern was as irrelevant now as Christmas decorations to a child in January. She had found her way in there. How on earth would she find her way out?

When she reached the outer clearing, she was still wondering. If she could get to Kumana, she could follow the jeep track out of the park. The river would take her that far. But how? The Kumbukkan Oya drew danger like a magnet. In the dry zone, water ruled and in August, the water holes were dry: every animal for miles would come to the river to drink.

Jan walked slowly towards it. She had seen a man killed by an elephant once: its massive foot had rolled him into an unrecognizable bone-crushed mess. The memory made her shudder. If she walked down that flood shelf on the edge of the trees, might she not meet one coming out to drink?

She eyed the bank distrustfully, unable to go on. There might be snakes: cobras, a Russell's viper; both deadly, both common in that terrain. Or some animal might already be drinking at the water's edge. If she unwittingly cut off its escape, what then? Wild buffalo charged on sight, especially with young in the herd. A full grown wild boar could snap her leg in half.

But bears worried her most. They could hardly see, hear or
smell and when not up a palu tree looking for berries, they spen
their time rooting around in antholes. They were too easily
surprised. Garuwa had lost an arm; another man an eye and one
side of his face; a third his scalp.

She swallowed, reminded herself that few animals attacked
unless provoked. But how could she fail to provoke them? She
could not even stay downwind: the bank of trees on each side of
the river produced a strange turbulence, unexpected eddies in
the breeze, its direction changing constantly.

She was growing desperate. She should have stayed in the
van, let Quincey take her back. She clutched the guard's torch,
thought of going back for his knife or gun, couldn't face the sight
of him again. Setting fire to some wood might scare the animal
away, but she dared not be seen by Quincey's men. She even
considered marching through the jungle trusting to animal
paths, yet she knew each path spawned a dozen more, weaving
labyrinth from which she might never escape.

She would have to stick to the river. She flashed the torch at i
as if it might respond. The water level was low, most of it flowing
in deep channels along each bank. The central ridge was barel
ankle deep. The torch beam trembled as she realized: that ridg
was the safest path she could find.

She struck out into the water before she could change he
mind. At the centre, where the sandy backbone rose, she turned
downstream. She told herself firmly that her splashing footstep
would warn any animal ahead, frightening it back up the ban
into the jungle. She had heard tales of bears trundling down tha
central ridge but decided to discount them, walking faster as
that made them more unlikely. Crocodiles she discounted, too
the evaporation of the deep pools they liked should have sen
them elsewhere long since; just as well too since so many ha
found a taste for human flesh during the insurrection. But eac
time her feet landed on nothing more fearful than sand, she wa
overwhelmed with relief.

Far above, the moon began to sink, setting beneath the eart
horizon of a jungle that reached up with grasping branches t
take it down. Sparks fell from the sky, shot through minute hole
pierced in an inverted bowl. Below, the jungle was alive.

Giant kumbuks at the water's edge, roots deeply flanged, pink-grey bark peeling off a polished skin. Rukattana, stately, handsome. Halmilla with heart-shaped leaves and six-winged fruit like propellers. Fluted timbiri stems. The spreading tamarind elephants love. Scaly ebony, its crown dense with leaves. Sculptured satinwood. Jan's torch illuminated each one. Smaller trees, too, not beautiful but dwarfed and ugly, knotted branches, spectacular grabbing thorns. Overhead hung nets of creepers, climbers, tendrils, epiphytic orchids, waiting like living traps.

Matted jungle walls gave a cathedral's acoustics to the whispered wild. Branches stretched and scraped and moaned. Unseen things rustled. Animals called. Every footfall beckoned.

Jan's eyes swept the water, probed the dark passages at its edge, straining bloodshot. She was alert to every twitching shadow, every nascent sound. The slightest breath was enough to make her use the torch, release the light at its command.

Once, it bounced on the snout of a porcupine with fifteen-inch quills displayed: a white patch waved as it fled and the quills rattled. Once, it surprised a wild boar scratching its bristles on a rock and sent a sounder of nuzzling little ones squealing up the bank and away. Several times, it framed the heaving bulk of a buffalo as it rose snorting from the squelch of mud. Or spotlit a troupe of grey langurs drinking inelegantly on all fours.

Jan listened to the sounds vibrating in the night and tried to trust them, tried not to use the torch each time. Then she heard monkeys cursing in the trees and stopped: a leopard. A minute later, a spotted deer sang its high-pitched warning call and the staccato grapevine of fear passed into the distance. She moved on.

Fireflies hung in the air beckoning, flickering on then off then on again, undecided what to do. The sky's dome hunched lower, leaning inwards. Darkness breathed down on her, sometimes urging her on, sometimes weighting her steps, always a heavy cloak that suffocated breath. She walked with her mouth open now, gasping in claustrophobic fear.

A bend in the river took her too near its edge and the jungle clawed her face. Hostile eyes peered. Leaves rattled in the rasp of the kachan. Serpentine creepers coiled. Fear oozed from every thicket, borne on the stagnant air. Death hovered in the chequered shade.

A colony of bats took flight with rushing wings. Startled, Jan stopped to listen: they were circling, dipping in and out of the trees. Then silence and a chill isolation crept over her. She made herself walk on.

Sounds joined forces in a crescendo of malice. Nameless crashes in the undergrowth. The weird moaning of nocturnal birds. A sucking splash as an animal left the water ahead. The brittle scrape of hoof or claw on rock. Irregular fleeing thuds. Harsh breathing close at hand and closer still, the stilted beat of her heart.

Jan fought back her tears. The jungle at night was evil, a place of black magic, of hideous sacrifices to gods in whose fear the stones shook and bats took flight. A choked cry: something fought and lost. She imagined the grey opacity of crocodile eyes watching, waiting. Evil eyes everywhere. The jungle alert in every leaf and twig. She walked faster, heard the minutes thudding by, felt the menace. Her sweat ran cool in the humid night as she hurried on, compelled yet sick with fear.

She stopped. A few feet ahead, claws shuffled dry earth. A sloppy sucking sound: something large was drinking. A grunt unbearably near. She switched on the torch. A bear frozen in the light, black and huge. Angry eyes squinted through a fringe. Nostrils distorted at her smell and lips drew back to roar a challenge as it reared and lunged. Jan screamed. The creature paused confused, its head turned sideways to the light. Then it fell on all fours with a splash. White fangs shone, a parting snort and it lumbered up the bank, the torchbeam stabbing vainly as it passed.

She began to laugh. Blessed, curative laughter bubbled up to exorcise the fear – only to be stoppered in her throat, cut as with a knife by that fearful scream. An unearthly rising shriek shattered the hushed jungle, broke the last tense cords of her reserve and sent her fleeing for her life along the river. She ran on and on, unheeding of all but escape, leaving the river, bursting through thorns, past ticks jabbing needles at her knees, on and on until she had left the screaming behind or it stopped, she could not remember which.

Later, she knew what it was: nothing more than an owl, the forest eagle owl, flesh and blood counterpart of the 'devil bird' of Sinhalese legend. Each teller embroidered the grisly tale: a vengeful drunkard killed his daughter, gave his wife the flesh to cook; transformed into the 'devil bird', those tortured shrieks were hers.

But it was over now. Jan found herself in a clump of trees. Through the darkness, she could see the lanterns of Kumana. She longed to creep up on them, cling to those solid walls, listen to the sounds of people sleeping, turning over, snoring perhaps, talking in their sleep. She wanted to inhale their humanity, their normalness, and know she was not alone. But she did not dare. Someone might be awake.

A nightjar whooped softly to itself nearby. Behind her, all around, the jungle deliberated, threatening her idly still. She pulled herself together and turned to go.

A shattering noise made her jump. A tractor had started up its engines in Kumana. It steamed towards her, pulling a trailer loaded with grain. Was it leaving the park? She stepped back to see. The driver was alone. She ran behind and hauled herself aboard, her shadow merging into the sacks of grain.

She looked at the sky. They should be in Panama soon after dawn. With luck, she might catch the first bus to Pottuvil. Breakfast with Mohan and Wolfgang. She smiled shakily. What would she tell them?

The thread that had run so easily before was in knots. Heroin, yes; but guns too. Financial motives; political ones as well? A Chinese murdered, but none at the cave. If the arms were for a revolution scheduled for the twenty-first, why were they not distributed to the rebels who needed them? Quincey, Andrews, Sando da Souza, too; but a Buddhist monk? And who was the key figure in Kandy who might spoil everything? What everything?

Questions whirled haphazardly like kittens chasing their own tails, each intent on itself. Jan closed her eyes. For a while, her mind ticked on, slowly winding down. At last, exhausted, she slept.

When she woke, the sky blushed with amethystine delicacy.

Undergrowth began to appear. Scattered pates of bald rock heaved into shape, flicked aside the night. Dimly visible, Bagura rock lowered at the dawn while inland the soft blue haze of hills lay rumpled with sleep. They were approaching Okanda.

Jan rearranged the sacks until she was enclosed by grain. Shouts heralded their arrival at the barrier. The driver yelled back. The barrier lifted and they were through.

As they approached the right-hand turn that led to the Pottuvil–Panama road, a man poked his head out of an isolated hut and beckoned. The driver stopped the tractor and jumped down.

She took her chance, ducked behind the hut and ran, threading her way along raised footpaths that zigzagged between the paddy, cutting across the corner. When she reached the main track again, she settled into a steady jog towards the sea. Ten minutes later, she heard the tractor roar and slowed to a walk. A crazy foreigner out for a morning's stroll. She turned her head towards the sound, the matted hair away. As the vehicle approached, she signalled for a lift. The driver nodded and grinned.

By the time they reached Panama, the sun had burst from the horizon and the world was ablaze. A crowd of would-be passengers surrounded the Pottuvil bus. Before the tractor could stop, Jan jumped clear, waved to her benefactor and ran to join in.

She found herself wedged in a complaining mass in the aisle, trying to see over their heads. In the front seat customarily set aside for the clergy sat a yellow-robed figure. She tried to see his face. Was this the same bhikkhu? And what had Quincey said? That he must not travel north?

Pottuvil was north. She scanned each face, searching for the tracker on the bhikkhu's trail. Then she began to work her way forward to the front. If it was the same monk, she had to warn him.

The bus lurched on, stopping at intervals to add more passengers to its impossible load. Jan studied each new face. Another priest climbed in and made for the front bench. The villager seated beside the first stood up and offered him his seat.

Jan's eyes followed automatically. The stranger's head shone as if it had been recently shaved and oiled. She hesitated. Newly shaved? She moved forward more violently, using her elbows. She had to check that second monk's face.

But they were on the outskirts of Pottuvil and the bus slowed down. Before Jan could see what had happened, the second monk thrust a path to the exit, jumped from the top step, knocked over a child and ran. The other crumpled against the window, turning slowly in his seat before he fell. His forehead struck the metal bar in front and stayed there, holding the limp body awkwardly halfway to the floor.

Pandemonium broke loose. A woman screamed. People rushed in panic for the exit, desperate to escape that accursed bus in which a holy man had died. As they pushed past her, Jan slid into the front seat, felt for the absent pulse, saw the blank eyes and blood fast staining the ochre red. Then she ran too. A glimpse of yellow disappearing round a stall was enough, but when she followed she found only a heap of cloth lying in the dust and footprints that merged into the rest.

Mohan and Wolfgang found her there. Wolfgang had walked all night and only just got back: he had gone straight to Mohan. They were in Muhammad's, trying to decide what to do, when they heard the screams. They rushed out, saw Jan leap out of the bus and turn the corner, and followed. They found her on her knees in the dirt, her clothes speckled with blood, her hands clutching a yellow cloth.

She looked up and saw them. Her eyes drifted from one to the other, glazed. Wolfgang moved first. He knelt and took her in his arms. She leaned on him like a child, exhausted, beaten, close to tears. No one spoke. Behind them, Mohan's face was creased in distress. His hands clenched, but his mouth trembled to find her still alive and there were tears in his eyes. Wolfgang held her until she was strong enough to speak.

PART FOUR

19th August 1975:

Colombo

When they returned to Mohan's bungalow, they found Baby
Singho's son cowering in the bushes at the back. He had
brought a message from his father. On hearing it, Mohan
announced that all three of them had to leave Pottuvil at once.

Quincey could have no more doubts about who was ranged
against him. He knew now that Jan had lied by the fish van. He
had seen her and Wolfgang drive away on Mohan's bike.
Andrews would have reported meeting them at Moneragala,
followed by the break-in at Maitland factory precisely when the
tea-maker was concealing the drug-filled battens. Quincey had
already let them force his hand at the hospital. Now, last night,
he had returned to Okanda to discover that a foreigner had been
on his trail. He would have put two and two together; he was no
fool. Which explained why, on his return to Ulle, the disabled
landrover had made him suspicious.

'He came with some men in the night.' The boy snivelled as
he told them. A bruise almost closed his right eye. 'They
shouted at us. Then they took my father outside and beat him.
When he did not speak, they beat us too. They said they would
burn down our home.'

So Baby Singho had told him. He told him of Mohan's bribe,
how the two foreigners had been hiding in the van, how long
Mohan had needed to cripple the landrover. Quincey had
struck him with cold violence to the ground, and left. Jan felt sad
for Baby Singho and his family, unwittingly caught up in the
plot. But it made her doubly anxious on their own behalf should
Quincey find them now.

It was too dangerous for any of them to stay. Quincey had
only to send a man to the cave to learn that his guard had been

killed. The opened crates would suggest that someone had found the guns. The foreman's intervention at Maitland might have prevented Jan's discovery of the heroin, but Quincey could not be sure. He would not waste time finding out: whatever it was, there was too much at stake for that. He had killed Christine for less.

They caught the first bus to Colombo. The journey would take all day under a baking sun. Mohan slipped the driver something and tied his motorbike on the back: he preferred to sit inside with his friends. He also realized that Jan needed all the support he could give. She was exhausted and scared. All she wanted now was to hand the problem over to someone in authority. Until Quincey was behind bars, she would not feel safe. Mohan and Wolfgang agreed. But, unlike her, they still wanted to find out what was going on.

She listened as they talked. She had said little since her return from Yala. Her voice empty of expression, she had outlined what had happened, telling her friends all they needed to know. The details and the emotions that went with them she had kept to herself as if not sharing them might make them go away. Now, her body needed sleep, but her mind did not dare let go.

Through the bus window, 19th August seemed ill-omened. Cloth streamers fluttered from tree to tree beside the road, tearing in the wind; pale green strips from banana stems, knotted into shapes, lined the paths funeral processions would take later that day; and men built bamboo pyres to be set aflame. The heat was demoralizing too. But her companions hardly noticed.

'It can't be a revolution,' Mohan was saying. 'Quincey's already one of the most powerful men in the country.'

'Perhaps he's tired of waiting for the prime minister to stand down,' Wolfgang replied. 'Or perhaps we've misjudged him and he's really a socialist at heart!'

Jan let her mind run idly over the thought. Quincey a revolutionary in disguise, a second Wijeweera? Certainly, the constitution as it stood offered no solution: either party would produce an identical royal family, another elitist rule dependent on maintaining the status quo. Had Quincey, like Wijeweera, decided this would not do? Mohan was shaking his head.

'Unlikely,' he said, 'but either way they wouldn't stand a chance. After '71, the armed forces have been strengthened beyond recognition. Quincey knows that.'

And they still had the international weaponry which was rushed to their aid in '71. British arms and helicopters; American spare parts; arms and more helicopters from India and Pakistan; Yugoslavian mountain artillery; nine tons of Russian weapons, with six Mig-17s and twenty armoured cars; and from China, a Rs 150 million loan plus guns, ammunition and five military speedboats equipped with rockets! Now, Jan was thinking, Sri Lanka could take on India if she chose, let alone a rebellion within her shores.

'I wonder where he got the stuff,' Mohan muttered. 'Even Russia and China were on the other side in '71.'

'That's easy enough,' Wolfgang replied with crisp cynicism. 'Politics don't come into the arms trade.'

'"All faiths, all follies, all causes and all crimes",' Jan quoted tonelessly from Shaw.

The subject usually made her angry. The United States was the largest arms merchant, her customers including a range of nationalities, religions, colours and creeds so varied as to stretch belief. The Soviet Union offered the highest credit at the lowest interest rates. Britain and France competed for third place, followed by West Germany (officially not manufacturing arms) and Italy. Sweden and Switzerland came next, both risking their neutrality. Everyone did it. Even South Vietnam sold arms abandoned by American troops.

The two men were looking at her, waiting. But she said no more and they resumed their discussion.

'They're all too busy peddling for profit to think of the consequences,' Wolfgang said. 'If war flares up in the Middle East again, American arms will be fighting on both sides. It's happened before: in '65, with Pakistan and India; in '74 with the Turks and Greeks in Cyprus. Why not here?'

'Now I see why you don't have much respect for politicians,' said Mohan with a smile.

106

Wolfgang laughed. His face was tired too but real fatigue had not caught up with him yet. Eyes ablaze, he seemed far too excited by their discoveries to rest. Jan wished she could join in. For them it was still an adventure, thrilling, dangerous, but something to be joked about nevertheless. For her it had gone too far. She had killed a man. The guard's face kept returning to her mind. She remembered the smell of arrack on his breath, the drunken malevolence in his eyes, the touch of his hands on her skin. The next sequence was a blur. Jan shook her head to clear it. She needed something to keep the images away. She tried to follow her friends' discussion.

The bus had stopped and a voice called to her from outside. A beggar with shrunken legs tied across his lap swung himself along on his arms. She handed him a coin. There were far more beggars than she remembered: in every town now, cripples had been joined by the starving, all casualties of the current crisis. It seemed ironic that while Sri Lanka was short of foreign exchange to import essential food items, she bought billions of dollars' worth of arms. Depressed, Jan turned her attention to her friends.

'Who do you suppose would back a revolution here?' Mohan was saying.

Wolfgang shrugged.

'That's anyone's guess,' he said. 'The US might want another base in the area. Or the Chinese might be striking a blow for the oppressed masses. They rage on often enough about Indonesia's Suharto or Ferdinand Marcos of the Philippines – why not the Bandaranaikes of Sri Lanka?'

'Even when they backed them in '71?'

'Who knows.'

'Well, that would make nonsense of your Chu Chow theory,' Mohan laughed. 'I doubt if the two factions would work together.'

Wolfgang laughed too. Speculation did not seem to help. Jan looked away, discouraged. Outside, the world continued at its own leisurely pace. Two elephants swayed majestically on the bridge ahead. Another lay on its side in the water below, its eyes closed as a mahout scrubbed its hide with a coconut husk. On the far bank, a banyan tree spread branching arms while aerial roots hung down, curling from giant armpits to the ground; children had tied some roots together and were using them as swings.

Jan envied their unconcern. If only the journey were over, their problems handed over to someone else. Her eyes felt hot from lack of tears, her throat tight. Then she realized that her friends were looking at her. Wolfgang placed a hand on her knee and spoke again.

'I'm sorry, Jan,' he said, 'but couldn't you tell anything from the guns?'

She forced herself to think back, shutting her mind to the memories waiting at the edge. She shook her head.

'Not really,' she said at last. 'There was a bit of everything – from brand-new machine-guns to old shotguns, various styles and makes.'

'Perhaps they're from a private dealer, then.' Wolfgang turned back to Mohan. 'I've heard some of them could equip an army at short notice.'

Jan nodded, glad they did not need her any more. Her eyes watched an old lady carve pieces off an areca nut to add to her plug of betel. She knew the guns might have come from any-where. Political scientists were always describing the dangers of selling sophisticated weapons to unstable military elites. How long before an Amin or a Gaddafi turned upon the West the nuclear force their victims had provided? Or would Quincey beat them to it?

The pessimistic chain of thought stopped with a jolt. The bus stormed into the Colombo depot, barely missing a manic performer crunching up a tube of glass. The journey was over.

They wasted no time. Mohan was left to deal with the luggage, to untie his bike from the back, and then to find a room for three in a nearby hotel. He had insisted they stay together that night; there was no knowing what Quincey might do. But now Mohan's face betrayed no such concern. He waved cheerily as Jan and Wolfgang found a taxi to take them to the British High Commission. Jan was fingering the card Saunders had given her at Christine's funeral.

By the time they got back, Mohan had had a shower, a meal and a rest. Jan had asked him to phone her father too but the lines were still down. When they opened the door, he held out his arms towards them with a massive grin.

'Well, can we celebrate?' he said.

They did not respond. Wolfgang closed the door and stood preoccupied. At last, Jan spoke, but her voice shook.

'I don't think so,' she said.

Mohan let his arms drop. He could see she was near to tears. She watched him cross the blurred room to her side. Awkwardly, he put his arms around her. Jan rested her head against his chest, inhaled his clean smell. But her fists were clenched. Why couldn't it be over now? Hadn't they done enough?

Mohan held her away from him so that he could see her face.

'What's wrong?'

She did not answer. He led her to a chair and she lowered herself heavily into it. She was so tired, and now she was even more confused. After all their efforts, it seemed unfair. Mohan turned to Wolfgang then, hands on hips.

'Well?' he said. 'Tell me!'

Jan watched him, wondered what he would say about the decision half formed in Wolfgang's mind. She did not know what she wanted any more, except to be out of it. She was scared of what Quincey might do, for time was running out. Fatigue echoed in her voice, as she tried to explain.

'We'd almost reached Saunders' office,' she said, 'just at the point where the corridor meets the back stairs, when we saw his door open.'

'Yes?'

She shrugged vaguely.

'Wolfgang made me hide. He pulled me with him down the stairs.'

Mohan's eyebrows rose, his body turned for confirmation. Wolfgang shrugged too.

'Don't ask me to explain,' he said. 'I was jumpy, that's all. Dealing with Quincey has made me nervous.'

Mohan's eyebrows sank once more but he looked none the wiser. He turned back to Jan.

'And?'

'Two men came out,' she continued. 'Saunders and da Souza.'

'What? Are you . . .'

'I'm certain,' she said sadly. 'I couldn't forget that smile if I tried.'

Her chin dropped to her chest and her shoulders hunched forward. What she really needed was sleep. But how could she sleep with Quincey at their heels and ugly memories in her mind? And now this. She remembered what Wolfgang had said, prayed he had changed his mind. It was a crazy idea, and after all they had been through already, a bloody dangerous one. Mohan was watching her with concern.

'Well,' he said, 'did they say anything?'

She shook her head.

'Nothing I could catch. Then they shook hands and da Souza left.'

'And you went in.'

'After a bit, yes.'

Mohan waited.

'Well?' he said. 'Did you tell him?'

She did not answer at once and when she did, her words stumbled.

'I told him about the heroin and how it was probably being shipped to London in Maitland tea.'

Wolfgang cut in suddenly.

'He said he knew all about it.'

'He knew?'

'Yes, it seems there's been a new influx of heroin into England recently. Rumours connect it with Sri Lanka and a committee has been ordered to look into it. Saunders is in charge.'

'So why doesn't he do something?'

'They're waiting until they know who is involved at the London end so that they can catch them all.'

Mohan nodded, taking it in.

'What about Yala and the guns?' he said at last.

Wolfgang looked uncomfortable now.

'Didn't you tell him?'

Wolfgang's response was slow.

'I said there'd been a commotion last night at Arugam Bay and that, as far as I could make out, it had involved Quincey, Andrews and a man called da Souza.'

'That's all?'

'Yes. When I said the name, he stared at me hard.'

Wolfgang hesitated but Mohan was waiting for him to finish.

'He thought for a while, drumming his fingers on the desk, then he pressed the bell. He told his secretary to bring him all the information she could find on da Souza. Then he told us he would alert the police.'

'Did you ask him why da Souza was there?'

'No.'

'So you told him the rest?' Wolfgang shrugged.

'I told him the carts were carrying arms. I didn't mention the cave, or the guard – I didn't want to get into that.'

He glanced at Jan. Mohan's eyes followed and he nodded again. She could see that he was worried. But there was more to come. Wolfgang explained.

'I was all on edge,' he said urgently. 'Here we are, trying to find out how Christine died. We watch Quincey and find da Souza too. We go to Saunders for help. And again we find da Souza. And Saunders just sits there, drumming his fingers on his desk. We need more evidence, Mohan! Who else is involved? What are they up to? We can't stop now!'

'But Wolfgang!' Jan's voice sounded angry. 'Whatever it is is about to happen. In two days, Quincey said. So did Christine's letter.'

But she knew then that Wolfgang had not changed his mind.

'That's why I must go tonight,' he said quietly.

Mohan was lost. Jan watched his face as he struggled to keep up. She hoped he could dissuade Wolfgang.

'Go where?' he said helplessly.

'To da Souza's. Then perhaps we'll have some facts to get Saunders moving.'

Mohan looked horrified. Much as she had thought he would. She agreed. At that moment, she could think of nothing worse than a visit to da Souza's. The thought made her shiver.

'Oh, but it's a horrid place,' she said almost to herself. 'Like a nightmare, a cross between a hospital and a graveyard – and all the time, that awful smell.'

She stopped in surprise. For Wolfgang's face was alive with a sudden realization. One hand slapped against his thigh.

'Of course!' he said. 'Why didn't I think of that?'

'Think of what?' Mohan was lost again. This time, so was Jan.

'What she just said: the smell.'

'What smell, for heaven's sake?' Jan had rounded on him too.

'The one you noticed by the Mudalali's van. The one we both noticed in that fish. The one at da Souza's. It's formalin, a preservative. All undertakers use it.'

Jan was thinking hard, remembering.

'Yes,' she said slowly. 'I think you're right.'

'Which takes us back to da Souza,' Wolfgang said. 'Again. Don't ask me how. Formalin means a mortician and that, as far as I'm concerned, means da Souza.'

Mohan laughed, his head shaking with disbelief.

'Well,' he suggested, 'Andrews would look a bit silly with a special order of decomposing fish – and August is hot.'

But Wolfgang was not laughing. His face was lined with fatigue and resolution.

'So, you see,' he said, 'someone must go.'

The three of them were silent for a moment.

'Then it had better be me,' Mohan said quietly at last.

He turned to Jan. She saw that his face was set. She knew that expression: it meant he had reached a decision it would be impossible to budge.

'You'd better get some rest,' he said. 'You've hardly re-covered from last night.'

She did not bother to protest; she knew she stood no chance. Mohan did not even pause for her response. He was gazing across at Wolfgang still waiting by the door. The German looked so tired standing there, his body like a crumpled scarecrow propped up on a stick.

'And that goes for you too,' he said.

Wolfgang hesitated. She watched him think. He was clearly exhausted, deep shadows round his eyes. Like her, he had not slept for two days. Mohan laughed suddenly.

'You're so sleepy da Souza might find you dozing in one of his coffins in the morning,' he said with a smile.

That gave her a shock. She could not help remembering the last time she had seen Christine. She had no desire to have similar visions of Wolfgang. Or Mohan, for that matter. The policeman regretted his joke at once. He reached out a hand to touch her cheek.

'I'm sorry,' he said. 'I didn't mean to upset you.'

Jan smiled shakily.

'I know,' she said. 'And anyway, I think you're right.'

He smiled back.

'I know I am,' he said. 'Just look at us. I'm rested, washed and fed, with all my faculties – for what they're worth – intact. You two need a bath badly, food even more, and most of all twelve hours' uninterrupted sleep. So I'm obviously the best bet. Besides,' he concluded with a jaunty grin, 'it's my turn.'

'I could come with you,' Wolfgang said. 'Just to see that you're OK.'

Jan gave an involuntary start. Mohan was at her side at once. She felt ashamed.

'I just didn't expect to be left alone,' she said in a low voice.

She did not need to go on. Mohan understood.

'My poor Jan,' he said. 'We wouldn't dream of leaving you alone.'

Wolfgang's resistance collapsed. He wanted to help Mohan but he could see Jan needed him too. And for all he knew, she might be running the greater risk: she should not be left alone with Quincey loose. Jan thanked him with her eyes.

When Mohan had gone, they ordered a meal in their room, and showered while waiting. The cold water stung Jan awake. Her attention returned to every cut and graze; she had not realized how many there were. Wolfgang helped wash the blood from her hair, cleaned up the gash on her head. Then she wrapped herself in a hotel towel and washed all her clothes. At last the food arrived. They sat close together on one of the beds, the tray on a chair.

They ate in silence. They were following Mohan's journey in their minds, wondering how far he'd got. Jan's head throbbed. A drop of water trickled from her hair down her back, carving a cool path through the heat.

She watched their images in the dusty mirror on the wall. They were both wearing hotel towels now, Wolfgang's bronzed skin accentuated by the yellow cloth. They looked tired but clean. Her body seemed pale beside his, her limbs slender and smooth. The light overhead tossed shining arcs into her hair as it moved. Beneath those dark damp curls, her eyes were bright.

The fan droned monotonously. Jan noticed that the ends of his hair were almost dry. Then she saw the swollen cut across his knuckles and remembered. Her mind sped back to his altercation with the barrier guard, the desperation with which he had fought to reach the van before it snatched her away. Back to the previous night, when he had swooped out of the darkness on Mohan's bike to pluck her from her pursuers. Back still further to the evening they had sat together above Maitland watching the sun go down.

Her mind stopped there. She remembered how close they had been, how warmly he had responded to her tentative kiss. She felt that same closeness now. Wolfgang seemed to sense it. In the mirror, she saw him look at her and smile.

'Safer now?' he said.

She nodded. It was good to be near him. But she did not tell him how afraid she was of the night. All day she had struggled to keep those memories from her mind; now she felt them gathering again. She shivered suddenly. Wolfgang put his arm around her. She dropped her head against his shoulder and breathed in his strength.

'It's nothing,' she said. 'At least, nothing real. Just nasty things in my head.'

He seemed to understand. He put one hand under her knees and lifted her on to the bed. Then he unwound her towel and slipped her naked body between the sheets. His movements were strong and deft.

'There you are, my sweet,' he said softly. 'Let me just get rid of this tray. Then I'll come back and keep the bogies away.'

She nodded, smiling. He placed the tray in the corridor outside, then locked the door. Turning out the light nearest her, he pulled a chair closer to the bed beneath the fan, and sat down.

'Now you relax,' he said. 'I'll stay here till you sleep.'

But he was too far away. Without his touch to comfort her, she was frightened to let go. The fear she fought against in her mind built up into a physical pressure and her body began to shake again. She buried her face into the sheets. Bloody memories were lurking in the shadows of her mind. The smell of sweat and arrack. Fear driving her knee into his groin. The bubble at his chin. She fought them back. Tension sent shivers back and forth across her skin, incomprehensible in that humidity. She clenched her fists in panic. Alone in the jungle once more, she had forgotten Wolfgang.

She felt a firm hand on her back. He was sitting beside her, stroking the fear away. His hand passed repeatedly from the nape of her neck down her spine, lightly over the curve of her buttocks to the hollows behind her knees. Slowly, his touch reached her mind. She felt the shivers subside. The images dispersed. Her fists began to unclench, the muscles in her legs to relax. Tightened eyelids fluttered free. His fingers explored the stiffness at her neck, released the rigid barriers she had placed against the night, then resumed their soothing journey down her spine. Her mind followed it, pacing out the easy rhythm of that hand, forgetting the guard, forgetting Quincey, forgetting even Mohan too. Soon the fear was gone. She was barely aware of that room, the bed, the heat. His touch was all she knew. Her breath came easily, rhythmically, like a child's, her whole body in harmony with his hand.

Then it paused. He must have thought she was asleep. For his weight lifted slowly from the bed as if to go. But she roused herself and stopped him.

'Don't go,' she whispered.

For she did not know if the spell would last when he was gone. Without speaking, he removed his towel and slid his body down the length of hers. There was not much room. She moved over to give him space, and felt his hand slowly soothing her back once more. Her eyes closed. Again, she felt that hypnotic touch, wishing the nightmares away.

But something changed. She did not notice why or when. Only that her spellbound mind followed his hand with a new intensity. The feeling took a long time to register as an idea, longer still before she recognized it for what it was. She wanted him. She thought of Paul, far away in England. Then she turned her body round.

He seemed surprised. His hand stopped as if uncertain of its role, his face anxious not to misunderstand. So, to make things clear, she took her own hand and passed it slowly from the nape of his neck to the hollows of his knees. For good measure, she kissed him too, and he understood. His hand descended to her breast. They made love gently at first, then with a rising passion that surprised her. She did not think of Paul again. All the fear and hatred of the night before, the ferocity of her own reactions, was burned up in the stabbing violence of making love. And afterwards, as she lay curled warm and damp against his chest, his arm across her waist, she knew she had won her battle with the dark. She could sleep at last.

She woke at 4.0 a.m. The far light was on but Mohan had not returned. She found Wolfgang's wrist and checked his watch again. He was fast asleep, his skin softened, his lips apart. She leaned on one elbow to watch him. Her gaze traced the lines sketched round his mouth by laughter, round his eyes by the sun. She wanted to kiss him but was afraid he might awake. She bent her head anyway. His lips responded, arms winding round to pull her down, but his eyes stayed closed. She lay against him, nuzzled kisses into his neck, and waited till he relaxed in sleep once more.

She was worried about Mohan. Stronger now, she was ashamed that her weakness had sent him off alone. She remembered the look in his eyes before he left. She had always taken his friendship for granted. Now she prayed nothing had happened to him. She could not bear to think that he might have been in trouble while they made love.

Then she heard the roar of a motorbike down in the street. That would be him. Carefully, she disentangled herself from Wolfgang's limbs and slipped out of bed. She dressed quickly. Minutes later, she was running down the stairs.

But the street was empty. The motorbike she had heard faded round the corner to her right. A lamp glared straight ahead. Jan stood there undecided. Now that she was dressed it seemed foolish to go back. She ought to check that Mohan was all right.

She half turned towards the stairs again, thinking to tell Wolfgang first, then stopped. He needed that rest. Besides, she had no intention of going into da Souza's alone. She only wanted to reassure herself that Mohan had come out. He had said he would leave his bike behind the big tree at the top of the drive. If it had gone, she would know he had slipped off somewhere else. There might be a dozen reasons why he had not returned. Perhaps something he had found had sent him to Saunders at once, regardless of the hour. Perhaps he had gone somewhere else to sleep: he may have tried to wake them and failed; he may have decided not to disturb them again; or perhaps his absence was proof of tact, of his knowledge that they would end up making love. She smiled at the thought. Then she woke a taxi driver asleep in his cab and commanded him to take her to da Souza's.

The bike was exactly where Mohan had left it. That meant he was still inside. The realization worried her. She wished now she had woken Wolfgang. She glanced at the taxi still waiting on the road. She could go back for him but it would take too long. And anyway, she reassured herself, she was not alone now: Mohan was still in there. She did not give herself the chance to change her mind. Paying the driver quickly, she sent him away. Then she left the open drive.

She followed the shadows of the garden wall towards the house. She wanted to get as close as possible, close enough to eavesdrop in case there was anything to hear. But she still did not mean to go inside. For all she knew, Mohan was simply taking his time.

As she drew closer to the house, she prayed there were no guards. And yet, if da Souza were involved, the lack of them was odd. The building loomed above her, both a business and a home. The family lived upstairs; downstairs was the reception room where Christine's body had been and, at the back, the embalming rooms. Not a single light was on. She made a detour through the garden, circling the house to reach the back. That was where Mohan would have gone.

The open window came as a surprise. She hesitated. Had Mohan opened it? Was he still inside? Or had he left and forgotten to close it again? She listened carefully. A breeze ruffled the foliage in the garden behind. No sound from within. Had Mohan been and gone? She half believed it, then remembered the bike propped behind that tree and knew she was wrong. With deepening apprehension, she climbed in. Then she tripped on something and almost fell. Her fingers closed around a torch: it was Mohan's. But why?

She paused to listen, heard only her own fast breathing, the stampeding beat of her heart. Then she switched on the torch. The room was empty. The torchbeam slithered over two marble slabs, a tiled sink, two heavy bottles left upside down to dry, a tray of lethal-looking instruments and two doors. She held one hand over her mouth as if to stop her own breath and listened again. Nothing. She slid towards the nearer door.

In the half light of approaching dawn, she recognized the parlour where she had seen Christine. There were the steps from the front door; there the brocade curtains framing the entrance and, at the top of the steps, the matching urns. In the middle of the polished floor stood the table that had held her casket and, apparently asleep inside, Christine.

She gasped and the ray of light scrabbled on the ceiling. Then she steadied herself, brought it slowly down again, back to the shape that made her wonder if she was in a nightmare of her own unnerving memories. The casket was real, beautifully grained and varnished, lined with silk. But it was empty. Jan stared, then with an effort unhooked her eyes. She would find no clues there.

She retraced her steps and tried the other door. It opened onto a storeroom filled with caskets of every size, every design: some ornate with gilt handles, others with plaques where a name might be engraved; and plain rubberwood coffins, mummy-shaped.

On the far side, shelves rose to the ceiling, each supporting a row of earthenware pots. She lifted one and read the label: 'Ashes, Gomez D. C., Borella, 29 July 1975'. She replaced it hurriedly, then paused. It might hide anything, even heroin, for who would break those seals to peer at a dead man's bones? Jan searched for an excuse, her eyes racing over an assortment of religious symbols: elephant tusks set in ebony; brass oil burners for Buddhists; statues of Hindu gods and goddesses; plain crosses for Protestants; ornate figures of Christ crucified for Catholics; and an array of gilt-framed prints.

The plain coffins lay in one corner apart from the rest. If she were hiding something, Jan reasoned, she would choose those. She turned her back on the earthenware pots with relief. Balancing the torch to shine onto the coffins, with both hands she slid open the clasp on the first lid. Each one was the same. Despite her expectations, she was shocked: da Souza possessed an armoury comparable to that in the cave.

She sat back on her haunches to think. She understood Mohan's absence now: these guns linking da Souza indisputably with Quincey must have sent him straight to Saunders to explain. It was odd he had lost the torch; odd too that he had left his bike; but the rest made sense. All she had to do now was go before she wrecked everything.

But she wanted to check some of the more expensive caskets first. She tried the nearest. The front opened up like the doors of a cabinet and remained propped outward for display. She was scared now. Neither guns nor ammunition lay inside. Nor heroin. She wanted to laugh but checked the sound in her mind; the feeling of hysteria prevailed. There she was in a mortician's, surrounded by caskets and coffins, the smell of death in the air; and yet she was surprised to open a casket and find a corpse. It was absurd.

Slowly, Jan drew the shroud down. She did not recognize him at first for someone had turned his face into a joke; but then she knew.

'Mohan!' she breathed. 'Oh, my God!'

She knelt in disbelief. Blank pupils stared past her, their sightlessness ringed in white paint with daubs of yellow radiating from them like twin brown-centred suns. The mouth hung slack, unstapled, a garish scream. The moustache had been brushed upwards as if electrified and neat blobs of red sat in each brown cheek, symbols of impotent rage.

Her hand reached out. But when her fingers touched his cheek, they jumped back in shock. Beneath the soft skin lay the hardness of the embalmer's art.

Her brain refused to register what she saw. Her face was blank for the thoughts had gone, no emotions to display. She was numb. Seconds dragged as she fought to understand. The grotesque vision, evidence of a mind too sick to contemplate, began to seep into her mind: Mohan, and he was dead.

Her body thawed. Reactions followed swift upon each other, all substitutes for tears: disgust, anger, fear; then anger again, a rage that made her shake. She scooped a handful of grenades from the coffin beside her and tucked them under Mohan's shroud. When they cremated him, those bastards would get a shock.

She was still smoothing the cloth down when she heard a noise. She tried to turn but it was too late. Something crashed into her skull. A black cloud invaded her mind and she fell. Her last thought was that she was a fool: she should have known it was a trap.

When she came to, her head ached. Her hair felt wet: the blow must have broken open that cut again. She opened her eyes and quickly closed them again: the bright light hurt. She tried to sit up but her arms and legs were pinioned. She began to panic.

A cordial voice greeted her:

'Ah, so you're awake at last.'

Her eyes slowly came into focus. On the wall in front of her, a bronze figure danced in an aureole of fire. One leg kicked the air, the other crushed the squirming dwarf of ignorance. Two hands celebrated the jig of life; a third beat the awakening drum; a fourth held the fire of destruction. In the supreme symbol of evolution and decay, Shiva beat his drum and the world danced; then, in the midst of man's folly, he applied the cauterizing fire. Symbols, legends and dark omens passed in confusion through Jan's mind. Which part of the cycle was she in, awakening or the final sleep? She shook her head to clear it and sent red sparks of pain into her eyes that confused her more.

She tried to concentrate. She was lying on a hard slab. Beside her was another, da Souza bent over it, working. With a jolt that lifted the sparks into a whirl, Jan saw that he was embalming a corpse. She closed her eyes quickly. The image of Mohan's cruelly painted face swung down behind them and she groaned in despair.

Da Souza seemed to understand.

'Did you get a shock when you saw him?' he asked. 'I wanted

to fix a spring at his back so that he'd sit up and stare at you like in a horror film but I didn't have time.'

A rigid silence was all that showed of Jan's struggle for control. Her fragile sanity did not encompass words. But da Souza needed no prompting.

'He was much easier to embalm than this autopsy case,' he said, 'or your drowned friend.'

She roused herself from her sea of pain. Had they been right about Christine's death? Da Souza saw that he had caught her attention and chuckled.

'Oh, your friend drowned all right,' he assured her lugubriously, 'but she wasn't in the water very long. What you might call a freak accident. I suppose I should have sealed her into a coffin with a zinc lining all the same – a drowned body is usually bloated and decomposing fast – but it seemed a shame not to show my handiwork.'

He chuckled again and Jan knew they'd been right. She tried not to think about it. She had to be in control; there was no knowing what might happen with this madman, what chance she might still have to get away. She blinked hard. For her own sake, she had to concentrate.

'Sorry I can't attend to you,' da Souza was saying with exaggeratedly British courtesy. 'But I've rather an urgent customer here – booked for a splendid funeral later this morning. I'm sure you understand.'

She blinked again, unable to find anything to say. Da Souza embarked on a rambling monologue unperturbed.

'Nice to have someone to appreciate my work, you know. The relatives usually take one look and burst into tears. My wife's no better, she gets quite nervous when there's a corpse down here. It's pretty disheartening sometimes.'

He smiled warmly in Jan's direction, an actor's warmth, heavily laced with malice. He seemed to expect an answer so she said the first thing that came into her head.

'I sympathize with your wife.'

'Ah, but she's no ordinary Chinese,' da Souza replied mysteriously. 'I was disappointed when she turned out to be squeamish.'

What had he said? Jan had been too unnerved to listen

121

properly. Chinese? Yes, she knew that; yet the word hung in the air, taunting her with what it did not say.

'Before we married,' da Souza said in the same teasing conversational tone, 'she was called Wu. Ling Wu, her father was. I expect you've heard the name.'

This time there was no doubting his intent. Ling Wu was notorious, well known to narcotics agents in South-East Asia in the sixties, a key figure in the Chu Chow. In early 1972, he had disappeared. It was said he had changed his name; or retired to Manhattan to enjoy his wealth; or had died in an accident. Who would have guessed he had come to Sri Lanka? Da Souza was enjoying her consternation.

'He brought his daughters with him,' he explained. 'My wife is the eldest.'

'Is Ling Wu still alive?' she asked.

'No.' He smiled, watching her think it out.

'So you've inherited the family business?'

The question was crucial and they both knew it. Da Souza gazed mockingly at her. In the given situation, his expression seemed to say, why not tell the truth?

'That's right,' he grinned. 'Explains a lot, doesn't it?'

Jan exhaled slowly. So they had been right about that too. The Chu Chow were operating in Sri Lanka to the orders of this arrogant Burgher and his squeamish Chinese wife. This was exactly what they needed to know. If she could tell Saunders, she thought desperately; if she could only escape. But her bonds held. Her tormentor returned to his work and their earlier topic of conversation.

'Tonight I can share my skill and artistry with you,' he said. 'Now you see this fellow here?' He paused. 'No, perhaps you can't.'

He pushed a cushion under her head to raise it the necessary few inches. The rough movement made it throb unmercifully. She closed her eyes to let the swirling pain subside.

'There, that's better,' da Souza was saying. 'Well, have a look at the poor chap yourself. He's not very pretty, is he?'

For want of an alternative, Jan looked. It was an old man's body, showing the gashes of a recent post-mortem. The skin had been drained of blood to the colour of wax. Coarse stitches marked where the knife had gone, marching down his chest; from the base of his stomach to a point beneath his chin, the corpse was a gory mess. She stared in revulsion as da Souza dug his hand into the old man's side, found a wad of cotton wool and rags, and threw it into the incinerator. Then he proceeded to wipe away the blood that had dripped from the corners of the dead man's mouth. The skull had been sawn through and the wisps of white hair were matted with red.

'"The way to a man's heart is through his stomach",' da Souza quoted, 'but in this case, it's literally true.' He patted the grisly belly. 'His heart's right here. So are his brains, his lungs and his liver, all duly inspected by the coroner.'

The cheerful laugh suited neither his profession nor his blood-reddened fingers. She stared at those hands. The skin was excessively dry and small pieces flaked off like scales. They were an old man's hands, death seeping into his skin. But his movements were quick and neat. She shuddered. Panic rose into her throat and she fought to keep it down. She dared not lose control now.

'By the time I've finished,' da Souza was saying, 'his hair will be washed and combed to hide the broken skull and there'll be a neat square of sticking plaster just here.' One finger rested under the corpse's chin where the last stitch dug cruelly into the flesh. 'His clothes will hide the rest.'

Jan was reminded of the sticking plaster Wolfgang had worn the day they first met. The memory stung. Why had she not woken him? But she remembered the trap. Would it have been better if he had been caught in it too?

Da Souza stood back as if to visualize the finished effect. His detachment was that of an artist contemplating his canvas before making the first brushstroke, aware even then of its final form. He shot another teasing glance at Jan.

'You can wait, can't you?' he said.

Da Souza prattled on. Perhaps he knew that the constant talk of death was the most unnerving torture he could have devised; perhaps, innured to it, he was unaware that she might not be. Jan tried to extract more information but even pointblank questions were ignored. He continued his macabre chatter.

'A mortician can't be glum all the time,' he said briskly.

He had a store of gruesome tales to tell. Some balanced precariously on the edge of crime; others toppled headlong over it. There was the one about the foreign ambassador who had shot his wife for infidelity and bribed da Souza to embalm her at once. From a graphic description of the bullet wounds, da Souza constructed his own inventive account of the shooting. The cemetery had been literally crawling with police – behind every gravestone, he insisted with glee – but they could do nothing and both ashes and ambassador left on the next available flight.

Stories like this terrified her. The police seemed to have no jurisdiction over da Souza's kingdom of death: a mortician might murder with impunity. Where else was a body so acceptable a part of the furniture? Where else could one find an array of coffins and caskets designed specifically to hold and therefore conceal a corpse? She could see through the open storeroom door a pile of rectangular shapes, each awaiting an occupant. One held Mohan already; any of the others would do for her.

The memory of Mohan under that shroud assailed her again. The thought of how he had died was almost more than she could bear. And it was her cowardice that had sent him to his death alone.

Da Souza had stopped talking. Jan glanced at him with apprehension. His task was almost complete. Into a vein in the corpse's upper arm dripped a pink liquid, its recipe engraved on Jan's mind: formaldehyde, a pickling agent like vinegar, da Souza had said; glycerine and phenol to eject blood from the arteries, to guard against infection and to reduce the hardening effect; and red eocin to preserve a natural skin colour in the absence of blood. Jan inhaled that familiar sickening smell. The bottle was almost empty.

'You foreigners are most peculiar about death,' he continued, warming to his theme. 'I did a marvellous job for an American once, but the wife was quite mad. There was only one flight to the States a week then and when she learned that she, her husband and her dog would all have to go on the same plane, she flew into a rage. And why?'

He chuckled merrily. Jan gave a constricted shrug to show she was listening but he did not notice.

'Because her poor dog would have to travel in the luggage compartment with her husband's body. Can you believe it? I told her he was perfectly embalmed and the casket sealed but she refused to listen. It was unhygienic, she said, and cruel. So she and the dog took the first plane and her husband had to wait for the second – in the hot season too!'

Jan gave an unconvincing grin. The bottle was empty. Da Souza was completing the finishing touches on the old man now. She watched, her nerves stretched taut. She wanted to scream at him to stop his nonsense and get on with it for she could take no more. He straightened up with a sigh.

'There we are,' he said, grinning across at her. 'Any questions?'

She was taken by surprise. She shook her head, her body tensed. But da Souza seemed to have something on his mind.

'That's odd,' he mused deliberately. 'I was sure you would have.'

The taunting tone made her want to know.

'Like what?' she said.

'About heroin perhaps?'

Jan was astonished. After what seemed like hours of morbid chit-chat, this was the first reference to why she had come. But da Souza was teasing her.

'I thought you might have read how American troops smuggled heroin home from Vietnam,' he said. 'In polythene bags neatly stitched inside their fallen comrades. Did you think we were doing the same?'

'Are you?'

'Sorry, no,' came the smug reply. 'Our game is much more complicated. A beautiful mosaic in which each tiny piece has its place. Just a few more pieces to go in, a few mistakes to be thrown out, and we're ready.'

Da Souza gave the corpse a final pat on the shoulder.

'That's that, my friend,' he said. 'A suit of clothes and you can go into your casket.'

Then he turned to Jan and his expression changed. The artist had found a defect that needed correction.

'You're one of the mistakes,' he explained. 'So I'm frightfully sorry and all that, but you'll have to go.'

He was standing at the head of the slab, staring down at her. Even upside down, the malice in those hard grey eyes was unavoidable.

'In two days, we'll bring our mosaic out into the public eye – without mistakes.'

Da Souza frowned as if she were guilty of some serious misdemeanour. Then he reached back to adjust a large bottle high on the wall. Her bottle. The waves of malice grew stronger, more specific, sending complementary waves of fear through Jan's mind. He selected an instrument from the tray.

Was this how Mohan had died? A controlled stabbing like a doctor giving an injection. A sharp pain in the upper arm. Excruciating agony like a tidal wave across his chest. Pink liquid surging through his veins, replacing blood and life with artificial death. Was this how Mohan had died? Jan waited, her eyes clenched tight, her body rigid in panic and anticipated pain.

But nothing happened. When she opened her eyes, da Souza had moved to one side and was gazing down at her, a new expression on his face: it was a mixture of admiration, cruelty and desire. With a shock, Jan saw her vulnerability. She had not thought of that. A hand reached out to touch her and she flinched. A flash of anger darkened da Souza's face, then he began to smile. Deliberately, he laid the metal instrument aside and turned towards her.

'It's a pity really I don't like my women stiff,' he said. 'There's plenty of scope for that sort of thing in my job.'

He was running one hand slowly down her leg. The palm was scaly, dry.

'I assure you I have tried,' he told her earnestly, 'but it always seemed rather boring. I need some kind of resistance, I suppose.'

His hand had reached her ankle and began to rise again. It moved slowly, da Souza's eyes gazing mockingly into Jan's. The change of tack was too much for her. Repelled by the touch of those hands, she lay there, unable to speak or scream.

'I told you we'd soon have them both,' a steely voice interrupted.

Da Souza's smile vanished. Jan closed her eyes in relief. Those loathsome hands had gone.

'What a funeral!' she heard da Souza say. 'Three bodies instead of one!'

'It should have been four.'

Jan opened her eyes. She knew that voice. But first she had to breathe, then to focus. At last, her eyes found Quincey. For the first time in her life, she was glad to see him.

But as she watched his face, she knew the feeling would not last. He was leaning against the doorway, black eyes fixed on his colleague. His smile was far from friendly. Da Souza had the sense not to reply. The silence deepened, accentuating the hierarchy of power. At length, his point made, Quincey turned that hard gaze to Jan.

'My dear girl,' he drawled, 'you're even worse than that silly bitch, Christine.'

But Jan was still too shocked to speak. Quincey gave her time, then tried again.

'You came to find the guns, didn't you?'

She swallowed, forced herself to answer, her voice to work.

'I came to look for Mohan,' she said.

The name started a whirlpool of grief within, like a pebble thrown into her heart. She closed her eyes until it subsided. She knew she could not cope with that now.

'But you knew about the guns, didn't you?' Quincey repeated. His face was beaded with sweat. He daubed a handkerchief at it absent-mindedly, but his eyes never left hers. 'You killed my guard.'

She nodded. It was too late to argue.

'We found the heroin at Maitland too,' she said.

There was no bravado in her voice, only weariness. It seemed so pointless now that Mohan was dead.

'It's all over anyway,' she added in the same dull tones. 'The police know all about you. Whatever it is you're plotting won't succeed now.'

Quincey's expression changed. But it was not the transformation she expected: the hard look was replaced by a beaming satisfaction.

'And what do you think we are plotting, my dear?' he asked.

The sudden affability puzzled her. She shrugged.

'A revolution, I suppose, but I don't see how you could hope to succeed.'

'And why not, may I ask?'

Jan was beginning to find his avuncular tone irritating.

'Because in April '71,' she shot back with some asperity, 'the JVP failed.'

But Quincey was unimpressed.

'Perhaps I'm more realistic,' he countered equably. 'I have years of political experience behind me that Wijeweera never had.'

'He wasn't related to the prime minister,' she retorted.

Wijeweera called himself a 'modern Bolshevik'; after years spent living in the Soviet Union and studying both Russian and Chinese Communism, he had the right to do so. Quincey's head bowed in apparent agreement, but his eyes glinted.

'I see your point,' he conceded. 'None the less, I am a revolutionary, and a successful coup will take place in exactly thirty-six hours.'

He pulled a chair from the edge of the room, placed it in front of her and sat down. He settled back against the wooden frame before gesturing to da Souza to help Jan sit up. His reluctance obvious, da Souza obeyed. Jan knew Quincey had deliberately spoiled his colleague's fun. She wondered now if he was contemplating having some of his own instead. She hoped it would take none of da Souza's forms.

She sat upright now on the marble slab, her wrists and ankles bound. It was a definite improvement. Quincey waited till he had her full attention.

'First of all, my dear,' he said, 'Wijeweera's cause was just.'

Jan's mouth opened to protest but Quincey made an imperative gesture so she listened instead. Da Souza was listening too. He leaned against the other slab, arms folded, a smile playing about his mouth.

'I didn't see it at first,' Quincey admitted. 'But when I saw how large the JVP following was, I looked at our government – its premises, its progress, its goals – from their point of view. And I saw what they meant.'

From the corner of her eye, Jan saw da Souza's smile: it bothered her. Quincey continued.

'Those rebels fought heroically against enormous odds and were massacred. Hundreds are still in gaol. And yet, after mass arrests of innocent and guilty alike, after torture, executions and all kinds of terror tactics, morale is high. A strong underground movement has developed.'

Jan was confused. Quincey was referring to government reprisals that had officially never happened. Why else except that they disgusted him? Had he really been won over to the rebels' side? It seemed impossible. She struggled to work out why.

'This isn't 1971,' she said slowly. 'You can't just try again.'

'Why not? The grievances are still there. Unemployment is still rising. The upcountry peasant is predominantly landless; the wet zone peasant loses both crops and possessions to monsoon floods; the dry zone peasant suffers drought and famine.'

She nodded vaguely but Quincey did not stop. Either his words or his feelings had carried him away.

'In the north, it hasn't rained for four years: that means starvation-level survival. And disaffection increases month by month. You've seen it yourself!'

'Yes, but . . .'

'But our government – mine, if you like – is doing nothing about it!'

The resounding phrases drew her into the argument. Quincey's eloquence troubled her but her desire to understand brushed doubt aside. She was remembering the discussion her friends had had on the bus.

'The armed forces are stronger now,' she said 'and the government knows from experience which nations it can count on for support. It will be an even bloodier massacre than before.'

'Revolutions are never easy, my dear, but this one will work.'

'Why should it – when Wijeweera failed?'

But Quincey was unruffled by her scepticism.

'First,' he said, 'the JVP appeal was merely ideological. Those five or six years of preparation – classes in elementary politics; reminders of our past glories; explanations of the economic crisis with popular insurrection as the answer to it all – they met a deep-seated psychological need, but they weren't practical.'

He paused, watching Jan's face.

'The net was spread wide but there was no time to tighten it up. When the crunch came, there was no cohesive unit to fight back: each group reacted differently. When Wijeweera was arrested, dissension broke out among the rest and potential success collapsed.'

'Could you do any better?'

'We shall,' Quincey corrected her gravely. 'We know what revolution means. Unfortunately for the JVP, Che Guevara's death sparked off a suicidal heroism. They saw the Cuban path like a John Wayne film: ten strong men behind their leader and the battle's won. That kind of adventurism no longer exists.'

Jan nodded sadly. She remembered the reports of insurgents captured and killed: eight hundred students in the Colombo district alone, some only fourteen or fifteen years old. The average age was twenty. A students' 'Suicide Squad' had been operating in the bitter fighting in the north. How many of those idealistic boys and girls were still alive? Quincey was right: the island had learned a hard lesson in 1971.

'Secondly,' he continued, 'the JVP had no independent supply of arms. Robberies provided some. For the rest, apart from some Chinese-made weapons, some 303s and Belgian FNs smuggled in by the North Koreans, they had to rely on guns handed over by sympathizers and homemade bombs. Before they could even block communications, they had to seize the police stations for arms. No wonder they were massacred!'

Jan recalled the staggering collection of weaponry in de Souza's storeroom and in the cave. It was beginning to make sense.

'Whereas you have enough,' she said.

Quincey bowed his head again. But she was still not satisfied.

'The JVP had a huge following,' she argued. 'The official number arrested was over ten thousand.'

Quincey laughed complacently.

'Numbers are meaningless,' he said, 'without the right distribution. Ninety per cent of those insurgents came from the Sinhalese Buddhist peasantry, mostly from the central and south-west rural areas. But there was no following among the plantation Tamils; not much from the Ceylon Tamils in the north and east; little support from the urban working class; and no response at all from the trade unions – which was fatal!'

The criticism seemed just. Jan could imagine the forcefulness of the Jaffna Tamils if their allegiance was won. As for the estate labourers, their discontent might be exploited with impressive effect. And if Quincey had managed to reach the trades unions, the island could be brought to a standstill.

'But . . .' she began.

Quincey's hand rose to silence her. The persuasive flow continued.

'Here in Colombo,' he declared, 'they gave up far too easily. When that bungled Wellawaya attack alerted the island six hours too early, their leaders fled: one man with two hundred students and seventy-five hand bombs tried to capture the city! Even the attempt to kidnap the prime minister was a fiasco! As a result, the government controlled the entire military machine: the rebels didn't stand a chance.'

'And in your case?'

'In my case,' Quincey concluded in clipped tones, 'my headquarters are in Colombo, for the army and police must be paralysed first. Trained battalions are waiting for my signal in every major city. I know the procedure to be followed in the event of another insurrection and the exact locations of the government's arsenals and armed forces. Once the key points are under my control and the present leaders taken care of, phase two swings into action: all workers on estates and factories down tools. Economic production will halt. Communications will be disrupted. We'll have total control!'

The audacity of the plan took Jan's breath away.

'As simple as that?' she said at last.

'As simple as that. Remember, Wijeweera's hand was forced.'

She had to admit it. The JVP had faced a touchy strategic problem: they could not move before the masses were ready; but they had to strike before the government struck first. In March, with a disastrous economy and JVP popularity ascending to unprecedented heights, the government cracked down: it was then or never.

'Whereas we,' said Quincey, nodding his head with such emphasis that his cheeks quivered, 'have chosen the time and place that suits us best. We are acting, not reacting; manipulating, not being manipulated.'

Jan's disbelief crumbled. Some details still bothered her but she believed him now. She frowned in her effort to concentrate. Quincey waited.

'Something's worrying you, my dear,' he said. 'Is it the heroin?'

She nodded. His answer was simple.

'Arms cost money, Jan,' he said.

The use of her name made her start with distaste. Quincey did not notice. Jan remembered the packets of heroin at Maitland, and the discussion late that night on Mohan's verandah. Mohan had warned her about Quincey then. She remembered how his voice had shaken on her behalf. She would never hear that voice again. Never walk into Muhammad's and watch his eyes light up. Never see him smile. The grief she had been fighting so hard to suspend swung down. She bit her lip fiercely to hold back the tears.

'In '71,' Quincey was saying, 'the rivers of this island ran red with the blood of idealists needlessly killed. I'm a practical man, my dear. The end justifies the means.'

'Does that go for the people you've killed?' Jan demanded, angered by her pain. 'Mohan. Christine. The man in the hospital. That poor monk. "The end justifies the means" – is that it?'

Quincey's face was grave.

'Politics is hard, my dear,' he said, 'and revolution the hardest of its parts. But please remember, your friends died for a noble cause.'

His oratory left her speechless. Even before she saw da Souza's smile, she knew she was the victim of a cruel joke. They had splashed paint on Mohan's face and now in the same mean spirit they had staged a farce with her credulity in the central role. They were sick. With bitter fury, she kicked out at Quincey but could not reach. She set her face into a mask instead, determined to be mocked no more.

'I take my hat off to you,' da Souza spluttered. 'She really believed it! Right up to that bit about her friends' heroic deaths, she was lapping it up!'

Jan's head sang with rage. She glared at him with all the derision she could muster, but da Souza was in no state to notice. He was laughing so much he was in danger of falling over. Quincey laughed with him, evidently proud of the charade.

'No wonder,' he said. 'Some of it's true and the rest' – he gestured modestly – 'put it down to the skill of the natural politician.'

He turned to Jan with apparent solicitude. But his eyes glittered.

'Anything else you'd like to know?' he said.

But she had had enough of their games. Even the thought of playing for time did not appeal to her now. She still did not understand, but she was beaten.

'Well, I can't sit here chatting all day,' Quincey resumed briskly. 'You take care of things this end,' he said, making a vague gesture towards da Souza, 'and I'll go on ahead to Kandy.'

As he rose, the words filtered into Jan's closed brain. Kandy? Surely he had mentioned Kandy once before? Her mind raced to remember before it was too late. Quincey bowed his farewell but the irony was wasted: she had remembered.

'The bhikkhu was going to Kandy,' she said, feeling her way. 'That's why you had him killed.'

The urgency in her voice made him turn. He smiled, teasing her again, savouring his reply. His tone was condescending.

'Very good, my dear,' he said. 'And Kandy is where it all begins. I'm going to see my fellow conspirator, His Holiness the Mahanayaka of the Malwatta chapter, now residing in the Temple of the Tooth. And if you choose not to accept that, my dear, you may, for in your place I too would find it singularly hard to believe!'

He bowed again and left. The door swung shut behind him.

But the oppressive presence he had brought stayed with them in the room.

Jan was still staring after him. Her mind spun as she struggled to work it out. For the Buddhist monastic order in Sri Lanka comprised three sects. The oldest and largest of these had two chapters, both centred in Kandy, each with a Mahanayaka or chief monk at its head. The custodianship of that most revered of all relics, the Buddha's sacred tooth, alternated between them. That year, it was the duty of the Malwatte chapter to officiate at the Temple of the Tooth.

Jan had a vision of an elephant bearing a glittering howdah, then it was gone, her memory opaque. After all the lies and games, could this be true? She had to know.

'The twenty-first,' she stammered. 'The last day of the Perahera. Thousands of people will be there.'

The Esala festival, probably the largest in the Buddhist world, lasted twenty-one days. The first phase was a Hindu ritual in honour of the four guardian deities of Kandy: Natha, Vishnu, the goddess Pattini, and Kataragama. The second phase signalled the start of the Buddhist celebration of the sacred tooth. For ten exotic nights leading up to the Esala full moon, the temple tusker carried that sacred relic in a magnificent procession through the streets of Kandy. The last five nights, the third phase, saw the addition of the golden palanquins of the consorts of the gods. Each evening's procession was more splendid than the last. Crowds lined the streets, stood shoulder to shoulder on walls and pavements, perched on rooftops, windowsills and balconies, balanced in the branches of trees. On 21st August, when the moon was full, the festival would reach its climax. Everyone who could travel to Kandy, rich or poor, would be there; some two hundred thousand people. If Quincey started his revolution among that unsuspecting crowd, the death toll could be momentous.

Da Souza chuckled.

'That's right,' he said. 'A fitting start to our campaign, don't you think?'

Jan stared at him. So the joke was crueller than she had thought: much of Quincey's tale was true. But which parts should she discard, which parts retain? Only one thing was certain: unless a miracle intervened, 21st August would be a disaster.

Da Souza's hands recalled her to the present. Before she could resist, he had pushed her flat onto the slab and bound her down.

'Now where was I?' he asked.

He hesitated, as if uncertain which game he should continue. He seemed to decide. Reaching up to check the bottle on the wall behind her, he selected a suitable instrument and connected it to the tube. Then he seized her arm and jabbed.

She gasped as the metal pierced her skin. It had happened so fast. Her eyes opened wide in shock as she felt liquid being forced into her veins.

But da Souza was listening to something. Now Jan heard it too. A car had drawn up outside; people were getting out.

He swore and removed the instrument from her arm. It left an isolated throbbing pain. Then he shouted something and almost at once, two men ran in. Men with high cheekbones and slanting eyes. At a command from their boss, they brought in a plain rubberwood coffin and placed it on the floor.

As the two men straightened up, one fingered a knife at his belt, his hand resting on the ivory handle. He looked at Jan, black eyes without emotion, then at his boss. Da Souza was dressing the old man. He shook his head.

'No,' he said. 'We don't want any more mess to clear up. Just put her inside. The fire will kill her soon enough.'

Jan's eyes were fixed on his face. Strange hands lifted her off the slab, deposited her roughly into the coffin. When the two men stood back, her eyes had not moved. Da Souza smiled.

'You should thank me,' he admonished her. 'Not everyone has such a dramatic opportunity to make his peace with God. You have at least twenty minutes.'

A movement to her right disturbed her gaze. One of the men had picked up a hammer. He looked at da Souza and her heart stopped. Slowly, her eyes turned too.

But da Souza declined the suggestion. The edges of his mouth lifted in that hateful smile.

'She's bound,' he said. 'Why nail her down? And this way, I can say good-bye before I send her in.'

The three men laughed. Jan watched da Souza's face, saw the pleasure with which he anticipated that last encounter, and found herself imagining it too. Her nerves were stretched to screaming point, her body stiff with fear.

Da Souza's mirth subsided.

'I trust no one will notice the two extra coffins on the old man's pyre,' he said.

He seemed genuinely perplexed. Jan waited, unable to speak. He shrugged.

'I'll slip one of you in with him at the beginning,' he decided, 'and add the other later when the flames are high and the mourners too preoccupied to see.'

He was looking at her more closely now, gazing with professional longing at her features.

'I'm sorry we've run out of time,' he added. 'I could have done a beautiful job on you.'

Jan shuddered. She remembered the 'beautiful job' he had done on Christine; and Mohan. Applied to herself while she yet lived, the idea was even more grotesque. But before she could formulate an answer, da Souza nodded.

'Gag her,' he said.

She twisted her head from side to side, but it was no use. A cloth was forced into her mouth and bound in place. When it was done, there were tears in her eyes.

'Bye for now,' said da Souza, waggling his fingers.

There was a thud and all light was extinguished. Jan heard the rasp of the catch as it slid into place. Then she passed out.

An eternity later, she woke. The air was black. She closed her eyes and opened them again, but the darkness prevailed.

Cautiously, unable to accept that she was alive, she tried to move her arms: they were bound. She stretched her legs: they were bound too but her toes struck something hard. Groaning with the effort, she raised her head and found the same: wood above, wood below, wood on both sides. She was in a box. The blackness shuddered with her: she was in that coffin. How long had she got? She heaved at the lid, striking it repeatedly with her forehead, but it would not budge. The clasp was down. Awake in her own nightmare, sobbing with terror through a sodden gag, she strained in the dark.

Unaccountably, something exploded: Jan, coffin and nightmare rocked together. Smaller explosions followed, chased by screams that pierced the panel above her head. Their panic reactivated her own. With all her strength, she hurled herself to the right. The coffin fell several feet to the ground, landing on its side. The clasp gave. As the lid fell away, darkness vanished and she was staring at the morning sky.

A cemetery, the remains of one. Fifty yards away, enclosed by white flags and twisted coconut fronds, the remnants of a pyre. The ornate structure, white cloth stretched over a bamboo frame, had been torn apart. Inside that smouldering shell, something red shot flames into the sky. Figures dashed back and forth in frantic silhouette against a Dantean fire. Matchstick men gesticulated; women screamed; children wailed. The ceremony was over.

The grenades. Jan remembered in a daze. Mohan's casket must have joined the old man's on the pyre. She muttered a prayer of thanks: that moment must have been da Souza's last. Mohan was revenged. She only wished Quincey could have been there too.

As she struggled vainly to free her hands, Jan found herself gazing into the astonished eyes of a Sinhalese youth. He was staring at the rope that bound her ankles, the cloth that tore her lips, the tears trickling from her eyes into her hair. She froze, willing him to stay. The boy swallowed, looked round for support, found none. He stooped quickly, slipped a penknife from his pocket and cut her loose.

Seconds later, she was twisting through the trees, dodging behind gravestones, running for her life. No one noticed. She reached the glass-topped wall and followed it round. At the open gateway, she glanced back. The boy still stood there, staring. Behind him, flames fingered the air like a friend waving. A magpie robin sang the song that brings bad luck but for Jan each note meant life. A steam-train shrieked in sympathy. It was 20th August; and she was free.

PART FIVE

20th August 1975:

Kandy (1)

They caught the next train to Kandy. But, as the unlovely buildings of the Fort area receded, Jan wondered what they were playing at.

After leaving the cemetery, she had gone straight to the hotel. Wolfgang had been waiting. For a few fierce seconds, he had held her to him. Then he let her speak. She had told him about Mohan, about the guns, about da Souza's link with the Chu Chow, and Quincey's garbled claims; and she had watched emotions play upon his face.

As they talked, voices hushed, it had become clear that they had two alternatives: they could go to Saunders with their news, or take the train to Kandy. For they knew now that the Mahanayaka was the key figure who could still put a stop to Quincey's plans. There was something he did not know. If they could tell him that, perhaps the grim climax of the plot might yet be averted. But they would have to get there first; and Quincey had already left.

So they had gone. As Wolfgang gathered their belongings and found a taxi, Jan wrote a note to Saunders. It made sense to speak to him in person, but neither Jan nor Wolfgang wished to stay behind. If one was going to Kandy, the other would too. So Jan had written it all down instead. She told him everything, including their decision to see the Mahanayaka. Saunders' office opened at ten, at which point, Jan wrote in her letter, he would have precisely thirty-four hours before the revolution began. The rest was up to him. It was a relief to know that, whatever happened now, someone in authority knew. Then they caught the early train to Kandy together.

As they watched the land unfold beyond the window, they sat

linked by their hands, separated by their thoughts. The track cut through broken villages, tossed aside people, dogs and crows, and stretched into the rich green of paddy. Lush squares glistened in the light. The last mists rose like smoke from the shadows, disintegrating in the sun. Here and there, patchwork greens gave way to clearings, vegetable plots, a sturdy mud house. Then they too retreated leaving only the brushstroke beauty of rice.

Jan saw it all but could not relax and enjoy it. For one thing her arm hurt. Her head too. But worse than that, she could not stop the questions. How much of what Quincey had told her was fact, how much capricious lies? She had seen both guns and heroin, but the rest – the birth of a new order with Quincey as midwife and king – was that true too? Da Souza had mocked her credulity, but was it all a joke?

She stared helplessly outside. Banana groves replaced the rice, thick leaves heavy in the breeze, not yet split into lace or rags.

What were their motives? Andrews must be after the money. But da Souza ran no risk of losing his job; it provided both profit and pleasure. He had to be in it for kicks.

And Quincey? Jan was at a loss. She hated the man and feared him, but had never claimed to understand him. At first, he had seemed a typical Ceylonese politician: to some degree corruptible, fond of rhetoric, ambitious; only that streak of cruelty and the power to instil fear set him apart from the rest. The discovery at Maitland had turned him into a criminal, and there Jan's image of him had crystallized until the previous night when she had almost exchanged it for his: a man driven by the duplicity of his own party to insurrection. If da Souza had not mocked her belief, perhaps even now she might have accepted it.

She was caged in by doubts. Was Quincey fomenting a revolution to unseat his own government? Perplexed, Jan resolved to ask the Mahanayaka himself. It was a gamble, but she could think of nothing else.

Outside, the scenery changed. Dense vegetation threatened the track. Creepers climbed telegraph poles, clung to rocks. The train passed through forbidding gorges, between great boulders like elephants drawn up to repel invaders. The atmosphere was oppressive, as if infiltrated with Quincey's presence. Jan hoped it was her imagination running scared. A tunnel seized the train, played with it, then tired of the game. Giant ferns embraced its escape.

She sighed. In 1971, her sympathies had been with the rebels, so why did she insist on interfering now? True, she wanted to know what was going on, but it was more than that: once she knew what Quincey and da Souza hoped to gain, whatever their claims, whatever their justifications, she would do her best to thwart them. Her motives now were hatred and revenge.

At least she was not alone. Jan glanced at Wolfgang. His face was closed, his eyes fixed beyond the window pane, his mind chasing thoughts like hers. But the closeness remained. It lay in the silence spread between them, in the loose intimacy of their hands. For they were lovers now, a pact of friendship sealed. Her eyes followed Wolfgang's through the glass.

The train rumbled past trees netted with creepers. Daturas drooped, heavy with poison. Kitul palms dangled strings of seeds. Bamboo sprouted yellow jointed with black, while woolly tree ferns with trunks like bears' legs scuttled out of sight. Mohan's favourite, the cannonball tree, wore its fruit like giant baubles on a leathery neck. The sight of it made her blink. There were flowers too: cannas, lilies, fuchsias growing wild and the scarlet pincers of the crab's claw.

The fuchsias reminded her of McDair. She felt a sudden stab of longing to see her father. She had tried to phone him before she left, without success. It seemed ironic: he had had to wait so long for her to reach out to him again and now that she needed him he did not know.

She watched the river slide beside them for a while, dodging boulders, side-stepping spits of sand, exploding into ruffling falls. Women washed pots and clothes; men soaped lean bodies; children shrieked and swam. An old man sat on a fallen tree and fished, naked but for a cloth about his loins. In midstream, two boys clung to a rock and waved. Wolfgang waved back but Jan could not bring herself to smile.

She had swum in the river with Mohan once, at Lahugala.

They had taken a picnic lunch, rice and vegetables wrapped in banana leaves, and a basket of fruit. Afterwards, they had let the water take the weight off their swollen stomachs, gossiping in the sun. The memory gnawed at her mind, a physical pain. She pulled herself together and looked outside.

Twin chestnut streamers flashed into view: bellies white, heads metal-black, paradise flycatchers escorted the train, chestnut ribbons looping fairy-like behind as they twisted in the air and disappeared.

The river spun north. Blue convolvulus lined the track. Pagoda flowers, red with yellow tongues. Villages grew more closely together now and the train stopped more often. Peradeniya, site of university campus and botanical gardens, came and went.

As the train approached Kandy, they noticed the monks among the crowds. For Kandy was the heart of the Buddhist faith, the Perahera the highlight of the year. In nearby temples and monasteries, the ranks of devotees trebled as monks from all over the island and beyond made their annual pilgrimage to the relic of their lord. Jan recalled the young bhikkhu from Okanda: perhaps he too had hoped to come with his lacquered begging bowl, black umbrella and palm-leaf fan, and worship at the altar of the Tooth. But it was too late now.

As they stepped out of the station compound, Jan shrugged the morbid memory aside to luxuriate in that crisp upcountry sun. After the humid air of Colombo, the aridity of the east coast, Kandy's freshness was a delight.

Kandy. The city meant many things to Jan. Its religious atmosphere, temples and dagobas, the peacefulness of its lake setting. She had promised to show it all to Christine. It seemed odd to be seeking out the key figure of an insurrection instead.

Yet the city boasted a bloody history too. For centuries, the old Kandyan aristocracy had ruled with barbaric vigour: enemies executed with revolting display; maidens sacrificed on Devil's Hill. Then with myopic eagerness, those same Kandyans had collaborated with the British against the Dutch just as they had with the Dutch against the Portuguese a century and a half before. But Kandy straddled the roads to the tea country and in 1815 the British invaded: two thousand years of independence came to an end.

As they continued towards the lake, Jan recalled that Kandy was both Quincey's home town and the stronghold of caste. Unlike India's small brahmin hierarchy reigning over a horde of lower castes, the Sinhalese pyramid was reversed: a high-caste majority raised above a few thousand individuals of low caste. At the top stood the Goyigama caste led by the Kandyan chieftains, the Radalas, the island's aristocrats. Quincey, the prime minister, and all her cabinet bar one came from this highest sub-caste; and that token exception knew his place on the bottom rung. Yet this rigid set of social distinctions – ignorance of which still meant ostracism – was invalid by law.

They were halfway up the main street when the smell of food stopped them short: they had eaten nothing all day. And they still hadn't decided what they would do. Jan had an idea, but they had to discuss it first. They might as well eat as they talked. So they climbed the rickety back stairs and chose a table on the balcony overlooking the road.

But as Wolfgang ordered, Jan's anxious mind sped past the lake to the temple, trying to anticipate what she could find. She folded her arms on the balustrade, laid her chin against them and stared at the bustle below. Cars stopped reluctantly at the crossing, barely allowing pedestrians to pass before screeching on. Flanked by sniffing mongrels, a man sat cross-legged on the pavement beating a tattoo on a drum, his eyes closed, his hands independent.

Jan spooned food into her mouth in much the same way.

'We'll have to split up,' she said suddenly. 'We need to do two things at once: see the Mahanayaka, and get help.'

Wolfgang nodded. His thoughts had followed a parallel track. But his answer was slow in coming.

'You speak Sinhala,' he said. 'Perhaps you should go to the temple.'

The reluctance in his voice and eyes was obvious.

Jan spoke quickly, ignoring it. 'And you can go to Mohan's family for help.'

She gave him directions, wrote down the address. She was glad he knew Kandy so well. Then she smiled: it seemed so

142

simple. But when she looked across at Wolfgang's troubled face, she was not so sure.

His anxiety was well founded. Quincey had claimed that the Mahanayaka was a pivotal figure in his plot. They dared not reject the allegation out of hand. After all, even the JVP had relied on monks to propagandize in the villages, to conceal arms and ammunition in their temples, to link outposts to the cause. As Jan well knew, there was no strict division between religion and politics in Sri Lanka: Sinhalese Buddhism fostered political hotheads and even monks were not immune. Worse still, recent political history provided a graphic reminder of what they might expect.

Wolfgang was shaking his head. 'It's so hard to understand,' he said.

Jan agreed. The Buddha's teachings were simple: life was suffering, impersonality, impermanence, a fatal disease; the twin causes of suffering were ignorance and desire; escape entailed their destruction by means of 'the eightfold path', a series of eminently practical goals. By transcending the illusion of self, the true Buddhist aimed at something beyond the distinctions of pleasure and pain, let alone the crude ambitions of politics.

So what had gone wrong? How could a head monk of the oldest Hinayana school, the one closest to the Buddha's words, become enmeshed in politics? Impossible, yet it had happened before, giving rise to an alarming religious fanaticism.

Jan recalled what she knew of 1956. By coincidence, that year was the 2500th anniversary of the Buddha's death and of his consecration of 'Holy Lanka'. Buddhist orders flocked to join the United Monks' Front, a politico-religious organization founded by the now infamous Buddharakkhita, the former head monk of the key temple at Kelaniya. A founder member and patron of Solomon Bandaranaike's SLFP, Buddharakkhita sent his acolytes throughout the island to incite villagers to the cause, calling upon them to sacrifice their lives for the restoration of a truly Buddhist land. He also extracted large sums from the temple treasury, his contribution to party funds rising above a lakh of rupees. Solomon owed his victory to Buddharakkhita, for it was he who had known how to exploit the clerico-chauvinist character of Sinhalese Buddhism for political ends.

Jan frowned in growing alarm. Had Quincey studied 1956 as closely as he claimed to have studied 1971? Did he hope to emulate that mystical merging of religion and politics? Had he found in the Mahanayaka at the Temple of the Tooth a second 'Buddy Racketeer'? If he had, there was nothing she could say. If not, all she had to do was tell the truth.

'It must be the heroin,' she said, almost to herself. 'He couldn't have agreed to that.'

Was that Andrews' crucial blunder? It had to be.

Wolfgang reached across to hold her hand. 'Take care,' he said. 'See him if you can. If you can't, for God's sake, get out of there!'

The vehemence came as something of a shock; she had been so embedded in her thoughts. She closed his hand between her own and nodded her assent. She would not stay a moment longer than she had to.

Wolfgang signalled for their bill. As they paid, Jan remembered the rumours circulating at Solomon's death. It was said that Buddharakkhita's vast financial empire had made him greedy. When one of his deals was thwarted by government intervention and when that same government because of continued riots instigated a slow-down in the anti-Tamil drive, he became angry: in September 1959, Solomon Bandaranaike was gunned down on his own verandah by one of Buddharakkhita's monks; the messianic regime he had created fell. Assassination, Jan reflected grimly, was an end to which Quincey was entitled too. They rose to go.

In the main street once more, they kissed briefly, then separated. Wolfgang went quickly east. Jan walked on towards the temple, past expensive jewellers, past antique and curio shops, past banks and restaurants. With each step, she felt more alone. She looked back for Wolfgang but he had gone. The world seemed doubly hostile now.

The accumulated strain of the last few days began to tell. Slant-eyed waiters lounging at the door of the East China café produced in Jan's mind the death mask of the murdered fisherman; da Souza's insolent henchmen in Colombo; their persistent theory of the Chu Chow. Painted devil masks in souvenir shops recalled the hideous caricature painted onto Mohan's face. Smart young men were replicas of da Souza; red-faced tourists of Andrews; rural villagers of the guard. Everything she saw held a foul reminder, a pointed threat.

Each time it happened, she tore her gaze away, trying desperately to find some innocent object for her eyes. Since Mohan's death, she had forced herself to continue, refused to allow herself to break till she had done all she could, refused to acknowledge the great dam of tears building up inside. But the effort was too much.

A placard written in bold capitals over a bus shelter jeered:

'WELCOME A TOURIST:
"A SMILE IS WORTH A THOUSAND WORDS"!'

It was only an advertisement issued by the Ministry of Tourism, one Jan had often seen before, but it mocked her cruelly now. What a fine tourist's welcome she had found. A smile was worth a thousand words, was it? Half a dozen smiles played simultaneously on the mobile retina of her mind: the strangely stapled smile Christine had worn; Quincey's public beam; Andrews' sycophantic grin; the sneering derision of the guard; da Souza's smirk; Mohan's painted scream. Images chased each other in her head, whirled round and round, building up an intolerable pressure to her sanity. Something gave way at last and she began to cry. She had tried so hard not to give in but now she sobbed as if her heart had cracked.

She had reached the edge of the lake. Clinging to its scalloped wall, she urged the tears to stop. Nothing would be achieved by crying, she told herself shakily. Later, when it was all over, when Wolfgang was there, would be the time. Slowly, she gained control. The effort made her dizzy.

A sudden cackling announced that a kingfisher had taken flight. She wiped her eyes to look for it but the bird was nowhere to be seen. She took several deep breaths, inhaled the calm of the water, and moved on. The lake soothed her as it had always done and she gazed at it, trying to think of nothing else.

Stone steps led down to the water. At the bottom, a diminutive popcorn-vendor fed the fish: hundreds of pink mouths on sleek black bodies clamoured for his favours. Beside him, a couple washed their baby girl. As Jan walked by, the copper-smith's song rang out from a flame tree as if to encourage her. Flowering trees tossed pink and purple blossoms to the ground. An ancient bo reigned wild in someone's garden, its long-stemmed leaves set trembling by the birds: bulbuls, barbets, scores of parakeets and a pair of screaming koels.

By the time she drew level with the temple, her tears had dried. She stared at it. The thought struck her that Quincey might already be there, but she chose not to pursue it. Instead, she wondered how long Wolfgang would take to join her. She had a feeling she was going to need him. She inhaled the rich atmosphere: the acrid smell of elephants tethered in the temple courtyard, the freshness of lake water, the heady fragrance of frangipani crushed underfoot, and traces of diesel fumes from a disappearing bus. She sent up a brief prayer to Kataragama. Then she crossed the road.

The Dalada Maligawa, Temple of the Tooth. Built in the late sixteenth century, restored by the last of the Sinhalese kings and the first of the Tamils, its ancient splendour was protected now by a modern structure in pink and white. A pair of stone carvings marked the entrance. Above rose the startling octagon-al that housed the holy books, with a wooden railing hung like a belt outside and a roof rising to a golden point. Behind it, Jan could see the temple compound, each roof divided by red-brown tiles; beyond that, the dense vegetation of the Udawattakele forest, ancient reserve of Kandyan kings; and in front, reflec-tions in the moat. She passed through the pink gateway, left her shoes at the top of the steps, and entered.

Despite her trepidation, she was impressed; as she always was. For in all the island, Kandyan architecture was unique. The classical solidity of Anuradhapura had been rejected in favour of fine lines, light planes and soft materials. Outside, these found expression in wide roofs, peaked and laminated with tiles cut into squares and rectangles. Inside, it rested in carved and painted wooden columns, painted plaster on the walls, and the symmetry of painted doors.

Jan admired its beauty with misgiving. Was she walking into another trap? For something seemed to draw her on. She felt

Quincey's presence everywhere. She turned round suddenly to see if he was there but found only smiling devotees. The excitement of the Perahera urged them on, pulling Jan with them. She seemed to be moving in slow motion, driven by a distant beat.

She entered the main hall through a tunnel, its ceiling decorated with white flowers and geometric patterns, the walls with lifesize portraits of princes going to worship. Two men holding conches to their lips. On gilded doors folding in against the walls, mythical creatures – half man, half bird; half beast, half bird – were painted above lions roaring yellow flames. The princely devotees walked in profile, each bearing lotus flowers in outstretched hands: some wore oddly dislocated moustaches, others were smooth-shaven; some were clothed in transparent patterns displaying their physique, others in white sarongs edged in blue; while the leader of each line sported a skull cap embroidered in white and gold.

Jan emerged with the rest into a hall throbbing with sound. The music threatened to overpower her. A primitive oboe wailed. Two men beat hide drums with their hands while two more rattled a metallic tattoo on double kettle-drums. The muscles of their naked chests worked in rhythm while their deafening creation bounced off twenty pairs of stout stone columns. Jan was tense with apprehension. The compelling beat made her pulse race. Confused, she gazed at the object of their serenade: the sacred Chamber of the Tooth.

The yellow doors were closed. A sculptured guardian held his sword aloft on either side. Over the lintel, flanking a lion's face, swam two green and yellow 'makaras' to mark man's passage through the turbulent ocean of life. The mythical beasts combined all creatures: the elephant's trunk, the ears of a pig, the body of a fish, the lion's teeth and mane, eyes like Hanuman the Hindu monkey god, and the peacock's exuberant tail. But the doors they guarded opened only once a year.

A worshipping current of humanity carried Jan along. They threaded their way between carved pillars, through the sounds, towards the staircase leading to the upper floor. Joss sticks perfumed the heady atmosphere. A crocodile of children streamed the other way, bearing bowls of flowers in their hands. Helpless now amidst that festive gaiety, Jan was drawn up the steps.

Upstairs, music shook the wooden floor. Devotees sat or knelt, prayed together and alone. Women floated by in pink and red and orange, sarees fastened at the waist in the Kandyan frill. Children stared, hair brushed wet behind their ears. Babies lay on shawls kicking chubby legs while their parents tucked their heads to the floor. Bhikkhus in robes of every shade from crisp yellow to faded red wandered back and forth. Flowers scented the air: temple flowers for good luck, white and pink frangipani, scarlet tulip tree flowers and glorious hibiscus.

With a start, Jan recalled Quincey's plan. Tomorrow, when the festival reached its peak and the streets were filled with worshippers like these, his bloody revolution would begin. The thought was chilling. It strengthened her resolve.

She left the pilgrims to their worship, the musicians to their noise, and climbed the second flight of stairs. The corridor led her to a pair of ornate doors. A monk stood guard. Jan hesitated. Then she scribbled a message and asked him to take it to the Mahanayaka. The note contained two short sentences: 'The revolution is financed by heroin. Quincey had your bhikkhu killed.' The monk took it.

Jan waited. Rival strains of organ music drifted through an open window from the church across the way, kettle-drums rolled to a crescendo below, and the reeling citizens of Kandy were left to adjudicate.

She became uneasy, restless. The noise made it difficult to think straight. What else could she do but wait?

To steady herself, Jan studied the ornate doors through which she would pass. Four-foot guardians, features painted red on yellow skin, barred her path. Overhead, a splendid pair of 'makaras' stood watch: blue heads spotted with white, yellow tails flecked with pink, bodies of shiny green scales; and white fangs that seemed both to smile and snarl. Each door was adorned with lotus plants whose golden stems and white blossoms wound in intricate confusion. In the centre of each artistic knot stood a symbol: on the left, a red smile on a golden sun; on the right, a ghostly hare in the moon. Jan pushed against them. Suddenly, sun and moon parted company; the doors had opened.

Fear sliced through Jan's nerves. She entered, her throat

aching, her palms grown cold. An urgent beat throbbed in her head. The doors closed behind her of their own accord. The sudden silence was a shock.

The chamber was empty. She saw a chest encrusted with gems; two brass lamps five feet high, topped with peacocks; on the floor a bowl of flowers freshly picked. A ceiling festooned with painted blooms, walls vibrating with life. She gazed distractedly about her, her eyes caught by the more striking figures: a frieze of pink and yellow lions, front paws raised, tails curled up like flags; a wall of meditating monks; princes and nobles kneeling in a row, their garments richly embroidered; a seven-headed cobra on glistening blue coils.

Then she heard the sound of bare feet approaching and dropped behind the chest. The monk who had taken her message was crossing the room. As he opened those double doors, the sound of kettle drums dodged in. Then the doors had closed again.

Jan waited. The floor was cold marble. With a shudder, she recalled da Souza's slabs and her eyes fled to the far end of the room. There, high on the wall, hung three discs of beaten gold: the central sphere bore the face of the moon, the outer pair the radiating blaze of the sun. Before she could stop it, another image invaded her mind – the rays of yellow paint round Mohan's staring eyes – and was gone.

Startled, she looked again. Beneath that sacred triad, a large frame picked out in gold. Within that frame, a life-size portrait, a man in monk's robes. He had materialized without warning, without a sound.

Jan stared. Was this the Mahanayaka? He was not what she had expected. Here was no fierce austerity, neither the single-minded rapaciousness of Buddharakkhita nor the absent aloofness of the saint, nor even the grinning corpulence seen on mantelpieces in the West. Years of meditation and self-denial had left a disarming gentleness. His face was round and this, with the shaven head and smooth skin, gave him the appearance of an elderly doll. But as he talked, lines shot out from eyes and mouth to bring his face alive.

He had not seen Jan. He was talking to someone else. As she watched, he turned back into the other room.

'If this is true,' he was saying quietly, 'then I have been misled.'

Jan stiffened then, for she had seen her note held loosely in his hand. Had they been right about Andrews' slip? Had Quincey kept the heroin from the Mahanayaka?

The gentle voice continued.

'My part is over. I cannot help you now.'

The doll-like figure reappeared once more within its frame. Then stepped away. He was heading for the double doors. Jan held her breath and watched.

Something silver whistled out of nowhere. A knife quivered on a yellow cloth, embedded in the old man's back. The handle was carved ivory, rounded and polished with use, the knife of the paid assassin.

The monk paused. His eyelids opened wide then slowly closed. One hand lifted in protest or perhaps in blessing. As Jan watched in horror, the erect body slumped within its cloth cocoon. The whistling whispered on, echoed round the chamber, menacing. She stared at the ivory handle, unable to move, unable even to look to see who had set it and that fearful whistling loose. He was dead.

At last she looked round. A row of Chinese faces stared back, oriental impassivity gleaming from every pair of hard black eyes. Bewilderment checked her anger. Chinese in the Temple of the Tooth? Then she saw da Souza's taunting smile and understood.

Quincey materialized then but neither he nor da Souza spoke. They did not seem surprised to see her. Jan looked back at the crumpled figure on the floor.

The sounds behind her grew more insistent. There was a metallic click as a far door opened, another as it shut. Jan sensed an indefinable thickening of tension in the room. Someone new had entered. She shivered. Slowly, she raised her head and looked across the room.

A thrill of fear spun through her brain. Quincey was still there. So was da Souza and his band of Chinese thugs. But another man had joined them: a European, tall and pale, with neatly groomed fair hair and cold blue eyes. The man she had met at Christine's funeral. The man she had gone to for help. The same man to whom she had written that morning.

Saunders. But this was not the Saunders she remembered. He wore a cool half smile and one fair eyebrow rose to greet her. Only the upper class composure was the same.

She felt numb. Dimly, she realized all was lost. Even Wolfgang could not save her now. Saunders was on Quincey's side.

No knife to silence Jan. She knelt, head bowed to the blow. A distant pain, the world dissolved and her body fell to the floor. But as she fell, the dead monk's hand touched her cheek, a blessing from a misguided man.

She woke in terror. A shot had splintered the night. The darkness recalled another darkness that made her fling her arms and legs against the coffin she felt sure enclosed her. When she found only the solidity of night, she sobbed with relief.

Was it eight o'clock? That shot must have signalled the start of the Perahera. She dragged herself to the window to make sure.

The window was barred. The spaces too narrow for her to squeeze through. Her fingers measured them automatically while her eyes noted the twenty-foot drop to the courtyard below where the elephants were kept. But the yard was empty, ropes hanging loose from the base of palm trees, piles of fodder untouched. The elephants had joined the parade. Jan noted that the crenellated wall around the yard, like that round the main temple building, was for decorative purposes only, no more than four feet high. Two men lounged by the open gates. They appeared to be casual bystanders, curious enough to attend the Perahera but not sufficiently interested to keep up with the procession. But one of them glanced up at Jan's window and she knew at once that they were guards. Even Quincey could not post an undisguised armed guard on the sacred Temple of the Tooth. She wondered how many of them there were, and whether they were expecting Wolfgang. The thought depressed her.

She forced her eyes past them, to the broad steps leading up to the side entrance on her right and the same low crenellated wall cutting off the moat. Beyond, in front of the park, crowds marking the road, and the procession. Whip-crackers; flag-bearers; lines of torch-bearers on either side. Tom-tom beaters, frenetic kettle-drummers; cymbals and flutes. A double row of dancers bobbed and swirled, driven by that beat. Caparisoned elephants strode behind. Then they too passed, their places taken by more musicians, more dancers and officials in court regalia. The next temple group began: whip-crackers, flag-bearers, musicians and dancers, dignitaries, elephants; a continuous cycle of celebration churning through the night. That night at least, Jan thought. The next would be different.

A metallic thud made her spin round. A bolt was drawn back, then another. The painted doors swung open and Saunders switched on the light.

Two more figures appeared. Quincey and da Souza posed beside him. Jan watched as the three men ranged themselves across the far side of the room and gazed amicably back. Saunders' eyebrows rose at the unintended drama. A sardonic smile betrayed da Souza's mood. Quincey beamed. The only face on which no humour played was Jan's.

She stared stone-faced. Quincey held a bottle of beer in one hand while the other raised a glass to her good health; it was evidently not his first. When she failed to respond, he laughed without malice. He was confident enough now to be generous. Jan watched his hand lift the glass again. Despite the careless attitude, his clothes were crisp and smart. Their paleness accentuated his size. Casual elegance drew attention to solid sandalled feet, to the bare skin of chest and hands. For it was his physical presence that made him stand out, not his clothes. Caught by a camera out of context, he would have been more than handsome. Flanked by da Souza and Saunders, he was a disturbing sight.

At length Saunders tipped his head. Da Souza caught the signal and clicked his fingers raffishly in the air. A Chinese entered, set a tray of food on the floor. They all listened as he bolted the doors conspicuously behind him.

Jan's eyes darted from da Souza to Saunders to Quincey but kept returning to the rice meal waiting on the floor. She had not realized how hungry she was. The smiles grew broader.

'Help yourself,' said Saunders.

152

She hesitated, her hunger undeniable. If she refused, da Souza would simply click his fingers for the guard to take it out again; that decided her. She walked across, sat down and began to eat.

As if her decision had been the cue to move, the tableau broke up and the three men reassembled themselves for another: Saunders took Jan's place at one window; Quincey banged his bottle onto the sill of the other and seated himself heavily beside it; da Souza lounged against the door. They watched her eat. Only Quincey could not keep still: he needed to celebrate aloud.

'The gun will go off at eight tomorrow too!' he crowed.

The thought filled him with evident pride. His moment of triumph was due. Jan shivered. She had had a sudden vision of a tipsy Christine in Quincey's arms; of Quincey flushed with drink and sex boasting of the plot to come; of Christine laughing at such grandiose ambition, then meeting those cold black eyes. Sleeping with Quincey had been her last mistake: he had let his guard down and she had had to die to put it back. Jan tried to calm herself, but she had a nasty feeling her intuition was correct. She forced herself to listen.

'By five to nine,' Quincey was saying, 'all those marked for execution will be there. And I'll have precisely five minutes to get away.'

A barely perceptible smile slid over Saunders' aristocratic face, but the blue eyes did not flicker. He was watching Jan.

'The guns will be everywhere,' Quincey said, spreading his arms impressively. 'On both sides of the procession. Truckloads of armed men in strategic back streets.'

'And a fleet of hearses with mounted machine-guns in the back,' added da Souza with a chuckle, 'and my gangsters itching for a fight.'

Jan turned her head. Da Souza nodded politely.

'Thank you for your intervention in Colombo,' he said. 'It gave me an excuse to come to Kandy. I wouldn't have missed this for anything!'

Jan wanted to protest but feared his tongue and the untruths that slid from it so easily.

'I hoped you were dead,' she muttered.

'You did your best,' he said gaily, 'and two of my men won't

153

be seen again. That was some explosion! You should have seen how quickly the old man's relatives forgot their grief and ran!'

He too seemed to bear her no malice and Jan knew why: she would soon be joining Mohan and Christine in oblivion. She wondered why they bothered to feed her. Saunders seemed to read her mind.

'We've decided to let you live a little longer,' he said gravely. 'Not as a reward, I hasten to add. But it seems more sensible that your body should be found amidst the carnage on the streets tomorrow night bearing a recent bullet-hole like the rest. The day-old corpse of a foreigner just might be noticed. And when your demise is reported to me, I shall send you back to da Souza.'

Jan pushed the plate of food away in disgust. The threat disturbed her but Saunders upset her more. For he had spoken with the same friendly concern, the same reassuring accent, the same well-bred courtesy that had misled her before. Her trust in what he represented had been automatic, fatal. She had been a fool.

When she looked back at him, Saunders was beckoning. Shaken, she obeyed. Two faces grinned at her compliance.

'Let me show you,' Saunders said in an avuncular tone; he might have been pointing out ducks on a pond. 'You see the big stand over there?'

She nodded. In other years, she had stood there herself to watch the Perahera unwind. Then he pointed beyond the mass of costumed dancers and burning flares towards the lake.

'And those three large tulip trees opposite?'

She looked. Two elephants swayed between the vital points: on the right the illuminated outline of the VIP stand; on the left a phalanx of trees. They faced each other exactly.

'It's perfect!' Quincey exclaimed. 'A guard posted at the foot of each tree. Snipers in the branches waiting for the signal.'

'The ceremonial gun,' said Saunders. 'The Mahanayaka was going to fire it, but now he'll have to ride up front.'

Jan blinked. The Mahanayaka was dead, she had watched him die. That apart, the Perahera was always led by the Diyawadana Nilame, the sole lay custodian of the Tooth. No monks rode in the procession, not even the Mahanayaka. Was this part of the plan? A sign to the revolutionaries waiting in the crowd? But how?

'The mahout riding behind the second group of dancers will fire the gun,' Saunders continued. 'But as they finish their piece and move on, instead of following, his elephant will step backwards out of the line of fire.'

'The signal shot rings out!' exulted Quincey. 'A score of shots tear the leaves off the tulip trees and knock each target down!'

'The prime minister,' gloated da Souza over by the door, 'and every cabinet minister barring Quincey!'

If Quincey's appreciation was for the cunning of the plot, da Souza's was for the slaughter it would bring. Jan tried to imagine the bedlam that would follow. Dancers, musicians and spectators would panic and run. Perhaps the drums would mask the shots from those further away but soon horror would infect the entire town. What then? Would gunmen open fire on the crowds? Elephants stampede from the smell of death? How many people would die? But Jan felt her captors' eyes on her face and she drained her features of expression.

Saunders stood up, effectively closing the conversation. With the air of a chairman ending a debate, he looked round at his associates and then turned back to Jan in the centre of the room.

'And now, if you'll excuse us,' he said coldly, 'we three need our sleep. Good night!'

His eyes flickered automatically from the heavy doors to the barred window as if to ensure himself that this time their captive would stay put. Then he seemed to remember something. The blue eyes returned thoughtfully to hers.

'Oh, and you mustn't fret about your hippie boyfriend either,' he said. 'My men will have picked him up by now. His body will join the others on the streets: one more unfortunate foreigner caught in the crossfire.'

He did not wait to see the effect of his words. He called an order to the guard outside and left.

Jan was stunned. She was remembering Wolfgang as she had first seen him: a naked bronze except for the patch on his nose and cloth on his hair, proud to be alive. The tensions they had shared. And then the night before, when he had stroked her fears away, his touch turning into a caress that brought her body back to life. Pain clouded her eyes. The walls began to dissolve. She had to fight to keep control, forcing her awareness back into the room.

Quincey was looking disappointed. He was clearly torn between swaggering after Saunders and staying to brag. The greater vanity won. He threw back his head and drained his glass in one gulp. Then he looked at Jan.

'Who do you suppose will be the next prime minister?' he asked with deliberate provocation.

But Jan stared through him. She could not concentrate yet. He waved the empty glass in the air as if to encourage her.

'Why, me!' he exclaimed. 'Quincey Senevisuriya, lesser cousin to her ladyship, not strictly speaking in direct line of succession but an ideal leader none the less.' The empty glass caught his attention and he paused to fill it. 'For years, I've watched her brats fight among themselves to inherit her throne and I've known all along they were wasting their time.'

'As the Chinese say,' da Souza cut in, '"while tigers fight, the lion steals the booty away!"'

Quincey's smile was radiant.

'All important members of the United Front will die,' he said. 'And as a gesture of conciliation at this auspicious time, all leading members of the opposition will be in the grandstand too.'

The remark was directed at Jan but she found it hard to follow the words. Did Quincey plan to kill all the politicians in the country? Was this a revolution or a campaign of extermination? What the hell was going on? Pain receded as she tried to understand.

'The island will be in the grip of chaos!' da Souza chimed in, egging Quincey on. 'And who will be left to cope? Who will save the day?'

'Me!' said Quincey cheerfully. 'In the national emergency, I shall declare myself prime minister. One party rule, my rule, a virtual dictatorship! Insurrection quelled, ring-leaders pinpointed and killed. By the time the country wakes up, it'll be too late. All opposition in the grave, a new dictatorial constitution in force, and the Senevisuriya dynasty under way!'

Da Souza was watching Jan's face and burst out laughing. Quincey rumbled happily. But Jan was lost. Insurrection quelled? What did he mean? Bewildered beyond endurance, she blurted out:

'Whose side are you on, for God's sake? What do you want?'

She shook her head helplessly. Da Souza's expression did not help. On the eve of triumph, he seemed taller as if he thrived not on food like normal men but on fear and death, his face lit with malicious glee.

'You're a Triad leader,' she cried, 'head of the Chu Chow in Sri Lanka! Isn't that enough?'

There was a brief pause as da Souza considered whether to reply.

'When old Wu died three years ago,' he said with a closed smile, 'the little power still attached to his name died with him. I've had to build it all up again from scratch: name, prestige, fear, everything! The Bandaranaike regime has been helpful but it has its limits.'

'Whereas Quincey's won't?'

Da Souza inclined his head modestly.

'That's right!' Quincey boomed. 'We'll be a pair of terrible twins, patting each other on the back!'

'Our combined power within the island,' da Souza added, 'will be boundless!'

'And the heroin . . . ?'

She stopped short, shocked by the expression on da Souza's face.

'Ah, the heroin!' he sighed. 'Apart from making me enormously rich, it has brought me a following among the Chu Chow that, not being Chinese, I might otherwise not have earned. This in turn extends my powers even beyond the island!'

Jan stared. The essence of the man had come into focus at last: gross ambition, ruthlessness and greed. Da Souza placed his palms in the traditional gesture of farewell and bowed low over them.

'Good night,' he murmured. 'We'll meet again – after the revolution!'

With a parting chuckle that threw his gravity to the breeze, da Souza walked out. Almost at once, the guard reappeared, stooped to retrieve the tray of unfinished food and retreated.

As the doors closed behind him, Jan turned to Quincey. Surprised to find himself suddenly deserted, he was trying to decide if he should leave too. But she could not let him go yet. First she had to know the truth. Now that she was so close, she was determined not to lose track of it again. Not until she had understood.

'And you?' she said, willing him to stay.

'I'm a born ruler,' Quincey replied with pompous condescension. 'I intend to rule.'

'Constitutional methods don't suit you?'

She had not meant to sound sarcastic; but the words slipped out that way and she let them be. Quincey laughed. He was sipping complacently at his beer, the thought of following da Souza evidently forgotten.

'There's a photograph in the PM's front room,' he said. 'It shows Solomon, his wife and their three children with Jawaharlal Nehru, his daughter, Indira Gandhi, and her sons: four prime ministers in one snap – and,' his voice rose suddenly, 'one is compelled to ask, how many potential ones? What chance have I, a mere cousin by marriage, and not even one of the better connected ones?'

'You could have formed your own party.'

'Why bother?' Quincey was genuinely amused. 'Why waste my energies and jeopardize my image in competition? This way, I eliminate all opposition at once. What could be more efficient? As Wijeweera proclaimed at his trial, "more buds will bloom" – unless we cut them down!'

Satisfaction streamed from his eyes, shone on the flushed mirrors of his cheeks. His body seemed swollen by drink and victory.

'When I've finished,' he crowed, 'there'll be such revulsion against insurgents that parents will educate their children to abhor the very idea!'

He laughed merrily.

'Because my revolution is going to fail dreadfully!'

The enormity of the betrayal left Jan's face blank. Blinded by Quincey's oratory, intoxicated by weapons they had lacked before, encouraged by the Mahanayaka's blessing and their own ideals, those vulnerable rebels were marching into a trap. She felt tired, disgust and indignation spent. If only Quincey would tell her the truth and be done. He obliged. His eyes were suddenly sharp again.

'Tomorrow night,' he said, 'rebel bands all over the island will be gathered in secret, listening to the radio commentary on the Perahera, waiting for my voice to declare the start of the rebellion. And they *will* wait – no one wants a repeat of the Wellawaya fiasco – but as they do so, traitors planted in each group will mow them down. And that fool Andrews will be among them.'

Quincey's face tightened as he spoke. Jan saw now that his drunkenness, was a kind of game: when he chose, cool self-control could override all else. Just as it had overridden affection when he decided to kill Christine.

'And here in Kandy?' she asked.

Quincey's reply was slurred but clearly put.

'Infiltrated by da Souza's bad boys, the rebels will be seen to go too far, killing indiscriminately. My men will shoot them. I'm no fool, my dear. Too often a revolutionary defeat becomes the proof of heroism, the spring-board for victory. This time they must be slaughtered in disgrace. And, as Saunders promised, I shall emerge as the hard-fisted saviour the nation needs!'

She struggled to take it all in. Da Souza consolidating his position within the Chu Chow. Quincey reaching for the premier's throne. But Saunders? What right had he to meddle in the island's affairs? Why was he raising a rebellion against the government he was officially meant to support? Why was he encouraging the heroin operation he had been deputed to stop? What was he after? She remembered his apparent solicitude, then the shock of realizing that her trust had been betrayed, and anger she thought had died surged back.

'What's Saunders got to do with it?' she spat.

Quincey grinned, amused by the violence of her reaction.

'In '71,' he explained airily, 'with a fraction more ingenuity from the JVP and the aid they deserved from either

China or Russia, this island might have become a Communist satellite. So when unrest began to build up this time, the West intervened.'

Jan's face went blank again.

'Where does the West come in?' she asked.

'That question,' he replied, 'shows how little you know of international politics.'

But Jan was determined not to be provoked.

'Why not support the United Front?' she asked. 'They're as right-wing as you can get for a socialist government.'

'But they signed an agreement,' said Quincey. 'That the Indian ocean was to be a zone of peace; that it should harbour no military installations; in short, that the West should keep their dirty hands out of there.'

He paused. His body was still slumped in drunken self-abandon, but his eyes seemed independent. Clear and hard, they watched Jan's reactions with amusement.

'Unfortunately for them,' he added with a grin, 'the United States had reached the opposite decision: after Cambodia and Vietnam, Sri Lanka seemed the ideal place to make a comeback.'

Jan knew he was laughing at her but she was finding it increasingly difficult to keep up.

'Saunders is British,' she said stupidly.

Her naïvety made him burst out laughing. His large body shook.

'He has two masters now,' he said.

Then his voice took on a clipped archness in mocking imitation of Saunders.

'"The British have had their day, but does that mean I've had mine?"' he retorted on Saunders' behalf. '"When fascism threatened, America stepped in, heir by right to the empire Britain could no longer defend. Now it's Communism and again America defends the West."'

But beer had ruined his gift for mimicry. Quincey saw it and laughed. Jan now understood where the explanation was heading and felt depressed.

'Is assassination part of American policy too?' she said sadly. She had heard the rumours, especially in recent months.

That Eisenhower had approved the attempts against Castro and Lumumba, and the murder of Trujillo. That Kennedy had been behind the death of South Vietnam's Diem. That Nixon and Kissinger had agreed to the anti-Allende revolt leading to Rene Schneider's death. She knew it was possible. Circumlocution was the order of the day: nothing officially endorsed, nothing definitely recorded.

She was struck by the irony of her situation. If Saunders' involvement in this affair ever came to light, it would be in the interests of both Britain and the States to cover it up. Her knowledge was futile, understanding an end in itself.

'So Saunders came to me,' Quincey was saying. 'I put him onto Sando whose only stipulation was the heroin deal. It fitted so neatly with everything else, providing us with a much greater bargaining power than mere dollars would have done that, as Saunders put it, it seemed churlish to refuse.'

But Jan had remembered the question she had asked Wolfgang that morning in Ulle and the bitter sorrow of his reply.

'So because of you,' she snapped, 'hundreds of young people will die!'

Assassination was bad enough but those distant squalid deaths shocked her more. Quincey was no longer amused.

'My dear girl,' he expostulated, 'we aren't forcing the stuff into their veins!'

'A British diplomat involved in heroin!' she muttered.

She was disgusted. But as she already knew, the drug trade was no morality play, law enforcement personnel no shining-armoured knights, and South-East Asian dealers not the only dragons.

She also knew that Saunders' heroin deal fitted perfectly with American anti-Communist policy. It had happened before. To restrict post-war Soviet influence in Europe, the US had recruited from Sicilian and Corsican mafias, boosting their drug smuggling operations in return. In South-East Asia, they had supported Nationalist Chinese guerrillas who were incidentally transporting a third of the world's illicit opium. In Laos, they had created a mercenary army of opium growers whose commander ran his own heroin labs. In Thailand, they had supported General Phao who monopolized Burmese opium; an

American airline even flew opium from northern villages to heroin labs in the south. Was it surprising it suited them now to encourage da Souza and Quincey?

'And the guns?' she pursued.

Quincey shrugged carelessly.

'Quantities of arms have been shipped into South-East Asia over the last few years,' he said. 'It was easy for Saunders to siphon some off for us.'

The stratagem clearly appealed to him.

'The guns found their way to Saigon. Da Souza's men removed the identification marks, added various oddments of their own so that it no longer looked like an American shipment, and brought them here.'

But beneath his nonchalance, Quincey was becoming bored. Bottle and glass were empty now. He rocked slightly on his heels as if preparing to leave. Jan leaned forward quickly.

'What happens to the heroin at the other end?' she said.

Quincey looked smug. He gave her the answer with a flourish, like a gambler dealing the ace of spades from the bottom of the pack.

'All tea-chests from the London auctions end up in a used crate business owned by Saunders' brother,' he said. 'He dismantles the ones Andrews has marked, extracts the heroin and no one's the wiser.'

He grinned complacently. Jan was silent, her questions at an end. The last one she did not bother to formulate: was there a toilet in the Temple of the Tooth? She said nothing; they were unlikely to let her out of that room. Quincey clapped his hands together to signify the end of their tête-à-tête. Their chat seemed to have left him well disposed towards her.

'And now, if you don't mind,' he said, 'I shall leave you. I do hope you enjoy the show.'

Still smiling, Quincey made for the door. The chamber echoed with the sounds of bolts shooting home. Jan listened till the silence returned. Then she crossed to the bowl of flowers and tipped the contents onto the floor. It would have to do. It struck her as vaguely amusing that when all was lost, her body still demanded attention.

PART SIX

21st August 1975:

Kandy (2)

The ninth night of the Perahera was over; 21st August had begun. But Jan could not sleep. Her fingers traced out figures on her gilded cage: a gentle-faced Buddha under a makara arch or descending a golden ladder; a frieze of pot-bellied dwarfs; a pink and yellow lion waving one paw; a stylized flower.

Dazed, she relived all that had happened since her arrival eight days earlier, imagined what the next day would bring. Was Wolfgang cooped up somewhere like she was, waiting for the right time to die? Did it make it any better that they would die together? She wondered what her father would do when the news of her death reached him; perhaps he would go to Saunders for advice. The thought stirred a pool of melancholy in her heart. Defeated, she waited for the dawn.

Her fingers found a dagoba covered in gems: a copy of the casket that held the sacred Tooth, solid gold with jewels – rubies, emeralds, pearls – that stood out from the wall with three-dimensional force. The original was too valuable and too large ever to be removed from the inner sanctum. During the Perahera, the Temple tusker carried a smaller one, also of gold, instead.

But the night was quiet now. Dancers and musicians had left a jaded city. The last revellers straggled off to bed or lay serenely comatose by the side of the road. Back in the courtyard below, half hidden by the trees, elephants snorted gently in the dark. Their mahouts slept with them in the hut inside the gate. Outside, two figures skulked in the shadows or walked back and forth to keep awake. From time to time, they looked up at her lighted window. Sometimes, a third man joined them; once there were four. Their vigilance made them conspicuous now.

Jan switched off the light and watched the darkness past the window come alive. The lake shone: streetlamps marched along the nearer edge, snaked through the trees beyond; and within this iridescent ring, water smooth and calm. Four sharp ovals of reflected light paid court to the moon. On the far hill, a row of lamps struggled through black vegetation, an orange gleam suggesting a household still awake. Brash headlights marked a driver ambling home, slowly tracing the last miles from the east coast to the hills, the road that started in Pottuvil. Jan thought sadly of Mohan, watching it approach. Each headlight emitted elongated rays. Above, cottonwool clouds flicked across a dark grey sky. Stars switched on and off, winking over deep blue hills at the lights below.

She forgot the guards, lost track of the hours floating by. Textured night leaned in against her cheek. With each breath, she tasted the freshness of the lake air, inhaled hints of jasmine, elephant and frangipani. Her ears were attuned to a city half asleep: a yelp of boredom from a dog chained on guard; disjointed rattling from a bullock cart; one shattering blast as an elephant challenged the world; while the vibrant hum of cicadas hugged the scene. As the moon sank towards the western hills, Jan sighed. It did no good to brood. Kandy at night wore the unreal delicacy of a dream.

A vehicle erupted on to the lakeside road and the dream splintered. With vague irritation, Jan watched the headlights slice the dark. A car materialized, stopped. The glare of an overhead lamp cast deep shadows inside. Jan could see nothing of the driver. By the wall, one guard nudged the other. A moment's silence, then the cicadas remembered and started up again.

A figure detached itself, spilled into the light. Jan tensed suddenly. It was a man, tall and better built than most Ceylonese, and his hair gleamed gold. Her eyes closed for a moment, then opened again. He was still there. Her lethargy disintegrated.

'Wolfgang!' she whispered.

He was still alive. Then she remembered Saunders' words and glanced back at the guards. They would be expecting him. Her fingers clenched around the metal bars. Had he seen them?

They had slipped back into the shadows out of sight. Her knuckles began to ache. She had to think of something, quickly.

Wolfgang was walking straight towards the temple. He moved slowly, apparently admiring the floodlit building as he headed for the main entrance. His eyes measured the steps up the side, saw the closed doors. But he did not look up. The two guards still watched him from the shadows of the crenellated wall. Then, as he turned the corner, they followed, hands reaching down for knife or gun.

But a movement by the car had caught Jan's eye. Two men were climbing out on the other side, dark bodies merging with their host. Her fingers tightened on the bars once more. Had Wolfgang found help? With growing excitement, Jan watched.

The two men slid across the lighted road towards the wall. They wore the khaki uniform of the police. The two they followed were closing in on one. Five shapes all heading in the same direction, the gaps between them dwindling fast. Then Wolfgang turned. The two guards crouched ready. A weapon glinted through the night. A pause, then the last two shapes closed in. Brief violence and only three remained. Shadows had claimed the guards.

Jan breathed again. She ran to the switch by the door, flicked the light on then off then on, turning the window into a beacon of distress to draw their eyes. It worked. When she hurried back to the window, three faces gazed up. Framed in light, all sense of caution lost, Jan waved. Thirty yards away, an expression of such relief brightened Wolfgang's face that she laughed out loud. Then she switched off the light and waited.

Her eyes scanned the dark. But she did not have to wait long. A shadow flitted to the car across the road, then back towards the temple. Jan thought she saw a fourth man in the driving seat, but her eyes did not dare linger long. For, below her, the other three had cleared the wall and dropped into the yard. One of them was carrying a rope.

They stopped. Ahead of them loomed the dark forms of elephants asleep on their feet, the hut of dozing mahouts to their right. They hesitated, clearly worried. Jan prayed. But these elephants had been selected for the Perahera, chosen for their placidity among celebrating crowds, and they gave no trouble.

The three men skirted the yard until they stood directly beneath her window.

'Jan! Catch the rope!' Wolfgang's whisper pierced the stillness, urgency spinning through the dark. 'Tie it to the bars!'

But one of the mahouts was awake. Jan heard him scramble to his feet, shake his fellow, caution him. Wolfgang froze. His body merged into the heap of fodder against the wall, a dark lump beyond the elephants. His friends seemed to have disappeared. Jan pulled herself back from the window as two mahouts emerged from the hut. She saw with relief that they did not know what had disturbed them. One looked up the road towards the hill, the other down towards the park. They patrolled silently, in the yard, patting their charges, listening for sounds. Then they returned to the gate. Their suspicions had been allayed. One lit a beedi. The other talked. For a while, they stayed in desultory conversation. When the beedi went out, they returned to their hut beside the wall.

Jan's fingers relaxed their grip on the sill. In the courtyard below, Wolfgang grasped the rope more firmly. Carefully now, he unlooped it and threw it in an arc toward her. Nerves taut, she stretched her arms through the bars. An elephant shuffled irritably. Three times, the rope fell against the wall out of reach. Once the throw was perfect but Jan in her anxiety let it slip; she almost cried out with frustration. Each time the rope failed to reach her hands, it fell with a crack of dry leaves on to the pile of fodder below. But the mahouts heard the elephants move and did not think to check. Wolfgang began again without a word.

At last the rope swung into her hands. With sweating fingers, she tied it round the bars. She was breathing fast now. Both face and hands were damp.

'Ready!' she whispered.

But she was not ready for what came next.

For one of Wolfgang's friends was cautiously advancing on the elephants. The younger animals were restive but the older ones had long been unafraid of men. Slipping a knife from his pocket, the policeman cut the cords that tethered them to the trees. One old bull slept on undisturbed. Before he could wake to the threat, the policeman tied the rope firmly to his leg.

The old bull woke with a start. The rope bothered him and he pulled against it. As the cord tightened on the bars, Jan stepped back. But nothing happened. The rope had not bothered him enough. Jan heard herself praying aloud.

She looked down to see the third man pick up a dried branch and put a match to the leaves. When the flame was high, he thrust it towards the drowsy elephant, willing him to move.

He did. Then everything happened at once. With an ear-shattering trumpet, the old bull careered across the courtyard taking the bars with him. The other elephants, infected by his fear, pounded after him, ears flapping, trunks held high, blaring indignation. The angry shouts of half a dozen woken mahouts carried above their noise. They emerged at a run, faces tight with consternation. They could see the burning branch, knew a man was holding it, but dared not enter the scrum of frightened elephants. They shouted at each other to keep their charges calm, shouted again for the guards. Three men ran to join them from the other side of the building. Elephants continued to trumpet and plunge. Wolfgang's command cut across the din.

'Jump, Jan! Jump!'

But it was twenty feet and she was scared. The heap of fodder waiting below did not look soft. If she hurt herself, how could she escape those massive stamping feet? She gazed in terror from the steep drop to the elephants stampeding the courtyard she had to cross, and the growing row of guards beyond the gate. She heard Wolfgang's order but could not move.

A metal bolt pulled back behind her. In slow motion, she saw the painted doors swing open and a silhouette peering into the darkened room. Whoever it was had heard that trumpeting, the tearing of plaster from the temple walls. As hands groped for the light, Jan clambered onto the sill.

She heard a shout behind her as she jumped, an angry guttural and the clatter of footsteps across a marble floor. Then a whistling sound and a vicious pain in her upper arm. She was screaming as she fell. Banana leaves cracked in protest. She landed badly, tumbling to one side. The fall dislodged the knife. A scream of pain, a glimpse of ivory, and blood flowing down her arm. Then her hand was seized and she was dragged along.

They ran behind the elephants, the burning branch lunging

at their tails. The animals thundered trumpeting at the gate. Mahouts ran wild, desperate to escape those fatal footsteps. A careening beast trapped one of them against the wall, leaned into him as it passed. He was only a boy.

Wolfgang pulled Jan away. On the road beyond, the guards saw elephants coming straight at them, trunks aloft, and they fled. The gate disintegrated, chips of wood flying through the air. The elephants hardly noticed. One man running in the leader's path was tossed out aside: his body fell limp against the temple wall.

They followed. Jan heard the car start up. But as they reached the smashed gate, a figure emerged from behind the wall to face them. A tight Chinese smile; the glint of a levelled gun. The policeman swung his branch. As the gun went off, he rammed the flame into their assailant's face. There was a screech of pain. Wolfgang bent to retrieve the gun. They ran on.

Shots rang out as they hurried to the car. Several tore at the cement. They crouched lower and ran. The burning pain in Jan's arm grew more violent, her fingers wet with blood. But they could not stop.

They reached the car and tumbled into it. As the driver accelerated away, Jan tore a strip off her skirt and held it to her arm to stop the blood. Shouting in the temple made her look back. Lights were flashing on all over the building. Silhouettes at the window with the broken bars. More shots. She glanced at Wolfgang. With a jolt of dismay, she saw that he was hurt too, blood spreading across his shoulder. But he turned to her and grinned. Then they were away. Behind them, at the window with the broken bars, the silhouettes watched them go. The Perahera was not over yet.

They drove straight to Mohan's family home. While the others went in, Wolfgang paused. There, while a flame tree stood sentinel and the lake glowed beyond, he held Jan close. She felt the warmth of his body, his face in her hair. Only the pain in her arm and the deep red smear on his shoulder stopped her drifting away. She was dizzy from excitement and loss of blood. After a moment, Wolfgang helped her to the door.

There was a scurrying of feet indoors. Servants were fetching the head of the household. At last, Mohan's father appeared. Jan was startled. Even Mohan's tales about him had failed to prepare her. Lakshman Weeragama was a bizarre sight. With his single betel-reddened tooth, a tatty grey moustache and a dirty cloth wrapped around his head, the old fellow looked more like a pirate than a retired police inspector. Flanked by vases of scarlet anthuriums, each as shiny as a plastic mackintosh, he was totally out of place. But his eyes were bright.

'Glad to meet you, Miss Nicholls,' he said when he heard her name. He spoke with a plausible English accent. 'My son has often spoken of you.'

Then he saw their blood-stained clothes. Formality disintegrated as he ushered them inside. While they talked, he washed their wounds himself, the old hands gentle but efficient. He started with Jan, cleaning the deep cut, binding the edges of the wound tightly together.

They told him everything, from the beginning. Lakshman blinked, prompted them with questions, exploded in exclamation from time to time. When they came to Mohan's death, the hands stopped still. The lined face seemed older now, the eyes opaque with pain. Then they cleared and he asked more questions, his voice controlled, pinpointing responsibility. They told him what they knew.

'Right,' he said at last. 'Da Souza's mine.'

He threw a fierce glance at each of them and resumed his task. They told him the rest. In as much detail as possible, they explained what Quincey had planned for the final night of the Perahera. When they had finished, they waited for his response. The old man did not speak. He busied himself cleaning up the messy path a bullet had carved through the outer flesh of Wolfgang's shoulder. But he was thinking hard. His tenacious look was that of a man who could not easily accept what fate had meted out. The grey moustache twitched with emotion not allowed into his face.

When he straightened up, he had come to a decision.

'Well, my friends,' he said briskly, 'we seem to have a crisis on our hands.'

The beady old eyes turned to Jan.

'You must rest that arm and get some sleep,' he said. 'I shall alert my relatives. And your young friend here can help me.'

He raised both hands in front of him as if to ward off a storm of protest. Jan smiled. The gesture reminded her of Mohan.

'You go to sleep,' he repeated. 'Dream of Kataragama and – you'll see – everything will be all right! For our great god of war has already heard my prayer: I know he will revenge my son!'

But he would say no more. A servant showed her to her room and she obeyed.

She did not wake until Wolfgang kissed her. Instinctively, she threw her arms around his neck.

'It's past midday, you know,' he said, kissing her again. 'Well past.'

Then she remembered. She sat up quickly and looked at him. Wolfgang's eyes shone.

'Has Lakshman got a plan?' she said.

He grinned. He was clearly excited about something.

'Oh yes, he's got one,' he said, 'but you won't believe it. I've been sent to fetch you so that he can tell everyone.'

'Everyone?'

Wolfgang nodded. She wanted to ask more but he had placed a finger on her lips.

'You'll see,' he laughed.

She leaped up to dress. His eyes followed her but he would say no more. It seemed it was the old man's prerogative to explain. When she was ready, he led her past the bead curtains to the lounge.

'I'm sorry I'm late . . .' she began.

Then she stopped and stared. In a room full of people, Lakshman sat in state. She recognized only Wolfgang, Neemal and the old man. All the rest wore the khaki uniform of the Sri Lanka police. One sported the new outfit now on sale, the open-necked shirt, loose-fitting slacks and peaked cap making him look absurdly young. For the rest, until the old uniforms wore out, there would be no appreciable break with colonial tradition: starched shorts and shirts, flamboyant slouch hats with brims buttoned up on one side.

A rumble of friendly laughter greeted her surprise. Wolfgang laughed with them. With a regal gesture, Lakshman waved her

170

to a seat. Jan gave in. Wolfgang showed her to a chair beside his own.

'What on earth's going on?' she laughed. 'You seem to have the entire police force here.'

Lakshman replied with mock severity, 'This is my family.'

Jan remembered what Mohan had told her: that his father had always urged them to take advantage of the secure income afforded by a lifetime in the police. She had not realized how many of them had followed his advice.

'All of them?' she said.

'All of them,' came the satisfied response. 'On your right is my eldest son – he's a superintendent now and the most senior of them all.'

Jan turned to greet an upright man with his own version of the ubiquitous family moustache. She recognized him now as one of her rescuers, the one who had wielded the burning branch.

'Next to him is my second son.' Another familiar face from the bedlam by the lake.

'Then my daughter's husband. Then a nephew, he's up from Colombo for the festival. Next, my grandson – you can see by the new-fangled uniform that he's only just joined . . .'

Jan nodded politely as each man inclined his head in her direction or half rose from his seat. She was too surprised to speak.

As the introductions continued, she became aware that there was beneath the courtesies a cohesive energy drawing them all together: a single-minded determination for revenge. Mohan's death hovered over them, uniting the entire family. She glanced at Wolfgang and saw that he had been drawn into it too, his face as determined as the rest.

'The lady is Manel, Mohan's wife,' Lakshman was saying, and Jan found herself greeting a tearful face framed by thick black plaits; she too was in uniform. Jan was glad they had met at last.

'And over there in the corner,' Lakshman concluded, 'is my disreputable old brother who refused through all his wicked years to join the police.'

Jan turned to find a replica of Lakshman. The second old man gave a roar of laughter at her expression.

'Lakshman has never forgiven me for turning out so similar none the less,' he said. He even had the same unlikely accent.

Jan shook her head in disbelief and laughed. She turned back to Lakshman.

'Well, I hope this means you've come up with something,' she said.

'It certainly does,' Lakshman sounded complacent. 'And it's time I let you all in on it. Neemal, offer Jan some fruit and we'll begin.'

Neemal set a bowl of assorted fruits on a table beside her: Jaffna mangoes, avocado pears with purple skins, passionfruits, mangosteens, bananas: Kandy's market was the best on the island. Lakshman watched Jan choose a mangosteen before he spoke.

'I was as baffled as the rest of you at first,' he said.

He paused. A Dumbara mat hanging on the wall behind his head formed a gaudy spotlight; stocky birds marched across a geometric red-and-yellow world.

'Once that gun is fired, I thought, all hell will be let loose! That gave me the answer!'

He darted his fierce glare round the assembled company. Grief still shone in his eyes but now the lined face gleamed resolution. Revenge had set all else aside.

'If we want to stop them,' he declared, 'we must act before that gun goes off.'

'But how?' Jan could not help herself. 'We don't know who they all are, or where they'll be beforehand.'

'I know,' came the serene reply.

No one else had spoken. Wolfgang's hand reached across to Jan's, a gesture of reassurance. Looking down, she noticed a row of reddish swellings on his wrist and wondered what had caused them; she had not noticed them the night before. She smiled at him. His eyes were bright with excitement, unclouded by her doubts. She had forgotten he was in on Lakshman's plan. The old man cleared his throat to gain her attention.

'At five to nine,' he said, 'Quincey will leave the grandstand. The snipers will be in the trees. And hearse- and truck-loads of armed men will be waiting in the side streets. So precisely then, before the second group of dancers have finished their bit, before the elephant steps backwards and the deputy fires the gun – we must strike!'

Even his family were unable to refrain this time.

'What with?' asked one.

'They'll see us long before that,' objected another.

'As soon as they see our guns,' cried a third, 'they'll mow us down!'

'They're on the alert,' was Jan's contribution. 'Now that I've escaped, they'll be expecting us to try something.'

Only Wolfgang was unperturbed. Lakshman glanced at him and smiled. The reaction was evidently no surprise to either of them. He raised one hand for silence.

'I'm not as stupid as I look,' he remonstrated calmly.

The old moustache lifted with sudden confidence. His voice was stern.

'Guns,' he said, 'are too obvious. The weapons I have in mind are not!'

No one spoke. As Lakshman flicked a searching gaze from face to face, they waited.

'I shan't make you guess,' he said at last. 'I'll show you. Neemal!'

The boy jumped up, anxiety almost making him salute.

'Neemal,' Lakshman repeated, 'you'll find some boxes on the back porch. Wolfgang will help you bring one here. Handle it gently: the contents are explosive.'

All eyes turned with them as the two obeyed. Silence descended behind them. Footsteps passed through the house, paused and came slowly back. When they reappeared, the two carried between them a large cardboard box. Very carefully, they set it down in the centre of the room. An unmistakable buzzing came from within. Lakshman watched as incredulity struck them all at once. Jan was the first to put the astonishing thought into words. She had suddenly remembered Lakshman's passion. Her eyes dropped to the swellings on Wolfgang's wrist.

'Bees!' she exclaimed, turning to him for confirmation. 'They're bambaras, aren't they?'

Wolfgang merely grinned.

'You're mad, father!' laughed a deep voice to her right.

'Not bad, old boy!' came the genteel accents of the second old pirate in the corner, accompanied by a high-pitched wheeze.

'Bambaras?' asked someone else. 'But why?'

'Because as we all know,' replied Lakshman deliberately, 'bambaras make lethal enemies. Which sniper could be accurate if he's bothered by even one bambara? Which gangster will remember his orders? When we open those boxes, not even Saunders will stay cool!'

No one disagreed. The bambara was a giant among honey bees, as large as a hornet, and its sting was terrible.

'Only two creatures are brave enough to face bambaras,' Lakshman intoned. 'The honey buzzard whose face is protected by scales and the Veddah who knows their ways.'

'How will you do it?' Jan interrupted to ask.

'How will *we* do it?' Lakshman corrected her firmly. 'We need to know what makes them tick – or, should I say, sting. Like the Veddahs, we must know what upsets a bambara and what doesn't, and use that knowledge to our advantage. For example, why do the Veddahs always steal honey at night, never at dusk?'

Jan remembered the shot that had disturbed the bees at the cave, and how quickly the darkness had calmed them down again. But she let Lakshman supply the answer.

'Because bambaras are disorientated by the dark,' he said. 'But at dusk – or when dusk is simulated, let us say, by the lights of the Perahera – bambaras are at their worst.'

'What about noise?' asked someone.

'Secondly,' Lakshman continued quietly. 'Veddahs always hunt in silence. Because bambaras can't stand noise. Tonight's kettle-drums and trumpets will drive them berserk.'

'They'll be wild before we even let them loose!'

'Thirdly,' Lakshman proceeded over his son's exclamation, 'Veddahs never hunt at the full moon. Because bambaras are especially sensitive then and quicker to attack. And as we all know, tonight is the Esala full moon.'

Jan's eyes were rivetted to that box.

'Oh my God!' she said softly.

'Lastly, Veddahs always approach a hive from below. Because when bambaras are disturbed they fly upwards before they organize their attack. So think of the snipers in those trees!'

He stopped then and waited for their reactions. At first, there was only an astonished silence. Then the room filled with objections and exclamations of disbelief. Only Wolfgang remained silent: he evidently wanted the plan to work.

'By the . . . !' someone began incredulously.

'That's ridiculous!' declared another, shaking his head.

'Oh no, Lakshman, it can't possibly work!'

Even Manel's trusting face showed concern.

'And why not, may I ask?'

Lakshman's question was directed at Jan for she had been the last to speak, but she was not the only one to answer.

'Because they'll attack everyone,' replied his oldest son, the superintendent, 'not just the men you're after.'

'You can't expect the bees to know who they're meant to sting,' agreed someone else.

'There'll be a mass panic,' said Jan. 'The crowd won't know what's hit them!'

Lakshman waited for the excitement to subside. Their scepticism did not seem to bother him. Jan's eyes returned to their perusal of the box. Hadn't she read somewhere that medieval Danes had hurled bees instead of bullets at their foes? And wasn't it in World War I that hives had been attached to trip wires to make primitive booby traps? It seemed preposterous.

'If it's any consolation,' Lakshman said at last, 'you're absolutely right.'

Jan looked up, suddenly afraid there was no answer after all. She glanced at Wolfgang, saw the certainty unaltered in his eyes, then turned back to Lakshman. She sounded confused.

'What can we do?' she said. 'We can't set them loose, can we? It wouldn't be right.'

'Of course it wouldn't!' agreed the superintendent indignantly, his moustache quivering. 'It's hopeless!'

'Not hopeless,' Lakshman objected mildly. 'We must use a little ingenuity, that's all.'

Wolfgang smiled openly at this, but from the rest his tone provoked a hail of questions.

'What?'

'How on earth do we do that?'

'Yes, how?' cried a spattering of disbelieving voices.

Lakshman took a deep breath.

'We have five main targets,' he said slowly, marking them off on his fingers. 'One, the snipers in the trees opposite the grandstand. Two, the hearses with machine-guns mounted to spray the crowds. Three, the truckloads of armed men. Four, the toughs guarding the trees. And five, an unspecified number of individuals mingling with the crowd and causing trouble.'

'Hopeless,' repeated the superintendent. 'Far too many of them and in too many places – we can't stop them all.'

'It won't be easy.' Lakshman planted gnarled hands square on his knees and stared round the room. 'Neemal, you and Jan can help Wolfgang deal with the snipers.'

'Me?' gasped Jan with a start. 'But they'll be looking for me! I'd wreck the whole plan!'

Lakshman's voice was reassuring, but firm.

'We must have you there,' he said. 'Besides, tonight isn't any night, or even any one night of the Perahera: it's the final night; the pavements will be packed. Those men guarding the tulip trees couldn't keep people away if they tried – their only concern is to stop anyone climbing up. So keep out of their way, out of the light, and you'll be fine – just one more tourist among the crowds.'

'But . . .'

Wolfgang smiled encouragement and Jan subsided. She did not want to seem cowardly nor was she unwilling to take her part with the rest, but she still could not see that her participation was worth the risk. Lakshman continued with the main thread of his argument.

'So,' he said with heavy precision, 'let's take our targets one by one. First, those snipers. Jan, Neemal and Wolfgang will each take a box and find a place under one of those trees. At the right moment, each will give his box a shake and open it – the bambaras will take care of the rest!'

Jan felt she should say something but nothing came to mind. The discussion had become unreal. Neemal bit his lip and nodded. He looked as if he wished he were someone else. Wolfgang merely stared, concentration tight.

176

'Secondly, the hearses. They should be easy to spot. A box of bees thrown into each vehicle and the gunmen dealt with as they emerge. The same method should work for the trucks of armed men.'

He paused and looked round the circle of faces.

'Who wants to take care of that?' he said briskly. 'The dangers can be avoided with the right approach.'

With a shrug, the superintendent volunteered.

'I can do it,' he said. 'If I have the men and enough time to pinpoint the vehicles.'

'I'll help,' offered a brother. 'We'll need a dozen men at least.'

'More, I think. Five or six on bikes to check the streets. Then one man with a box of bees for each hearse and truck. And one or two men per vehicle to deal with anyone who tries to escape. Two dozen to be safe.'

'Right,' agreed his colleague. 'And anyone who isn't needed elsewhere can join us too. We need some way to get close to them, near enough to throw the bees inside. And once the men are disarmed, we must get the vehicles away so that they can't be used again later.'

'We could drive them up here – there's plenty of room in the compound – or to my house behind the temple.'

Objections forgotten, the men were absorbed in the problem. Their discussion of tactics triggered a wave of excitement through the room. Lakshman's face beamed satisfaction.

'Fine,' he said. 'That takes care of targets one, two and three. It also accounts for most of us. But there are still two problems left: the men guarding the tulip trees, and those ordered to mingle with the crowd and kill indiscriminately to discredit the rebels.'

'You keep looking at me, old boy!' his brother wheezed, eyes narrowed with suspicion.

Jan looked from brother to brother. The likeness between them was astonishing.

'That's right. Feel like helping us out?'

'Why not?' The single tooth caught the light. 'What do you want me to do? Shake bambaras at them?'

'Not bambaras, brother. Arrack.'

His sons' exchange of strategies was silenced.

177

'You said the bees don't know who to sting so I've found a way of telling them.'

'A way of . . . ?' Jan echoed faintly.

Lakshman placed his interlocked fingers across his middle and explained.

'Alcohol sends bambaras crazy!'

'You want me to throw arrack at the gangsters?' his brother asked with a distinctly piratical leer.

'Throw or spill, whichever you like,' Lakshman replied. 'I'll join you, and a few others too. We'll approach as many of the individual targets as possible and spill arrack liberally all over them. Then the bees will know exactly who to sting.'

'And how will we know who to spill it on?'

'That's where Jan and Wolfgang come in. I know some of the men – da Souza and Quincey – but they will recognize more.'

He turned to Jan.

'If they knew what was going to happen tonight, they'd be the ones afraid of being recognized, not you,' he said. 'We'll keep in the shadows and watch for them. If you see someone you know, tell us.'

He paused. 'And we'll also need some people on the look-out for armed men.'

Hands flew up in the room, including Manel's, and he nodded with approval. Jan wished she had been as keen.

'They can be given the same treatment,' he said. 'When the bees are let loose and the gangsters unable to defend themselves, those guns must be removed.'

He waited but no one spoke.

'Right,' he said firmly, 'that's settled. All five targets accounted for and every one of us with a job to do. If all goes as planned, there'll be no one left to start the revolution when the gun is fired! Any questions?'

There was one.

'How do we stop the bees from stinging us?' objected Neemal.

A murmur of agreement ran round the room and heads nodded anxiously. Lakshman complied.

'Remember the honey buzzard's scales,' he said, 'and wear protective clothing. Something on your head, two or three shirts on your back, two pairs of trousers, socks and shoes instead of

178

sandals. You'll be hot but it'll be worth it. And I have a dozen face guards for the men disabling the trucks and hearses; that part must not go wrong. I'm sorry there aren't enough for all of you.'

He paused and gazed round the room. Every face looked back. The only sound was of the bees still buzzing in the middle of the room. Lakshman stood up.

'Before you go,' he said, 'wash thoroughly: sweat acts as a homing device for an angry bee. Don't drink for the same reason. Those of you carrying arrack, take care you don't get drenched yourselves; if you do, get as far away as you can before the bees are released.'

Everyone nodded gravely. Lakshman's old brother wheezed in the silence.

'And don't shout even if you are stung,' Lakshman added. 'Noise only makes them worse. Let others draw their attack.'

The heads nodded again. Jan was thinking of the din made by tourists at Sigiriya rock and the recent outbreak of bambara attacks: the Ministry of Tourism had had to instal wire mesh cages to protect people from the bees.

'Wear dark colours so that you don't attract attention – from bees or men,' Lakshman continued.

He paused once more.

'And most important of all,' he said earnestly, 'whatever you do, whatever happens, don't kill a bambara yourself. Not even by mistake. If you do, the rest will follow you to the death!'

He stopped, placed his palms together and bent his head over them. When he looked up again, his eyes burned.

'It is Kataragama's idea, not mine,' he said. 'How can we lose with the god of war on our side?'

His confidence was infectious. But now the old man's face had changed. The eyes grew sombre.

'Kataragama promised something more,' he said. His gaze flicked almost coldly over his friends. 'That da Souza is mine.'

In an atmosphere of grim resolve, the meeting broke up.

As the sun sank in the west, in the east the moon began to rise: the full moon of the Esala Perahera jealously obliterated all but the brightest stars.

By seven-thirty, they were in position. The procession started at eight. The revolution was scheduled to begin at nine. There was plenty of time.

Jan stood by the lake, not far from the tulip tree to which she had been allocated, and tried to calm herself. Everything conspired against her. The crowds were already thick and noisy, men and women chattering excitedly, gesticulating, laughing, waiting. The air vibrated with expectation. She looked for Wolfgang but could not see him any more. Alone and apprehensive, she drew her headscarf closer to her face. Her only companions in that busy isolation were the bees, an angry army trapped in a box that hung from her shoulder. As the density of the crowd increased and the box was repeatedly jolted by mistake, the buzzing grew more insistent. She was sure someone would hear it. She forced herself to look relaxed. With what she hoped was the right glazed expression, she leaned against the scalloped wall, a tourist enjoying the scene.

Behind her, fire ringed the lake: streetlamps, burning flares and strings of bobbing coloured lights. The reflections in the water shifted as the ripples from the breeze above or a swirl of fish below spun their brightness into catherine wheels or shot sparks like rockets to a reflected moon.

In front rose the iridescent splendour of the Temple of the Tooth; illuminated from within, spotlit from without, an octagonal jewel blazing in a fiery crown. Jan's eyes wandered past the pink lobes of the outside walls, past the clump of palm trees in the courtyard, to a window with broken bars. It seemed so long since she had heard Quincey describe the revolution he had planned. Was he expecting them to try to stop him now?

The grandstand stood exactly opposite, against a light-filled park. The front seats reserved for the prime minister and her colleagues remained conspicuously empty. Jan looked away.

The crowd was gathering fast: women promenading in their best sarees; smart youths displaying tapered trousers and vivid batik shirts; boys selling nuts and sweets, yelling their wares in professional raucous tones; businesslike little girls trailing balloons on a string. Overhead, a loudspeaker belched announcements in three languages, interspersed with Sinhalese folk songs and ten-year-old tunes from the West.

In that eddy of humanity, Jan's courage failed. Wolfgang materialized twenty yards to her right and she tried to catch his eye; but he was busy. He gestured to someone in the crowd. An old fellow lurched as if drunk, stumbled and, before Jan realized what had happened, fell heavily against a passer-by. The impact loosened the old man's grip on his bottle: his victim was doused with arrack. As the pair separated, Jan recognized the inimitable Lakshman and da Souza, the latter daubing angrily at his clothes. One down, she thought triumphantly, but how many more to go? Methodically now, she checked each face.

At first, she recognized no one. Then among the bobbing heads, an unforgotten Chinese face emerged. Jan signalled to Wolfgang and at once, as if connected by an unseen string, Lakshman ambled from the crowd. She did not see what happened next for another familiar face had come into view. In sudden panic, she tried to run but found she could not move. The man drew nearer, turned his head in her direction and winked. She smiled weakly: one of Lakshman's nephews patrolling the crowds.

The realization gave her confidence. She was surrounded by friends: Wolfgang to her right, Neemal to her left; the old man and his cronies laying their alcoholic trail; trained policemen weaving through the crowd on the lookout for trouble. How could she be in danger? Reassured, she kept her back to the light and resumed her task.

A commotion in the grandstand made her turn: the VIPs were assembling. It was almost eight. The prime minister's red and gold saree drew all eyes. Quincey leaned over to speak to her and she smiled vaguely as if she had not understood. Quincey laughed anyway, looking around.

Jan glanced up at her tree. Were the snipers already there? The foliage was too thick to tell. She looked anxiously at the other two trees. Had Wolfgang or Neemal seen them climb?

A sudden blast startled her: the ceremonial gun. With one movement, men, women and children, VIPs and commoners, all turned towards the Temple of the Tooth. The Esala moon was full. The final night of the Perahera had begun.

But Jan did not turn with them. Something in Wolfgang's expression alerted her and she sank back against the wall to watch. As the crowd surged forward with a muted roar of pleasure, a band of men slunk along the dark margin at the back unseen. When they came level with Neemal's tree, a few men detached themselves, shinned up the trunk and disappeared among the leaves. Neemal darted a conspiratorial glance at Jan, then looked away.

Another handful vanished up the second tulip tree – her tree, Jan muttered to herself – and the rest scurried on. Each man nodded to someone waiting at the base; the last even had a helping hand. More important, each carried something long and bulky swung across his shoulder.

Jan glanced at Wolfgang. He had melted into the shadows of the wall, but she saw his gleaming head of hair and could have sworn he smiled.

As the last man slid into hiding, an unexpected altercation broke out in the branches of the third tree. A child's voice protested, then a small figure fell out and scuttled away in tears. It was over in seconds and only Jan and Wolfgang noticed.

She ran her hands anxiously over her box. The three tulip trees now harboured da Souza's men. At that moment, they were drawing preparatory beads on the politicians opposite. Jan remembered Lakshman's words and prayed to Kataragama to make their plan work.

The next moment, Lakshman stood before her. He had popped up out of nowhere like a bedraggled jack-in-the-box, his clothes sodden with arrack, the cloth on his head askew. But as his face crumpled into the drunkard's decomposing grin, his eyes were hard and clear. Any orders, they seemed to say? She gestured to the man standing guard at the base of her tree, his back towards them. Hazy blinds dropped over the old man's eyes and he turned to obey. It was soon over: an angry Chinese dripped arrack while a drunk tottered away.

A gasp of appreciation rippled through the crowd. Whip-crackers cleared the way, sizzling and spitting their ancient warning. Flag-bearers held aloft their standards. On either side, torch-bearers walked with lighted braziers, each one emitting flames and a hail of sparks. Then came a costumed official carrying the mandate for the Perahera.

A strange sound pierced the air. The first troupe of the

evening, the dancers and musicians of the Dalada Maligawa, were about to perform. Jan turned with the crowd to watch.

A single figure stood alone. Above a white sarong and scarlet cummerbund, his naked torso was oiled, gleaming in the light of the flares. Haughty features were accentuated by a white cloth that concealed his hair. A murmur rose from the crowd. Proudly, he raised the conch to his lips once more and the mournful call echoed over their heads, evoking the spirits of the dead.

The night disintegrated into sound. Two dozen pairs of hands descended on to stretched hide. Fluid wrists propelled rigid fingers in a tattoo so fast Jan could barely hear the rhythm she knew she could not see. Two dozen heads rose proud on shining necks. Two dozen sets of shoulders worked together, rising and falling, muscles sending spasms across taut skin. Two dozen pairs of feet executed a staccato four-step that moved their bodies back and forth and turned their fierce profiles a hundred and eighty degrees left, then right, then left again. The temple drummers were possessed. Excitement rolled from them to infect both the swaying crowd and the dancers waiting for their cue.

It came, and set a glittering stream of silver into dance. Each whirling figure wore the same outlandish costume: loose folds of white falling from a scarlet belt; red-edged frills bunched at the hip and trailing an embroidered tassel; a vest of silver circles; silver ornaments at wrist and ankle, arm and throat; shining disc-like earrings and a conical hat with scalloped brim swinging a tassel from its tip. Compelled by the drums, they threw themselves into the famous Kandyan dance.

Every movement splashed silver. Jumping silver circles glittered like animated fish scales. Feet stamped. Shoulders rolled. Ankle bells clashed and tinkled. Arms snaked out and back, fingertips flicking into place. Heads tilted to send long tassels arcing over their shoulders. Eyes and teeth flashed white.

As impassioned as the rest, a boy twirled with closed eyes, bent knees, his face entranced. Beside him, wiry and supple, an old man set up a pounding rhythm in memory of his youth, his jaw dropped in concentration, his lips curved in an ecstatic smile. The crowd burst into spontaneous applause.

Jan was finding it hard to think. All around her, dazed faces followed the drums. She pulled her eyes away to look for Wolfgang. He winked and calmly indicated it was not yet time.

The dancers roused themselves for their finale. Each in turn leaped backwards in astounding somersaults. White robes shone and silver clinked. Again and again, like hand puppets tossed in the air, the figures rose, turned and fell neatly back on to their feet, back into the syncopated rhythm, back into the swirling vision of red, white, brown and silver revolving at the mercy of the drums.

They stopped. The spell broke. Frenzy was replaced by a brisk tattoo and the troupe drifted on down the road. When they had gone fifty yards, the beat changed again and the dancers prepared to entertain a new audience. For a while, the heads of the crowd followed them; then, one by one, they turned.

Three magnificent elephants with gold-sheathed tusks paced towards them. But it was Rajah, the Temple Tusker, who swayed the crowd. Men ran ahead of him to spread lengths of white cloth down the lakeside road. His forehead, ears and trunk were adorned with red velvet on which gold and silver ornaments had been sewn: a row of gold-edged silver suns straddled his brow; gaudy lotuses covered his ears; and a stylized bo tree with golden branches and silver leaves ran down his trunk. His back was draped in a massive ornamented cloth that brushed the ground as he walked while a silver howdah holding the casket of the Tooth balanced on top. Both howdah and tusker were liberally hung with electric lights that flickered with each step and overhead, supported by retainers on foot, swung a gold and crimson canopy. As Rajah carried his sacred burden past, men and women fell to the ground in awe.

The cavalcade drew level with the grandstand. Jan turned with the rest to watch it pass. Men in traditional Kandyan costumes with flat-topped hats accompanied the tuskers: two sat astride each of the outer pair, holding bronze shields on lacquered staffs and honorific umbrellas fringed with silver leaves; some marched beside the elephants' feet with instruments to prod and guide; others ran busily in front or stumbled in the rear as if they had been left behind. All were lit by the torch-bearers' blazing flares.

Then Jan saw Saunders. He was watching from the far side of Neemal's tree, his fair hair conspicuous above the diminutive Ceylonese. She whirled round for help but Wolfgang had already moved. He spoke to someone by his side and gestured with his chin. All she could see was Saunders' pale face floating above an ocean of heads.

He glanced down angrily and tried to brush someone or something off. On the point of losing his temper and hitting out, he changed his mind and wheeled away in disgust. Jan felt only relief that he had gone away.

She turned back to the procession; and gasped. For there in the howdah on the back of another elephant, eyes closed, hands clasped in his saffron lap, sat the Mahanayaka.

'No!' she cried. 'I saw him die!'

Two women turned to stare but they had heard only the tone of her voice, not the words. She fought to stay calm. As the line of elephants approached, their fragile burden seemed poised above the turbulence of men. She wanted to call out to him, see his eyes open, but as the light from the flares shone onto his face she stood quite still.

There was something wrong with his mouth. A shudder shook her body; it made the bees throb. This was da Souza's work. For without the Mahanayaka's presence, the revolution could not proceed; alive or dead, he had to play his part. So this was what Saunders had meant. Jan felt sick.

She spun round to tell Wolfgang but he already knew. He was watching her, understanding, warning. She remembered where she was, and why.

She checked her borrowed watch: twelve minutes to nine. Wolfgang stood ready in the shadows; Neemal too. Out of sight, the others waited. In the grandstand, Quincey shifted in his seat. Jan watched him, morbid thoughts jangling in her head, and drew revenge like a blanket over pain. It was almost time.

A new troupe moved into position. Behind them, with his lancers and parasol-bearers, waited the Diyawadana Nilame, the lay custodian of the Tooth. Behind him, on a massive elephant, rode the mahout with the gun. As Jan's eyes searched for the weapon, the drums erupted into a cacophony of sound. Dancers jerked and spun. In unlit back streets, Mohan's brothers burst into action, their conflict obliterated by the din. Jan stared at the mahout, thought of the marksmen in the tree above her head, and waited.

Quincey looked at his watch. Jan looked at hers: five to nine. For both of them, it was time.

In the grandstand opposite, Quincey's face distorted in a grimace of pain, his hands clutching at his belly. Those nearest him turned in sympathy. The prime minister's lips formed a question. Quincey shook his head. Fixing her eyes to his face, Jan held her bees ready.

An interminable moment later, Quincey rose. Jan waited no longer. She gave the box a vigorous shake. When the bees' anger rivalled the drums, she held the box high in front of her, averted her face and flipped open the lid.

Furious black forms spun out and up, buzzing demons in a rage. Two more black clouds unfurled on either side. Like smoke signals on the opposite pavement, smaller ones rose against the moon. The effect was instantaneous. Elephants trumpeted, pushing out of line. The procession caved in, made way for their unthinking retreat. Drummers lost their drums. Torch-bearers dropped lighted braziers into the crowd. Someone screamed. Then everyone began to run.

Beside Jan's tree, one man turned. Slanting eyes pierced hers in recognition: the man with the ivory-handled knife. Jan stared back in terror. His hand reached up inside his shirt but the whistling never came. The knife began to swat the air instead. A horde of striped black bodies swarmed over his face and chest. The hands flapped more wildly. The knife clattered to the pavement but still Jan did not move. She knew she should but was paralysed with shock. As she struggled with herself, a figure sprang from the receding crowd, snatched the knife from the ground and flung it into the lake.

'Get back!' Wolfgang shouted. 'Go on – get away from the bees!'

Then he vanished and left her there. Horrified by the plague she had unloosed, Jan watched the man's strangely silent battle. It was right that he should suffer, she reminded herself, but she felt ashamed.

A loud yell came from the tree to her right, Wolfgang's tree.

Another yell, followed by a resounding slap. Jan held her breath as cry after cry erupted from above, from her tree now and Neemal's.

Branches shook. Something heavy fell to the ground: a rifle thudded down, then another. Seizing the weapons as they landed, Wolfgang tossed them over the lake wall. The water closed over them before anyone might see what they were.

The branches above Jan's head shook more violently. Two men, apparently grappling together, fell from their tree. Wolfgang moved forward, shoulders set, face stern, and swung their heads together. As he propped their inert bodies against the wall, more men jumped or fell, yelling and slapping their backs and arms. But each sting seemed to find its mark and they screamed and ran.

One fell clumsily, let out a screech of pain, then lay rolling on the ground. He was clutching his ankle, moaning and swatting with his rifle at the bees. Wolfgang wrenched the gun away from him. He was about to toss it over the wall with the rest when he turned and hit the man across the head with it first. The moaning stopped.

As the snipers fled, piercing cries rang out on the other side of the road. The grandstand had collapsed. People fought to escape as what was left keeled over to one side. The crowd scattered in all directions. Jan noticed with dismay that some of the bees were attacking indiscriminately. A small swarm of them chased a group of people shrieking down the street. There was the sound of breaking glass as they crashed through the windows of the Queen's hotel. Shop owners bolted doors to keep the stampede out; others opened theirs to help. Some thought only of themselves, knocking people down in panic; some carried children to safety. Each man chose his role by instinct: hero, victim, rogue.

A harsh yell recalled Jan to her own side of the road. Two figures ran beside the wall, their heads and shoulders veiled in bees: Saunders and da Souza. For a moment, she wanted to cheer: their plot had failed; their men fled disarmed; their intended dictator lay in the shambles of a broken grandstand. The revolution was over.

'We've won!' she kept saying. 'We've won!'

Two more figures materialized: Mohan's brothers stood ready, arms bent to tackle, eyes hard. Da Souza came first but he was agile and desperate to escape. He dodged, seemed to slip, then shot past. Leaping up onto the lake wall, he plunged into the water. The policemen converged on Saunders. The Englishman was slow and never knew what hit him: within seconds, his head lolled in a halo of bambaras against the cement.

Then she saw Lakshman. The old man stood precariously on the lakeside wall, holding a revolver in his hand. The grubby cloth had slipped from his head, its place taken by a seething mass of bees. She gasped in horror. He must have been drenched with arrack. But something was more important. One hand brushed the bees away from his eyes while the other aimed at where da Souza would appear. Jan watched the curly head emerge, heard the shots, saw bullets scatter the bees to find their mark. Da Souza jerked, coughed red bubbles into the water, then lay still, the rest of his body rising slowly to the surface. A splash reminded Jan of Lakshman. His duty done, the old man had jumped into the lake to escape the bees.

But something was tickling her scalp. Her headscarf had slipped off. Without thinking she raised a hand to her hair. Something buzzed against her fingers. She tried to pull it out. She did not mean to be rough but somehow, between her fingers and the tangle of hair, the frail body was crushed.

At once, she was the centre of attack. She saw them coming, tried to cover her face. Black missiles, tiny kamikazi pilots diving to revenge. Pain pierced her scalp, her neck, her hands and arms, and poison spread. She cried out in agony.

'Jan!'

A voice cut through the pain. She was waving her arms blindly, hitting out at each new sting. She killed them by mistake, moaning at her stupidity, unable to stop herself fighting back. Each death bound her closer to her hell. She wanted to run, found nowhere to run to. Cowering against the lake wall, she bent her back into a vulnerable shield and screamed for Wolfgang like a child.

'Jan, you idiot! Jump into the lake!'

It was Wolfgang but she was too swamped by fear and pain to understand.

'Into the lake!' he yelled again.

The voice was close but she saw only the striped black mass of bees. Strong hands dragged her upright, lifted her over the wall, into the lake. She thought of da Souza's floating body and tried to resist. Wolfgang took no notice. She sank, water soothing her skin. But when she rose to breathe, the bambaras were back. As they closed in once more, she let out a wail of despair and went under.

Dimly, beyond the buzzing that filled her ears, she heard another splash. Then another, and several more in quick succession. One of them was Wolfgang.

'Take off your shirt!' he shouted.

Her legs kicked out to keep her afloat, her hands protecting her face. She hardly heard the words, let alone took them in.

'Your shirt is black with bees!' Wolfgang yelled again. 'Take it off – it's your only chance!'

She stopped kicking and sank, tearing off both shirts at once and with them the bodies of countless dead and dying bees. The rest waited for her to surface. The shock of their renewed attack made her cry out. She felt the tiny bodies on her skin, each one plunging a poison dagger into her face, her back, her breasts. She screamed again. Wolfgang seized the tangle of shirts and held it over her head.

'When I say "Go!",' he shouted in her ear, 'dive underwater and swim towards the temple, that way!' He gave her a shove. 'Understand?'

Her head bobbed vehemently.

'Are you ready?' he yelled. 'Go! Now! Dive!'

She dived. As powerfully as she could, she swam towards the temple. At last, her lungs about to burst, she surfaced. Her feet touched bottom.

The bees had gone. Her face and shoulders throbbed but no new stings added to the pain. Her ears were free of that maddened scream. But Wolfgang was nowhere to be seen.

She peered across the lake to where she had left him. Something floated in the opposite direction: as it drifted into a patch of light, she recognized her clothes, obscured by a shifting swarm of bees that swooped and darted to attack. There was no sign of her friend.

'Wolfgang?' she called, suddenly afraid. 'Wolfgang!'

His bronzed face erupted from the water beside her, eyes gleaming, teeth flashing in a cheeky grin. As his hand rose to push the hair from his eyes, his face glowed.

'You see,' he said, his head bouncing from side to side in mockery of the Ceylonese, 'it worked! They think you're still in there!'

He laughed delightedly, as if the spectacle of bambaras attacking an empty shirt was the greatest joke. His merriment reached out irresistibly to Jan. Soon she was laughing, too, gently at first but with increasing conviction. All the accumulated tensions of her so-called holiday, all the emotional and physical stress of the past few days and the crescendo of the final hours, exploded into laughter, evaporated in the clean lake air.

She flung her arms around his neck and kissed him.

'Oh, Wolfgang!' she gasped. 'Thank God for you and your sanity!'

'Thank Kataragama!' he retorted, returning her embrace, still laughing too. 'As Mohan would say, our god is a mighty tough bugger!'

'Thank you, Kataragama!' Jan called with feeling to the moon.

He was a tough bugger indeed.

POSTSCRIPT

The Daily News reported things differently. 'The Plague of
Bambaras', the incident was called, and there was much
speculation on the karmic justice of it all.

According to the report, hospitals had been inundated with
cases of bee stings and broken bones but few were serious. The
two who earned the most publicity shared the photograph on
the front page: the prime minister and Quincey. The text
related how, due to the unfortunate colours of her saree, the
prime minister had suffered numerous stings to which, had it
not been for Quincey, she might well have succumbed. An
attack of stomach cramp had caused him to leave the stand but
when it collapsed, he had courageously returned to help. Mrs
Bandaranaike was quoted as saying that she did not know what
might have happened if he had not been there.

Among the fatalities listed, there were two of note: a Colombo
mortician who appeared astonishingly enough to have died of a
series of bullet holes in the head; and a British diplomat who had
been with the High Commission for five years and would, the
report insisted, be sadly missed. There was no theory to account
for da Souza's death. Rumour suggested that Saunders had
been drinking, but the newspaper merely speculated that during the height of the attack the Englishman had slipped and hit
his head against the wall, thus rendering himself defenceless to
the stings. An obituary followed that would have warmed the
cockles of that cold British heart.

The last footnotes to the drama came in a later edition: in
hideouts dotted across the island, groups of men and women
had been found dead; judging by the spray of machine-gun
bullets, murdered. In each case, the victims were armed and

gathered around a radio. One such unfortunate group included a foreign planter named Andrews. Investigations, concluded the report, were under way.

*

There is no question that *apis dorsata* is the most ferocious stinging insect on earth. It is not unusual for one to five thousand bees to leave a nest within a few seconds to attack an enemy. The principal alarm odour in *apis dorsata* is iso-pentyl acetate. . . . *Apis dorsata*, unlike other *apis* species, may attack in large numbers. The attacking bees fly in a cloud, usually three to six metres in diameter; most of the bees fly into open, sunny areas; some bees search close to the ground, even in shady areas, for intruders; attacking bees are extremely sensitive to alarm odour and may easily pursue an individual for several hundred metres, especially when stings in the body of the offending animal or person are releasing alarm odour.

'Biology of *Apis Dorsata*' by R. A. Morse and
F. M. Laigo 1968
(unpublished thesis)